Creative Texts Publishers products are available at special discounts for bulk purchase for sale promotions, premiums, fund-raising, and educational needs. For details, write Creative Texts Publishers, PO Box 50, Barto, PA 19504, or visit www.creativetexts.com

CLAY BRENTWOOD: BOOK EIGHT: LORALIE
by Jared McVay
Published by Creative Texts Publishers
PO Box 50
Barto, PA 19504
www.creativetexts.com

The following is a work of fiction. Any resemblance to actual names, persons, businesses, and incidents is strictly coincidental. Locations are used only in the general sense and do not represent the real place in actuality.

ISBN: 978-0-578-44029-3

LORALIE

By

JARED MCVAY

An imprint of Creative Texts Publishers, LLC
Barto, PA

TABLE OF CONTENTS

CHAPTER ONE

-

LATE 1800's
Loralie Benson's Tennessee-Walker horse ranch, just north and
east of Cinch Mountain, Tennessee
Mid afternoon

The mountain air was cool and crisp, but the bright sun made the day tolerable as three young Cherokee boys, none of whom had seen more than fourteen summers, rode their ponies slowly across the pasture, admiring the fine-looking horses grazing there. Each one of them hoped to someday own a horse as fine as any one of these. They were waiting for the woman to break and train them. They had been here twice before and knew their way to the barn where the woman kept the horses, she was training, which were the ones they were here to steal. The two men who were paying them to steal the horses had been clear about that point. They wanted only the horses that had been broken and trained by this particular woman, and those were kept in the barn and corral.

Because of that, the horses they were after were already penned in the stalls and would not shy away when they put a rope around their necks to lead them away.

Trying to chase and rope a wild horse in the pasture would not only be very hard but also noisy and might raise the attention of the woman who owned them. None of the three boys had any idea what a scared, hysterical woman would do if she saw Indians stealing her precious horses, but they had heard stories and none of the boys wanted to die at the hands of a screaming, out of control woman with a gun in her hand.

The closer they got to the ranch, the more cautious they became. Coming up to the barn from the backside and being quiet had worked the other times, so they figured it should work this time too. The men who paid them to steal the horses would not be pleased if they came back empty handed and their families sorely needed the money the men would pay them.

-

Several years back the Mullins gang murdered Loralie's parents and burned the place down, leaving Loralie with nothing but the land and no money to rebuild - so Loralie did the only thing she could think of doing and headed to the gold fields of Colorado, in search for enough of the precious rocks to rebuild the mountainside property that was now hers.

Although she was devastated by the death of her parents, especially her father who had taught her to be self-reliant, knew life went on, and to say that Loralie, at the tender age of eighteen would not be able to take care of herself would be a gross understatement.

Loralie could sometimes be a bit headstrong and from time to time leaped into situations without thinking things through. With that being said, during her trip between Tennessee and Colorado, Loralie found herself in a life or death struggle where she had to kill or be killed on more than one occasion and each time by luck or fate, a Texas Ranger by the name of Clay Brentwood had come riding up like a knight in shining armor, although he wasn't actually wearing armor, nor did he ride a big white horse. His horse was black and he was dressed like an ordinary cowboy. But the bottom line was, he always seemed to appear when she most needed him - and, as things sometimes happen, an event occurred were she had saved his bacon. It was like the powers enjoyed throwing them together.

While their relationship was nothing more than brief periods during times of trouble, Loralie was drawn to Clay Brentwood and felt he was the kind of man she hoped to someday marry – and if it was in the cards, it would be Clay Brentwood. Being a woman who was inclined to speak her mind, she had written Clay several letters that in her own subtle way, let him know exactly how she felt.

Whether it was just beginners' luck or just plain hard work - panning for gold in the rivers of Colorado yielded far more of its treasure than Loralie expected it would. Within just a few weeks, she found enough gold to not only rebuild her ranch - but she had enough money to replenish the place with prime stock for the horse ranch she'd always dreamed of, with a small sack filled with nuggets, in reserve.

When she got back to Tennessee, she found the Mullins had taken over her land and was about to cut down all the timber and sell it. At first, she tried bucking them alone but found herself out gunned. Once again, fate intervened and brought Clay Brentwood to help her reclaim what was hers.

When it was over and the land was hers once more, Clay went back to Texas and Loralie hired a crew of four men to come up from town and cut down only enough trees from her vast forestland to build a new house, barn, three corrals and a couple of out buildings. The rest would never be cut down if she had anything to say about it. She loved her forest.

Her new house had four bedrooms in case she and Clay ever got married and wanted a family. There was a good-sized parlor, a dining room that would seat twelve in case there might be ranch hands, and large kitchen with an inside water pump. The kitchen floor had a trap door in the corner of the room that led down into a good-sized root cellar where she kept a large stock of food. Winters in the Tennessee Mountains had a reputation of being man killers if people weren't prepared, and Loralie didn't want to be one of the victims.

On a whim and because she could afford it, she had them build a wraparound porch that covered three sides of the house. She liked the idea of being able to sit out on the porch at whatever time of day she chose and look at her forest, her horses and maybe a beautiful sunrise or sunset. Being able to sit in a rocker and watch the children she hoped to have as they played in the yard was an added incentive to build the porch.

There were three corrals; each large enough to allow her to train and exercise her horses. The barn had sixteen stalls and a huge hayloft, plus a tack room and a grain room. Her horses would be well fed and draw a high dollar. Raising and breeding Tennessee Walkers had been a dream of hers since she was a little girl that was now coming true. At the front of the barn was a good-sized room that held a desk and chair, along with a bed in the corner in case she had to spend the night to be near a sick or injured horse.

-

At the rear of the barn, the Cherokee braves tied their ponies loosely to a railing in the corral fence and eased their way up to the back door. Looking around to make sure no one was nearby they proceeded with great caution. They were nervous. Each time they came here they were defying the odds of getting caught. Before entering the barn, they pulled flour sacks over their heads. On a prearranged plan, two of them would enter the barn from the rear and the other one would sneak around and enter the barn by the side door in case someone was in the barn. They might be young and inexperienced but they were not stupid. Each one crossed his fingers and hoped no one would be in the barn. They had been lucky so far and prayed their luck would hold.

The men who hired them said there would be no one in the barn at this hour. If there was, it would be a woman and she would more than likely faint from fright, or run for the safety of her house. That might or might not be true, but they didn't want to take any chances. People didn't take kindly to Indians coming up from North Carolina and stealing their horses and cattle. Even though the sun was warming up the day, it wasn't the sun that caused them to sweat – it was nerves.

-

Loralie Benson was in the barn cleaning out one of the stalls where she kept her prized Tennessee Walking horses. As she worked, she wondered if Clay Brentwood received the telegram, she'd sent him asking for his help to discover who had been stealing her horses. So far, she hadn't been able to catch them, and was at her wits end. If they kept stealing her stock she would soon be out of business. She figured the rustlers must have someone watching her place because she always seemed to be down in Cinch Mountain on business or busy elsewhere when they came.

If Clay wasn't off doing Texas Ranger business, she hoped he would be able to come.

Loralie wished the request for his help could have been on different terms, but as her grandmother had said many times, "Sometimes fate has a better idea about how to put two people together than people themselves do."

Over the years, several men had tried to court her, but the only one who measured up to her standards was Clay Brentwood. Besides, most of the men just wanted to get their hands on her land and her prized Tennessee Walkers. Not that they didn't consider her attractive or anything like that, they did, but a profitable ranch with some of the best horses in the country, along with six hundred and fifty acres of good timber was icing on the cake. Clay, on the other hand, didn't want or need her land or her horses. As she understood it, he had a good-sized ranch of his own in Texas that was doing quite well.

Before all the rustling started, Loralie had been tempted to take a trip to Texas and make her intentions perfectly clear to Clay that he was the one she wanted, but in the end, she had procrastinated, fearing he might not feel the same way. Why she felt that way, she wasn't sure - his letters had indicated he was tired of being alone and her being a woman, she read between the lines as women tend to do. She deduced that he had the same feelings for her that she had for him - but did his feelings include marriage? In her limited knowledge on the subject of love, men didn't seem to think about it the same way women did, at least that's what she'd been told by several older women down in Cinch Mountain.

Loralie grew up believing people should speak their minds and get things out in the open instead of skirting around the edges of their feelings like so many people did. And to be truthful, like most of the others, she too held back, not wanting to get hurt if things didn't turn out the way she hoped they would. Clay had lost one wife and he might be afraid that if he let another woman get too close, he might lose her too. Being a young woman in love was not an easy thing, especially when the man she had her cap set for lived over a thousand miles away.

Lost in her thoughts, Loralie had just tossed a pitchfork of fresh hay onto the floor of the stall and was spreading it around when she heard the back door of the barn make a squeaking sound as it was opened slowly. Standing the pitchfork against the wall of the horse stall, she pulled her thirty-two-caliber pistol from the holster resting against her hip and eased her way to the front of the stall and listened. Nervous sweat was already beginning to trickle down her back. If this was the rustlers coming back to steal more of her horses they were going to be in for a rude awakening. There was only one lantern lit inside the barn and it was near where she stood, making anything beyond its light hard to see.

From the rear of the barn she heard whispered voices and figured her guessing had been correct, the rustlers had come back. They had already stolen nine of her prized animals and she was determined she would not let them steal any more. She took a deep breath and waited. She wasn't afraid, she was angry. She could feel it beginning to well up inside her. The small pistol in her hand felt like it weighed a thousand pounds

and her sweating hand made it hard to hold. Transferring the pistol to her left hand, she wiped the palm of her right hand against her pant leg, then shifted the pistol back to her right hand and waited.

When the voices got within the far reaches of the lamplight, Loralie stepped out of the stall and leveled her pistol at two, what looked like, young men coming slowly toward her with sacks over their heads – holes cut over the eyes so they could see.

"Hold it right there!" she shouted. "You've stolen all the horses from me you're gonna get. Now, lift them peashooters outta, I mean, out of your holsters, and toss them over by that pile o' hay," she said, pointing toward a pile of dirty hay that had come from the stalls, "or I'll make holes in ya big enough to drive a team of horses through!"

Loralie knew she hadn't said it quite right, but she was getting better with her speaking.

Raised in the mountains like she had been, she knew she sounded like a hillbilly, but she wanted to speak more like the flatlanders, hoping the next time she saw Clay he would notice and think better of her.

Almost a year ago, she had gone down to see the teacher in town and hired her to help her learn to speak correctly, or as close to it as she could get.

Loralie made the teacher promise she wouldn't wind up sounding like one of those uppity New Yorkers who came looking to buy her horses. They always looked down their noses at her and tried to sound like they were better than she was. She told the school marm, "I just want ta speak like folks not raised in the hills - that's all."

The teacher, who had been raised in Philadelphia, gave a sigh. If this woman was anything like her other students, she would have a real challenge on her hands. Only a handful of them even tried to change their speech habits, but by the end of the year, she told Loralie that she was proud of her for the progress she was making.

-

Startled by Loralie's appearance, the two young Cherokee boys stopped dead in their tracks and stared at the woman pointing a pistol at them. Their worst fear was standing in front of them and they were wondering what to do. They had not expected her to be here, especially, pointing a gun at them. They were each wearing a pistol on their hip, but the guns were just for show. They had no bullets in them - but the woman pointing her pistol at them didn't know that. Both the boys raised their hands in the air, making sure their hands came nowhere near their empty pistols.

The two would-be rustlers looked exactly alike to Loralie. Both were close to her height, five foot six. Both wore Levi jeans, scuffed brown boots, flowered shirts that were sun bleached and worn. Neither had on a hat, but instead, their heads were covered with flour sacks with holes cut out so they could see and breathe. Each one had a pistol hanging on his hip, which made her nervous, but she tried to remain calm. If either of them went for his gun, she would have no choice but to kill him. She hated killing.

"And take them goofy looking sacks off 'en, I mean, off your heads," Loralie commanded.

Because of the flour sacks covering their heads, Loralie couldn't see the grins that were spreading across their faces as they continued to stand there without removing the flour sacks or tossing their empty pistols onto the floor of the barn.

After staring at each other for nearly half a minute, Loralie was about to restate her demands when she saw the shadow on the wall of the barn. Someone was sneaking up behind her with what looked like something long and round in his hands. It was raised over his head, ready to strike her from behind, and from its shape, it looked like a singletree from the harness rack.

Loralie spun around and fired at a man who looked just like the two rustlers in front of her. She heard him scream as the bullet drove its way into his left shoulder and out the backside. She'd been hoping for his heart, but she'd fired before coming to a complete stop, which had thrown her aim off slightly.

A rustling sound came from behind her and she spun back around just in time to see the other two rustlers rushing toward her. One of the rustlers had his pistol raised high in the air. He was intending to strike her in the head with the butt end, but just as he brought it down toward her head, she sidestepped and instead of being struck on the head, she took the blow on her right shoulder. Her teeth gritted together from the pain as she staggered backwards trying to stay on her feet.

-

Loralie Benson had been born and raised in the hills of Tennessee and was considered by every male she encountered, to be beautiful. She had fiery red hair, large blue eyes and a figure that filled out her clothes, nicely. They were also, mostly afraid of her. She was no stranger to a knockdown, drag out fight. Unlike many of the young ladies who were raised in town, Loralie had been raised like a boy - learned to shoot like a man, fight like a man and accept pain as though it was a normal thing. She had been breaking horses for her father since she was eleven. She could track and hunt and help provide for the family as good as or better than most of the boys in the area. She had been the son her father had wanted but never had. But that was all in the past. Since the death of her parents, she had worked hard to build up her horse ranch, and now had one of the top Tennessee Walker horse ranches in the entire eastern part of the country and had no intentions of losing it.

Just as things were beginning to look good for her financially, a new problem dropped out of the blue and landed squarely on her shoulders – horse rustlers – and now here they were, trying to steal more of her prized animals.

When one of the rustlers came at her with both his hands doubled into fists, she meant to lift her pistol and shoot him in the leg, but realized she'd dropped her gun when she was struck on the shoulder. Added to the pain in her shoulder, she was having trouble moving her right arm. It just hung limply at her side.

She saw his fist coming but couldn't duck fast enough. The rustler's fist connected with her jaw and sent her sprawling onto her back.

Thinking she was done in, they turned to look for what horses they could steal.

Loralie rolled over and came to her feet, then surprised them when she charged the tallest one and kicked him between the legs from behind. His high-pitched scream filled the inside of the barn. With her left fist she struck the next one closest to her in the face and heard his nose break. The young rustler staggered back, confused - eyes wide with astonishment at the blood staining the flour sack and dripping onto the front of his shirt. She was fighting like a man, not the hysterical female they were told she would be.

Loralie turned to face the one she had shot and saw the singletree coming toward her head. She tried to move to the side, but she was not quick enough and when the piece of wood struck her head, she felt excruciating pain, then nothing as she slumped to the floor of the barn. Her last thought was that she was about to lose her horses, along with the possibility of never seeing Clay Brentwood, again.

CHAPTER TWO

-

After the ordeal with the Marlow brothers, Clay decided it was time to retire from being a Texas Ranger and settle down to being a rancher, selling horses and high-quality beef. He'd had enough of long days in the saddle under unfavorable conditions. He couldn't remember how many times he'd been shot, knifed and beaten half to death by men who wanted him dead – men who were wanted for every kind of crime a man could think of, and killing him would make them big men in front of the other owl hoots they ran with.

Then there was that time he'd almost froze to death in that blizzard up in the panhandle. And how many Indians, and Mexican banditos had he gone up against? Clay shook his head. Each time, fate or whatever it was, had pulled him from the jaws of death by the skin of his teeth and kept him alive for some reason, only God knew. But how much longer could he keep defying the grim reaper? As it was, his body was covered from head to foot with scars. Enough was enough. He'd done his share at bringing bad men to justice and more. Bill McDaniel, head of the Texas Rangers and his boss, would just have to understand that he was going to hang up his gun and that was the end of it. There could be no argument.

On the day Clay returned home after several months of chasing the Marlow brothers, he announced his retirement to the shouts of joy from the people who worked for him; but the celebration they planned for him turned out to be short-lived.

Riley, his ranch foreman, walked up and asked, "You sure about that retirin' stuff, boss?" Riley looked at Clay with a mischievous grin spread across his mouth.

Clay assured him he was as serious as a shot to the head, but when he saw the gleam in Riley's eyes and the slight grin on his mouth, the hair on the back of his neck stood on end. "What are you up to and why do I get the feeling you know something I don't?"

"Might want ta look at this," Riley said as he handed Clay a telegram.

With building apprehension, Clay took the telegram from his foreman and read it slowly. After reading it, Clay grinned and shook his head, then read it again.

NEED HELP [stop]
HORSE THIEVES STEALING MY STOCK [stop]
HOPE YOU CAN COME [stop]
LORALIE BENSON, BENSON HORSE RANCH,
CINCH MOUNTAIN, TENNESSEE.

This was turning out to be the shortest retirement he'd ever heard about.

While this wasn't officially ranger business, he would still be dealing with outlaws in the form of horse rustlers and he would be doing it in a state where he had no authority to arrest anyone.

Everyone who worked for him, his ranch hands, his housekeeper, Mrs. McIntyre and her daughter, even the children of the people who worked on the ranch stood watching him. Riley had already informed them of the telegram and they all wanted to see how Clay would react.

There would be no question about whether he would go to Tennessee or not - Loralie was in trouble and needed his help. Officially, he couldn't go as a Texas Ranger, but he could go as a civilian – a friend, and hope he could get this cleared up without gunplay, which he knew was a pipe dream.

Clay sighed, knowing he also had another reason for going. Just before being sent to hunt down the Marlow brothers, he had sort of planned to take a trip to Tennessee. He and Loralie had communicated by mail for some time now, and after a lot of thought, and riding out across his land to clear his mind and make sure he would be doing the right thing, he was planning on asking her if she might consider being a rancher's wife – the good Lord knew she needed somebody to watch over her. Trouble followed that gal around closer than stink on a skunk.

From her letters, he got the impression she had the same kind of feelings for him and would be receptive to a proposal. The one problem that kept coming to his mind was, Loralie's ranch was in Tennessee and was becoming well known for the Tennessee Walkers she raised and trained - and his horse and cattle ranch in Texas was also doing well. It would be hard for them to live in Tennessee and Texas at the same time. Clay sighed again and decided he would cross that bridge when he got to it. Right now,

he had to consider her telegram and what kind of problems the rustlers might be giving her. Knowing Loralie, she would not have sent the telegram unless she was in way over her head. How long would it take him to get to Tennessee? And would he be able to get there in time to help her? So many questions that had no answers.

Clay Brentwood decided to give the black stallion a rest. The big horse had done well during the time they went from Texas to California and back, but he wasn't getting any younger. So, with that in mind, Clay rode an appaloosa mare into Seymour that had recently been broken by his ranch hands. Seymour was a small town fifteen miles east of his ranch and the closest town to him. The town had a telegraph office where he could send an answer to Loralie's message requesting his help. The telegram would inform her he would do his best to be there in four or five days and hoped she could meet him at the station.

When he arrived in Seymour, Clay found the town busier than usual. People waved to him from the sidewalks, and in the center of town Clay saw a banner high overhead stretched across the street by ropes proclaiming today to be the Founding Fathers Day Celebration.

As he wrapped his horse's reins around the hitch rail in front of the telegraph office, Clay was greeted and slapped on the back by several townspeople he knew. Even at this early hour, their celebrating had already begun and they were in high spirits and offered him drinks.

Trying not to offend anyone, he laughingly turned them down by saying, "Got some business to attend to, maybe later."

The telegraph operator greeted him and quickly sent the telegram, then asked if he would be hanging around town for the celebration.

"Probably not, Sam," he told him. "I need to be following that telegram, but I'm sure I'll be represented by the people from my ranch."

The telegraph operator nodded and wished him a good trip to Tennessee, then went back and sat down in front of the rapid firing machine that was clicking away. Sam picked up a pencil and began writing.

Clay found Harold, his train engineer, in the diner down the street, eating his breakfast. Clay was glad to see that Harold had not yet joined the celebration and was more than anxious to take a trip.

"You going to visit that pretty redheaded lady back there?" Harold asked.

"She's having a few problems and has asked for some help," Clay said, not wanting to get into a deep discussion about Loralie or his private life.

"Got herself into trouble again, did she?" Harold asked as he dropped his napkin on the table and stood up. "That woman sure is something. Yes sir, she's quite a woman."

"We'll be taking the train out to the ranch on that new spur I recently had built," Clay said, not wanting to discuss the subject any further.

Harold nodded, noticing his boss's reluctance to talk more on the subject of Loralie and decided to let it pass.

As the train made its way across Clay's land, he looked out of the window and was amazed at how much his herd of cattle had grown during his absence. He would need to take a trainload up to Wichita soon and meet with the buyer he'd recently met during his time chasing the Marlow brothers. The man had told him if the cattle were even close to being as good as Clay described them, he would buy all Clay had to offer and by what Clay was seeing out the window, he figured they would both prosper.

Leaning back in his seat and closing his eyes, Clay decided riding the train was not only much faster than traveling by horseback, but also a whole bunch easier on him and the horse he would be riding. The times were changing – some for the good, and other things not so good. Clay imagined a time in the near future when men no longer carried guns. Maybe not in his time, but someday, which he hoped would be a good thing.

As the train rattled its way toward his ranch, Clay gave the Loralie situation a great deal of thought. With the way the popularity of her Tennessee Walkers had grown, it made sense that someone would want to steal a few of them, but his gut told him this was something different. She hadn't mentioned how many had been stolen, but for her to ask for help, it had to be more than just a few. Knowing Loralie the way he did, she would fight back, with or without help. She was almost as good a shot as he was, and she was not afraid to stand up against people she thought were trying to do her wrong. She would even go without food or sleep if she had to. She was that strong willed.

If she was asking for his help, that meant she had exhausted all other means, like the sheriff, who in his opinion was as worthless as a one-legged man in a foot race. Asking someone from town for their help would also be out of the question. She wouldn't put any of them in danger.

His hope was to get to Tennessee before the rustlers overpowered her and... He didn't want to think about that. He'd already lost one woman to outlaws.

The following morning, after the train had been loaded with food and other supplies, Clay loaded Midnight into a boxcar attached to his private train just in case he needed a horse with sand to pursue the rustlers. Besides, he knew Midnight wouldn't want to be left behind.

Clay laughed as Midnight ran up the ramp and into the boxcar, nodding his head up and down.

Clay had already given his foremen instructions the day before and the only thing left was to say his goodbyes, which he did.

Standing next to the engine, he told Harold to head for the small town of Cinch Mountain, Tennessee. "Depending on the stops we'll have to make, I hope to be there in four or five days," he told him.

Harold grinned and said, "We'll do our best. I'll slow down as we go through Seymour just enough for my coal stoker, Andy, to hop aboard, then it's full steam ahead."

Clay smiled and stood for a moment, looking at the sky. It was proving to be a nice day. The sky had only a few slow-moving clouds floating around and the sun was shining brightly.

After a final word to his two foremen, who had walked over to see him off, Clay climbed aboard his train and waved to Harold up in the engine, signaling that he was ready to go.

When Ol' Son heard the train whistle and saw the train begin to move, he raced as hard as his three legs would carry him, barking - trying to catch up with the train.

Riley, knowing Ol' Son wouldn't be able to catch the train, pulled his pistol and fired it three times in the air.

Clay heard the shots and pulled the emergency stop cord.

Harold brought the train to a stop, which wasn't difficult since it was just getting started and was still a long way from building up a full head of steam. As he stepped down from the engine to see what was wrong and saw Clay lifting the dog in his arms and carrying him aboard the train, he laughed so hard his eyes watered.

Clay heard Harold's laughter and yelled, "Well don't just stand there, get this train moving. We've got a long way to go."

Harold wiped the tears from his eyes and turned back toward the engine after seeing the grin on Clay's face. As the engine began moving forward, Harold marveled at the friendship between this man, who chased down outlaws, and his horse and three-legged dog.

Once they were inside the train car, Ol' Son hobbled down the aisle until he found the seat he wanted, then hopped up on it and plopped down on his stomach, wagging his tail slowly back and forth.

Clay scratched Ol' Son behind his ears and said, "I guess you're not as ready for retirement as I thought you might be, are you?"

Ol' Son watched until his master settled down in his seat and began to read. Once the train began picking up speed, Ol' Son knew he wouldn't be left behind. At that point, if dogs can grin, Ol' Son grinned, closed his eyes, and settled down for a nap.

Five days later, around four in the afternoon, Clay's private train pulled into the Cinch Mountain train station and came to a stop – steam hissing from the engine. Except for the beauty of the land they crossed, the trip had been somewhat boring. He was glad he had brought along a copy of a book titled, The Time Machine, written by an English author by the name of H. G. Wells. The sheriff had given it to him the day he was in town sending off his telegram, and laughingly said, "This man sure does have a big imagination. Ain't no way it can ever happen, but it's a good story, I'll give him that."

Clay had to agree with the sheriff, Mister H. G. Wells had a very active imagination, but all in all, he had enjoyed the story.

Clay had finished the book and had been napping when they pulled into the station and he heard the steel wheels grinding on the iron rails. He opened his eyes and sat up. He was glad to finally get here. Except for the times when Clay would have to stop the train so Ol' Son could get off and do his business, the trip had been mostly uneventful

The problem with stopping the train for Ol' Son was, it slowed the trip down a good bit. Plus, Ol' Son enjoyed his freedom, and would chase anything that moved causing the trip to be further delayed. At one such stop, Clay had spent almost an hour yelling for Ol' Son to come back to the train, then finally decided he would wait no longer and waved his arm, signaling for Harold to move out.

Standing in the engine, Harold looked out across the land trying to spot Ol' Son and thought he got a glimpse of him in the far distance. He pulled the cord on the train whistle and let it give a long, loud blast before moving the train forward, slowly.

When Ol' Son heard the train whistle and saw the train begin to move, he raced as hard as his three legs would carry him to catch up with the train – barking as loud as he could.

Harold stopped the train, again, so Clay could help Ol' Son aboard, knowing he would not really have left him behind. Clay leaned out away from the train car and waved at Harold for his cunning.

A cloud was hanging low over the town of Cinch Mountain, creating a misty like rain.

Clay looked out the window of his private car, hoping to see Loralie Benson standing on the platform, but saw only the man who ran the station giving instructions to Harold.

Clay stood up and leaned close to the window and took a closer look, swinging his eyes toward the inside of the station house, but she was not there, either. Clay sighed. This was not a good beginning. Turning, he looked down at Ol' Son. "Well, boy, it looks like we've been stood up," Clay said, feeling his disappointment and trying to overcome the growling feeling in his stomach that told him something was very wrong. He was certain Loralie wouldn't intentionally not be here.

Knowing Loralie like he did, it wouldn't be like her to forget to come to town if she knew he would be there. Hadn't she been the one who asked him to come in the first place? He would ask the telegraph operator to make sure she got his telegram before letting his imagination run away with him. Clay took a deep breath and could only hope at this moment, she wasn't trading fire with the rustlers – or the thing he feared the most, the distinct possibility that she was injured, or worse.

As the stationmaster walked back into the train station, Clay's train began moving again and made its way over to a side track where it finally came to rest.

After putting on his coat and hat, Clay climbed down from his car and walked through the heavy mist, back to the station with Ol' Son trailing along behind him.

They found the stationmaster busy at his machine, sending a telegram. Clay reached down and scratched Ol' Son on the top of his head as they stood patiently waiting.

When the man finished, he stood up and walked back over to the counter. "What can I do for you, sir?" he asked politely.

"I just came in on that train now sitting on your side track. I was sort of expecting Miss Loralie Benson to be here to meet me. I sent her a telegram telling her I would be here today. Has she been here, or did she leave a message for me?" Clay asked.

The stationmaster stood looking at Clay for a long moment - attitude written all over his face. "I'm the stationmaster here and anything that goes on around here, goes through me," he said with a bit of a whine in his voice. Puffing himself up a bit, he said, "My name is Atwater. Sampson Atwater - and to answer your question, no sir, I have seen neither hide nor hair of Miss Benson in about a week or so. The last time I saw her, she was in here to send a telegram to someone by the name of Brentwood. May I presume that would be you?"

Clay had almost burst out laughing at the stationmaster's name – Sampson. The man stood barely five feet tall and didn't weigh an ounce over one hundred pounds. Instead, he held himself in check by coughing into his fist, then said, "Yes sir, Mister Atwater, I'm Clay Brentwood and that's my train out there. Are you saying she hasn't gotten my telegram yet?"

Sampson Atwater shuffled some papers around on the counter in front of him and then picked one up and said, "That would be correct. Right here it is."

Frustrated, Clay tried to hold his anger in check. "I thought you were supposed to deliver telegrams when they came in," he said, looking the stationmaster in the eyes.

Sampson Atwater glanced down at the telegram, then back up at Clay, a slight smile of indignation gracing his face. "For your information Mister Brentwood, I deliver telegrams only to the city limits. I am here alone and I am not required to traipse all the way up a mountainside to deliver a telegram to Miss Benson or anyone else for that matter. If Miss Benson wants to know if there was a reply to her telegram, it is up to her to come to this office and inquire about it."

Clay did not like this scrawny little excuse for a man, but knew jerking him across the counter and slapping him silly would do no good.

"What's the cost to leave my train here for a few days – maybe a week?" Clay asked.

"As I told your engineer, one dollar a day," the stationmaster said, staring down at the three-legged dog sitting next to Clay. "You can stay as long as you want. I can never remember ever having a private train in here before. Came close once. The head man of the railroad came through right after this place was built, but he stopped only long enough to stick his head inside the door, nod, then head on up north. The man was in my opinion, very rude. He didn't even introduce himself, ask my name or say a word for that matter."

Before Clay could say anything, the stationmaster said, "I've never seen a three-legged dog before. How did he lose his leg?"

"Not sure," Clay said offhandedly. "He just came home one day without it."

Clay almost laughed as he watched Atwater's jaw drop and the questioning look appear on his face.

To keep from laughing out loud as Atwater pondered his statement, Clay looked out of the front window. The fog was now so thick he couldn't see his train and that bothered him some. During the short time he and Ol' Son had been inside the station, the rain had turned to a heavy fog, which was getting thicker by the minute. It was like a huge cloud had descended on the town, soaking everything it touched.

It was already late in the day and nighttime was only a few hours away. Trying to go up the mountain at night would be difficult in good weather, but impossible in this pea soup fog. Clay gave a long sigh. His instincts told him he needed to find a way to go up the mountain. He needed to check on Loralie and make sure she was all right, but for the life of him, he didn't know how that would be possible.

"You heard anything about her having trouble up at her place?" Clay asked as he turned back to the stationmaster.

Sampson Atwater couldn't fathom how a dog could just lose his leg, but held his tongue. There was something in the man's eyes that told him he wouldn't get a straight answer.

Sampson made a big deal about rubbing and scratching his Adams apple before saying, "No sir, I haven't. I make it a habit not to pry into people's affairs. But because I have to read the information when it comes in, and then type the words on my telegraph machine, I do however know of their contents. In the case of Miss Benson, I recall her telegram mentioning something bout rustlers, yes sir, but, again, I didn't ask anything further."

Suddenly Sampson's eyes got big and he said, "You're that Texas Ranger that was here a few years back when Silas Mullins and his bunch were trying to take over her land. That was you, wasn't it?"

Clay looked at Sampson but said nothing.

"So, is that why you're back? She's in trouble again, isn't she? I swear, that girl can get herself in trouble quicker than a drunken cowboy on Saturday night. You think you'll have to shoot somebody?" he asked excitedly.

Clay reached into his pocket and pulled out twenty dollars and laid it on the counter and said, "This should take care of our stay - along with the coal and water we'll need for the train. If he hasn't already told you, my engineer's name is Harold, and he'll be around town until I get back – in case you need him to move the train."

"Is Harold his first or last name? He didn't say when we talked." Atwater said.

"I guess that's something you'll have to take up with him. I don't pry into people's private affairs," Clay said, as he turned and walked out the door with Ol' Son hobbling along right next to Clay's leg, leaving Sampson Atwater sputtering and stammering something inaudible.

As Clay stood on the platform pondering his situation, he took a cigarillo from his shirt pocket and lit it. Loralie not coming in to check to see if he'd replied to her telegram was not a good sign. This whole thing was giving him a bad feeling in the pit of his stomach. In none of her letters had she ever mentioned having any cowboys working for her, so he doubted she would have anyone to send to town in her place. She would be up there alone - and if the rustlers had come back, she could be having to shoot it out with them all by herself, which he knew she would do.

Clay stood there, smoking his cigarillo, feeling helpless to do anything until morning, when he hoped the fog would have lifted. He had no idea how many rustlers she would be up against, which suddenly became another concern to worry about.

When Clay walked out to his train, he noticed Harold had already gone into town – probably to get a room and something to eat. Clay lifted Ol' Son onto the platform of his private car, then climbed the steps feeling at a loss with himself. Ol' Son waited for him to open the door, then followed Clay inside.

When Clay sat down at a table he used for eating, writing letters and such, Ol' Son sat down next to him and looked up, making a small whining noise. Clay grinned and reached down and scratched his ears. "It's gonna be all right," he said, not really believing his own words. Clay continued to sit there for a few minutes while he thought about the situation. After sitting there, fidgeting for nearly thirty minutes, angry that he was not doing anything positive, he stood up and left the car with Ol' Son following along behind.

Harold had made sure he stopped the train so that the stable car was next to a ramp where Clay's horse could be unloaded easily. Clay made his way slowly up the slick ramp and slid the door back to the sound of the black stallion's whinny.

The black stallion stepped off the boxcar gingerly and onto the platform where Clay and Ol' Son stood. Midnight laid his head across Clay's shoulder, glad to be out of the car.

"I'll bet you're tired of being pinned up," Clay said, reaching into his pocket and pulling out an apple, which he fed to the black stallion. "Maybe tomorrow we can see about stretching those long legs of yours."

Out of the fog, Harold made his way up onto the platform where Clay, Ol' Son and Midnight were standing and patted Ol' Son on the head.

"Thought you'd already gone into town to see about a room and something to eat," Clay said with a grin.

"Nope," Harold said, shaking his head. "Had to make a visit to the two-holer out back of the telegraph office."

Grinning, Clay reached into his pocket again and pulled out another twenty dollars and handed it to Harold. "This should keep you and Andy in beans and a roof over your head until I get back."

"I hope there won't be too much trouble, and tell Miss Loralie hello for me," Harold said as he stuck the money into his shirt pocket. "I'm meeting Andy at the restaurant."

Clay made his way cautiously down the ramp, knowing the black stallion and Ol' Son would follow.

Harold watched his boss disappearing into the fog. "Now why didn't he wait for morning instead of wandering around in this pea soup? Makes no sense atall," he mumbled to himself.

Rather than trying to ride his horse down to the livery stable, Clay decided it might be safer to walk. By now, the fog was so heavy he couldn't see more than two feet in front of where he was walking.

CHAPTER THREE

-

Even walking was time consuming. Once, he had accidentally angled a little to his right and found himself up against the sidewalk. Embarrassed, he was glad no one had been nearby to witness his blunder. Easing back out into the street, the sound of a hammer striking iron and the small glow of lantern light led Clay the last half a block to the livery stable. When he stepped inside, he saw the familiar face of Hank, the blacksmith.

Big Hank looked up from his work and saw a man and a horse enter his barn. Surprised at someone being out in this weather, he put his hammer down, wiped his hands on a towel hanging on a nail and then walked toward them. He didn't notice the three-legged dog until he got closer, then looked up to ask the obvious question and saw a face he hadn't seen in some time but immediately recognized.

Hank's face broke out into a broad grin. "Clay Brentwood! What a surprise! I reckon you'd be the last person I expected ta see around here today," he said, extending his hand.

Clay shook hands with the big blacksmith and felt the man's power as their hands grasped each other. "Kind of surprised to be here, myself," Clay said.

"I see you've got Midnight with ya, but how did ya come by ah three-legged dog? I'll be wantin' ta hear that story!"

Ol' Son looked at the blacksmith and took an instant liking to him. He walked over next to him so the big blacksmith could scratch his ears and pat him on the head.

When he'd finished petting Ol' Son, Hank looked at Clay and said, "It's Loralie and those horse thieves, ain't it?"

"You know about that?" Clay asked.

"Not much ta know; It's ah dag-gum mystery," Hank said, shaking his head. "How about ah cup of coffee? Doubt you'll be doin 'any travelin' in this weather and I can tell ya what little I know."

"Coffee sounds good," Clay said. "And thanks for any information you can give me. All I got from Loralie was a short telegram saying she needed my help."

"That she does," Hank said, as he poured two cups of coffee and set them on the small table in his livery stable office. "Offered mine, but she turned me down. Said it was too dangerous and time consumin'."

"Yeah, that sounds like her," Clay said, taking a sip of his coffee and then raising his cup to indicate he liked it.

Before he sat down, Hank opened a drawer and pulled out a piece of beef jerky.

Before he offered it to Ol' Son, Hank looked at Clay for his approval. Some people don't like other folks feeding their animals.

Clay looked down at Ol' Son and saw his mouth watering and nodded his approval.

Hank held the piece of jerky out to Ol' Son and said, "Here boy, gnaw on this while me and Mister Brentwood do ah bit of catchin' up."

Ol' Son looked up at Clay and watched as Clay nodded his head, then took the jerky in his teeth and went over to the doorway where he layed down and began to work on trying to chew the piece of dried meat.

"That's ah well trained dog you got there. You teach him?" Hank asked, still wanting to hear the story about how he came to lose his leg.

Clay shook his head and grinned. "Actually, it's the other way around," Clay said as he began the story of how he'd come by Ol' Son, and when he finished, Hank shook his head and said, "Well now, I'd say that's some story. Yes-sir, by golly, it sure is, and I'd bet my last dollar both of you got lucky when you found each other."

Clay looked at Ol' Son and smiled. "I think you might be right."

Hank poured more coffee and said, "Don't reckon it's any of my business, but ain't you tired a' gettin' yerself beat on and shot all ta pieces? If outlaws out in Texas and them other places is anything like the scoundrels we have around here, you must have more scars that ah roadmap."

"I am, and I do," Clay replied. "Gonna retire as soon as I can get this rustling thing of Loralie's settled up."

Clay looked at the big blacksmith and said, "Now, about Loralie and the problems she's having with these rustlers. How many horses has she lost?"

"I'm not sure," Hank said. "The whole thing's ah mystery. Whoever they are, slips in whenever she's not around and steals three horses out of her barn and then disappears without ah trace. I went up there awhile back, but like I said, there weren't no tracks ta follow, so there wasn't much I could do. At that time, they'd stolen nine of'em, but I don't know if'n they've come back again since then or not. Our new sheriff went up there, but he couldn't find any tracks ta follow, either."

"New sheriff?" Clay asked, surprised.

"Yeah. He's been here less than ah year and I think he's ah good man. The folks here in town seem ta like him. From what I can tell, he's a square shooter. And like I said, he went up there and scouted around but the tracks disappeared once they when inta the woods, same as they did when I went up there. They just plumb disappeared. I scouted around fer two miles but didn't pick up hide nor hair of'em. I'll tell ya, whoever these rustlers are, they know their business, and they seem ta know when she ain't there so's they can come in and steal her horses at their leisure. Strange thing is, they only take three at a time and all of them from the barn. Not even one of the horses out in the pasture has been bothered."

"Are the horses in the pasture broke to ride?" Clay asked.

Hank thought for a minute then said, "Come ta think on it, there might be ah few of 'em that is green broke, but none gentled out or trained like the ones in the barn."

Clay took a sip of his coffee then set it on the table. "Seems like someone knows a lot about her business."

Hank nodded his head in agreement.

"She was supposed to meet me at the station today, but she didn't show up and I'm a little bit worried," Clay told the blacksmith.

"Maybe it's the weather that kept her home. You got ta admit, it ain't no weather ta be travelin' down ah mountainside in," Hank said matter of factly.

Clay sighed. "Maybe you're right. It could be that this fog kept her home, but my gut says it's something else. I don't think the fog rolled in until just before I arrived, so she should have been down here already," Clay said, staring at Hank.

Hank nodded his head and looked Clay in the eyes. "And I suppose you don't want ta wait fer mornin' ta go up there. That's what yore sayin' ain't it?"

An idea had been rolling around in his head ever since he got to the livery stable, but he had waited until now to say anything. Clay shook his head, giving Hank a sheepish grin and said, "I was kinda hoping you'd go with me. You know this part of the country a lot better than I do and just maybe know how to get up to her place in this fog."

Hank finished his coffee in one long gulp and said, "I'll hitch up the wagon."

-

Clay and Hank rode the wagon up the narrow mountain road with Ol' Son in the back. The black stallion plodded along behind. It was one of those high sided wagons farmers use to haul hay and grain in. The seat squeaked and bounced them around with every rock or chuckhole in the "so-called" road. Clay could barely see from time to time.

Hank couldn't see any better than Clay so he allowed the team to find their own way up the long, winding mountain trail. The going was slow, which irritated Clay, but at least they were doing something, which was better than sitting back in town getting himself all worked up even more than he was already.

The fog seemed even heavier on this part of the road, but Hank had traveled it many times and felt confident the horses would find their way. After a little over an hour and getting several hundred feet above the town, the fog began to lift a little, and within another hour, they could see the road well enough to no longer feel threatened.

"Well, I'm glad to finally be able to see where we're going," Clay said, glancing over his shoulder to make sure Midnight was still with them.

"Seems ta have settled over the town more'n up here," Hank said, looking back over his shoulder.

"How much farther?" Clay asked, trying to remember by looking for landmarks, but nothing looked the same as it did when he was here before. He'd been preoccupied then and hadn't taken the time to memorize the trail.

Hank looked around at their surroundings for a moment, then said, "Don't reckon it'll be more'n another half an hour, or so."

Clay lit a cigarillo to try and calm his nerves. "Can we go any faster?" he asked.

"It's ah uphill climb, all the way, Mister Brentwood, and I let the horses set the pace so's they don't tire themselves out too much," Hank replied, pulling an ancient looking briar pipe from his shirt pocket.

When Clay and Hank finally arrived, the air up on the mountain where Loralie's ranch was located was free of fog. The sky was full of stars and there was a half moon to light up the night. The area where the house, corral and barn sat had been cleared and looked well taken care of, but beyond that, it was nothing but forest.

Sensing something, Ol' Son stood up and looked around, trying to see over the tall side boards. Hank and Clay could hear a low grumbling emitting from his chest.

As Hank drove his team into the yard, they noticed the house was dark, which didn't surprise them since it was close to ten o'clock at night and long past most folk's bedtime.

Hank called out, "Hello, the house. Miss Benson - it's me, Hank. Don't shoot - I got Mister Brentwood with me." They waited, but got no response.

Clay poked Hank in the arm with his elbow and pointed toward the barn where a lone lantern shone through an open barn doorway. "Shouldn't that barn door be closed this time of night?" Clay asked.

"You're right, it should be," Hank said as he pulled on the left rein, turning the wagon in the direction of the open barn door.

When they got near, Clay jumped from the wagon before it came to a stop and hurried into the barn with his pistol in his hand and Ol' Son running next to him.

As Clay and Ol' Son entered the barn, Ol' Son immediately ran over to a body laying on the barn floor, and began whining.

Clay rushed over and looked down. It was Loralie and she was unconscious – there was a pool of blood under her head, mingling with her hair spread out across the floor.

"Over here," Clay called out as he knelt next to Loralie and checked to see if she was breathing.

Hank arrived and grabbed the lantern and held it up.

"She's alive, but barely," Clay said.

"We need ta get her inta the house," Hank said. "You wanna carry her, or should I?"

"I'll carry her," Clay said, picking her up in his arms and starting for the doorway. As he walked toward the house, he could feel her body losing its warmth and knew they had to do something, soon.

Hank raced in front of him, holding the lantern up so Clay wouldn't stumble over anything.

Inside the house, Hank lit a lamp, then lit a fire in both the fireplace and kitchen stove and put some water on to heat.

CHAPTER FOUR

-

Several miles up the mountain to the east of Loralie's ranch, the three Cherokee Indian boys sat next to a narrow stream of water that flowed through a shallow canyon running for a quarter of a mile, hiding them should anyone come riding by. In the glow of the fire, Lives in The Woods was trying his best to put a bandage torn from his own shirt, on Wolf's shoulder where he'd been shot.

Bullfrog was kneeling next to the stream soaking a piece of his shirt in the cold water, then holding it against his broken nose and try to stop it from bleeding and hopefully relieve some of the pain. Along with being scared over the fact that they could have been killed, they felt lucky to have gotten away with the horses and only a few wounds that would eventually heal.

The worst part was they had been able to steal only two horses. The men who hired them would not be happy. They wanted three horses, but how could they steal more than was in the barn. The men had instructed them, "No horses from the pasture, just the barn." They had done the best they could under the circumstances, but their mood was a long way from being joyous.

The water flowing downstream bubbled over the rocks and echoed through the canyon. Along with their ponies, two of Loralie Benson's Tennessee Walkers were standing nearby, nibbling grass under a sky filled with stars and a half moon to light up the sky.

"Do you think you killed her?" Lives in The Woods asked of Wolf.

Wolf had been the one who hit Loralie in the head with a piece of singletree he'd grabbed from the harness rack.

"I hope not," Wolf said, holding his shoulder. "I panicked. She was not supposed to be there and even if she was, she was supposed to stay inside her house, whimpering and crying like a normal woman."

"She is a hell cat. She fought like a warrior," Bullfrog said, shaking his head. "You saved us from her. I do not want to see her dead, either, but she might have shot us all if you had not hit her on the head."

Lives in The Woods looked down at the pistol resting on his hip and said, "Maybe we should not have worn these empty pistols. It made us look like we were armed and wanted to kill her."

"I agree," Bullfrog stated. "If you wear a pistol on your hip, it needs to have bullets in it."

"But we have no bullets and no one will sell them to us. Even full-grown braves have trouble getting bullets for their weapons, so how do three young braves like us who have seen only fourteen winters get bullets?" Wolf asked, grimacing from the pain in his shoulder.

"It is because the whites have made it illegal to sell guns, ammunition and whiskey to Indians," Bullfrog stated profoundly, dabbing his bloody nose.

Lives in The Woods sighed as he thought about their situation. "I am not sure we should wear these guns, empty or loaded. I do not think I could shoot anyone. I've never shot a pistol before and I'm not even sure I could hit whoever I was aiming at."

The other two readily agreed.

"I have never actually shot a gun," Bullfrog said, shaking his head.

"None of us have that I know of," Wolf said.

After an awkward moment of silence, Lives in The Woods, said, "Whether we have bullets for our pistols or whether we wear them or not is not our biggest problem right now. It is the men who pay us to steal horses for them. I am sure they will be upset with us for bringing only two horses when they told us to bring three."

Bullfrog nodded. "You are right. They will not be happy. They are very insistent about what we are to do and how we are to do it."

"It is true, they will be unhappy," Lives in The Woods said, "but what else could we do? There were only two horses in the barn and Wolf, you were shot, and Bullfrog, you have a broken nose. We did the best we could. They will understand that, won't they?"

Of the three, Lives in The Woods was always the most optimistic and tried to see the best in everyone.

"Humph. When did we ever matter? They could care less about us. All they want is the horses. They are not the understanding kind you'd like them to be. They think only of themselves," Bullfrog reminded him.

Lives in The Woods nodded his head in agreement.

After eating some of the nuts and dried berries and jerky they carried with them, along with drinking water from the stream, they talked long into the night, but found no solution to their problem. They could not go into her pasture and try to catch another horse to make the white men happy. Not only would it be risky, it had gotten too dark to see. Even if they were lucky enough to catch one, they had no idea which ones, if any, had been broken to ride and trained - which the white men insisted on. Plus, none of them were experienced ropers. They had done the only thing they could do; steal the trained horses from the barn like they were told to do and had always done.

The moon was high overhead when they decided there was nothing more they could do and more talk would accomplish nothing. They agreed to leave at first light and needed rest. It was a three-day trip and the men from Ashville, North Carolina would be anxious for them to get back. They would be waiting in the trees next to the river on the outskirts of town and they were not patient men.

As always, they would never actually see the men who paid them to steal the horses. The men wore masks over their faces and stood some distance off. They had been instructed to bring the horses to a certain place in among the trees next to a bend in the river, then walk away a short distance and wait. The men would inspect the horses and if they were satisfied, they would put ten dollars apiece for each horse on a nearby tree stump and leave, taking the horses with them.

So far, the white men had been pleased, but only because they stole the horses they were told to steal, and no others.

Since it was such a long ride, and they were in a hurry, they normally traded horses every few hours, taking turns riding the woman's horses, which allowed them to ride much faster. But this time they had only two horses to trade off with and decided not to bother.

Based on their sizes, they didn't need to trade off. They were each one close to the same size – five foot seven, one hundred forty-five pounds; an easy carry for their own ponies, who they noticed didn't seem get worn down from the pace.

-

Loralie had started the Walker breed with a single mountain horse her father had owned – a mare who stood fifteen and a half hands, which amounts to sixty-four inches from the ground to the top of her withers, or shoulder. The bay mare was born and bred in the mountains, and was tough as nails, but she also had a quality about her that spoke of thoroughbred somewhere in her background.

With some of the gold she'd found in Colorado, Loralie purchased a Morgan stud from a young man down in the southern part of the state who gave her a good price when he found out why she wanted him.

She bred the Morgan to the mountain horse, which threw a beautiful male colt. Next, she bought four, good-looking quarter horse mares from a man in Kentucky along with two thoroughbred racehorses. Within two years and a lot of hard work, Loralie had her Tennessee Walker breed started and was just beginning to become known when all the trouble started.

The great thing about Tennessee Walkers was the fact that they were all around horses that could be shown as fancy steppers in shows, used as all around ranch horses, and even racehorses. Their gait and ride was smooth for both men and women. They had a gentle nature and good endurance. They weighed between nine and twelve hundred pounds, depending on their height. Because of different studs, their color and size were each a little different, giving the new owner pride in having a one of a kind horse. But she would shortly be out of business if she didn't somehow stop the rustlers.

None of this information did the three young braves know anything about, nor did they care. All they knew was the two men they worked for were willing to pay them ten dollars for each horse they stole from this particular woman, which so far had been easy until this time. So far, they had earned ninety dollars – more money than they'd ever had before.

Money was hard to come by for Indians and when each of them brought home thirty dollars to share with their families, they were looked at with great pride. Lives in The Woods had no family, but shared his money with the elderly women who had no brave to take care of them.

Three days later, on a bright, sunny afternoon, the three braves topped over a hill, leading the two stolen horses. The outline of Ashville in the far distance created excitement in the young Cherokee boys. Even though they wanted to whoop and shout as they rode closer to the river, they held their silence. They did not want to be seen with the stolen horses. These horses were too grand for an Indian to have – people would talk and the sheriff would come looking for them – asking questions.

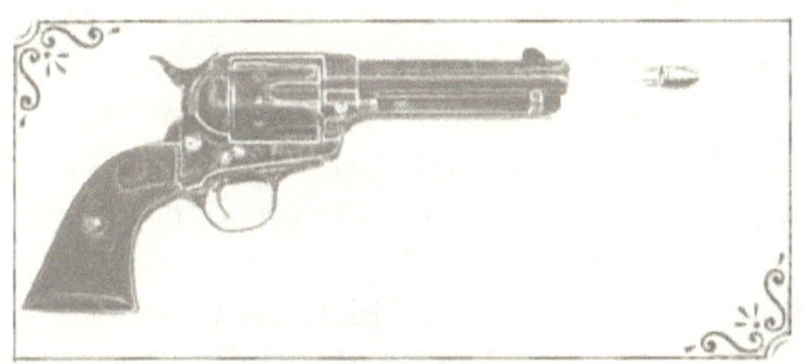

CHAPTER FIVE

-

"Should I take the wagon back ta town and get the doctor?" Hank asked after examining Loralie's head wound and got the bleeding stopped. She was still unconscious and her breathing was labored, but other than that they had no idea as to her condition.

Clay let out a sigh and said, "With a wound like this, she should be kept quiet and allowed to rest, but on the other hand, she needs a doctor to look at her. Head wounds like this can be serious. It will take somewhere in the neighborhood of a five-hour round trip to go fetch a doctor and come back. She could die in that time. But if we load her in the wagon and take her to town, she could see the doctor much quicker in case she has trouble inside her head and needs attention right away. You know, like swelling of the brain or something."

Hank looked at Loralie and then back at Clay. "What about the road and all the shakin' around she'll take? Won't thet be jest as dangerous to her?"

Clay looked at the floor and shrugged his shoulders.

"We'd need ta pad the wagon real good," Hank said. "On these mountain roads, such as they are; more like rough trails, it'll be ah rough ride in the back of that old wagon of mine, but I'll do whatever you think is best. It's yer call."

Clay looked down at Loralie and he felt helpless. Her skin was pale, and he knew he needed to make a decision, fast.

Clay bent over and put his right ear against her chest and listened for a moment, then stood up and said, "She has a strong heartbeat, but I think she needs to be seen by a doctor sooner, versus later. You start loading the wagon bed with fresh hay. We can use it for a cushion. I'll get all the pillows and blankets I can find."

Fifteen minutes later Hank was driving his team down the mountainside in the direction of Cinch Mountain, trying to find a speed that would hurry them along, but slow enough so Loralie wouldn't get shaken around too much. Ol' Son layed next to Loralie with his chin on her stomach while Clay rode along next to the wagon on the black stallion so he could keep an eye on her in case she woke up and needed attention.

It was close to five o'clock in the morning when Clay banged his fist against the doctor's door without stopping until he knew someone had heard him.

Lamplight appeared through the window, followed by the doctor's gruff voice. "Just hold your damned horses! And stop that infernal banging on my door! I'll be there as soon as I can get my pants on!"

"It's me, Doc. – Hank. We got Loralie Benson with us and she's hurt bad with ah head wound."

The door was jerked open and Hank carried Loralie into the office. The doctor led the way into another room and said, "Put her on that table, then step back so I can examine her. How did this happen?"

Neither man had an answer so they just shrugged their shoulders. Finally, Clay spoke up. "I think the rustlers may have come back and she interrupted them."

While Hank was laying Loralie on the table, the doctor lit another lamp and set it on a stand next to the operation table.

After a quick examination the doctor put some medicine on Loralie's wound, then got his thread and needle and sewed up the open cut on the top of her head toward the back. It took seven stitches and when he was finished, he turned to Hank and said, "What happened? And I don't want just a shrug of your shoulders and a dumbfounded look on your face, or some theory about horse rustlers. Didn't she say anything?"

Hank looked at Clay, then back at the doctor. "Not a word, Doc. I'm thinkin' them horse rustlers must 'a come back. We found her in her barn, unconscious and her head was bleedin' somethin' awful. And there weren't no horses in the stalls like there usually is. That's why I think it musta' been them rustlers come back. We put ah bandage on her head and hurried back ta town as quick as we could. She's gonna be all right ain't she?" Hank asked.

Clay walked over and took Loralie by the hand and stood looking at her. Even with the bandage on her head, she was beautiful and for the first time in a while, he was afraid.

The doctor took out the makings and filled his pipe and got it going before he answered.

"To be honest, I don't know. In cases like this... well, you just never can tell. Sometimes the patient wakes up and everthing is fine – then other times... the brain begins to swell and they never wake up."

"Anything we can do to help?" Clay asked, looking back over his shoulder.

The doctor looked at Clay and asked, "And you sir, are?"

"Clay Brentwood. Loralie and I are friends. She sent me a telegram asking for help with some horse rustlers she's been having trouble with. I just got into town a few hours back and Hank and I went up to her ranch. I needed help to find the place in all that fog."

The doctor looked at Hank and frowned. "You brought her down the mountain in that ole rickety wagon of yours, did you?"

Hank nodded his head. "Yes sir, we did; but we filled it with hay, pillows and blankets. She rode real comfortable like, Doc. Didn't she?" Hank asked of Clay.

"We were as careful as we could be," Clay said. "It was my decision to take a chance and bring her here instead of waiting for you to come to her. We weren't sure how bad her wound was. I've heard about times when the brain begins to swell like you just said and let's be honest, neither of us has any medical background, so we brought her here as quick as we could."

The doctor nodded and walked back over to where Loralie was laying on the table. With his stethoscope, he listened to her heart and put his fingers against her neck to feel her pulse, then looked back at Hank and Clay. "You did right by bringing her here. Let's just hope you got her here soon enough. She's going to need somebody to sit with her and put cool, wet towels on her forehead every hour or so until morning."

Clay pulled off his hat and stepped close to the doctor. "I'll stay and do whatever needs to be done."

The doctor looked at Clay and could see the concern in his eyes and said, "Well then, I guess that's settled. Grab that chair over there," he told Clay, pointing to a chair sitting against the far wall. "I'll get a pan of cold water and a towel."

Clay looked at Hank and asked, "Will you see to Midnight and Ol' Son?"

"Consider it done," Hank said, "And come mornin', I'll be back ta relieve ya."

When everyone was gone, Clay applied a cold towel to Loralie's forehead, then sat down on the chair and then, once again, took her hand in his.

"Loralie, it's me, Clay Brentwood. I got your telegram and I'm here. I don't know if you can hear me, but in case you can, I need you to wake up and tell me what happened so I can try to find whoever did this to you. They need to pay for what they've done."

He waited and watched her face for a sign she'd heard and understood him, but there was no reaction, nor any response – not even the twitch of a finger.

Clay sat next to Loralie throughout the rest of the night, applying cool towels on her head every hour and talking to her. He even told her about his last adventure with the Marlow brothers and finding a dog he named, Ol' Son."

When the doctor came into the room just after sunrise, Clay was having a hard time keeping his eyes open and smiled when he saw the doctor had two cups of coffee with him.

"Figured you might need a cup about now," the doctor said, grinning at Clay.

Clay took the cup and said, "I sure do. Thank you."

"How's she doing?" the doctor asked, setting his cup on the stand next to where Loralie lay.

"She needs you to figure that out," Clay said. "The only thing I can tell you is, she hasn't moved or responded to any of my questions. When's she going to wake up, Doc?"

The doctor took a deep breath and began examining her, leaving Clay's question for the moment, unanswered.

Clay stood up and walked over to the other side of the room and watched as the doctor examined Loralie. From Clay's point of view, the doctor looked to be a man nearing retirement age, if doctors ever retire that is. His hair was almost a silky white, and he could stand to lose some weight. He wore glasses and walked with a slight limp like he'd been injured some time ago. His hands looked as though he suffered from arthritis, the fingers and knuckles were out of shape, but his actions were quick and precise, like a man who knew exactly what he was doing.

When he finished his examination, the doctor turned from the table and stuck out his hand and said, "We haven't been properly introduced. My name is Hubert Roswell. I'm the only doctor within... well... let's say, two or maybe, three days ride on horseback, so folks are stuck with me. I came out here from Chicago twenty some years ago. I try to keep up with all the newest doings, but I fear I still lack knowledge in certain areas, like head wounds and amnesia."

Clay stuck out his hand, wondering why the doctor was taking this time to introduce himself and talk about his background. Was he trying to tell him something? Did he have bad news, and just delaying the inevitable? Clay looked at the doctor and decided to go along and see where it led. "Clay Brentwood, I'm a rancher back in Texas and a friend of Miss Benson. And like I said before, she sent me a telegram asking for my help."

"Brentwood? Are you the Texas Ranger that was involved with the Silas Mullins affair?"

Clay nodded his head. "Yes, that was me, but I'm not here as a ranger – this is a good bit out of my territory. I'm here just as a friend to see if I can help."

"I see," the doctor said, raising his bushy eyebrows. "And you say you just arrived yesterday?"

"Yes sir, about five yesterday afternoon. Do you know anything about what's been happening up at her ranch?"

The doctor scratched the back of his neck and said, "Not much, other than she was losing some horses now and then. Sheriff went up there but wasn't able to figure out who was behind it. Said the tracks led into the woods, then just disappeared about a mile or so north of her place."

"Anyone else having problems with horses or cattle being stolen?" Clay asked after downing the rest of his coffee.

The doctor thought for a moment, then said, "Not that I've heard of, but the sheriff is the one you need to ask about that, he would know if anyone would."

Clay gave the doctor a questioning look and said, "Hank said he was fairly new here."

The doctor said, "Yes, he's fairly new, less than a year since he came to town and took over. Unlike the old sheriff when you were here before, this one is a good man and the people like him. Was a deputy down in Dodge City as I understand."

Clay nodded his head and looked over at Loralie. Her breathing seemed to be a little less strained, but she still hadn't stirred since Hank put her on the table some seven hours ago, which made Clay uneasy.

"You still haven't answered my question, Doc. When's she going to wake up?"

The doctor looked at Loralie for a moment, then turned back to Clay. "You go get some breakfast, then get some sleep. I'll get ahold of you if her condition changes," the doctor said, patting Clay on the shoulder.

Clay looked at the doctor for a long moment, realizing this was all the answer he was going to get, which agitated him all the way down into the marrow of his bones. Was he holding something back, or possibly, didn't he know the answer? 'What if she never wakes up?' Clay thought to himself.

As Clay stepped out of the doctor's office, Hank was coming up the stairs and when he saw Clay he asked, "Any change?"

"No. She's still unconscious, but the doctor said her breathing is better and he doesn't think her brain is swelling."

Hank sighed. "Well, at least that's a good thing. You had breakfast?"

Clay shook his head. "Just headed that way. You?"

"No, but I'm as hungry as ah bear after sleepin' all winter. Mind if I join ya?"

"Not a bit. I could use someone to talk to," Clay told the big blacksmith.

"Don't know how much I can tell ya, but I'll do what I can," Hank said, heading back down the stairs. "I think the world of that young woman up there and God help the ones who did this if I get my hands on' em."

Clay knew that was also his sentiments exactly. Anyone who would do this to a woman was less than a man in his book.

Clay glanced up to the window of the doctor's office and saw the doctor looking back at him. The doctor raised his pipe at him and then turned back into the room.

CHAPTER SIX

By the time the three young horse thieves arrived at the place among the trees where they were supposed to meet the men who hired them, large, dark clouds had moved in making it seem almost like night time, even though it was not yet five in the afternoon.

"I don't see them anywhere," Wolf said as he slid off his horse and looked around.

Lives in The Woods and Bullfrog slid off their horses and also looked around, but saw no one, either.

"Are we late?" Bullfrog asked.

Wolf tried to look through the tops of the trees to see the sky and predict the time, but the dark clouds had it blocked out. "I cannot tell, but I believe we are where we are supposed to be and at the right time, or close to it."

"Maybe it is the white men who are late," Lives in The Woods said.

The gruff voice behind them made them jump.

"We ain't late. We've been waitin' on ya fer some time now. How come ya only got two horses? We tole ya three."

The three young braves turned and faced toward where the voice was coming from but could see no one.

"That is all she had in her barn," Lives in The Woods said. "Plus, she was there and shot Wolf in the shoulder and broke Bullfrog's nose with her fist when we tried to fight back. You said she would not bother us. You said she would be afraid and stay in her house, but she was not afraid. She is a strong woman who fights like a man."

"Maybe we got the wrong ones doin' the stealin'. Maybe we need men instead of boys who are afraid of a lone woman."

"We are not afraid of her, but she had a gun and was going to kill us. Wolf saved us by hitting her in the head with a piece of wood. Then we took the horses and came here."

"Did ya kill her?" the man asked.

"I do not know," Wolf said, stepping forward. "There was blood coming from her head when we left her on the floor of the barn."

There was a long silence, then mumbling, before the gruff voice spoke to them again. "We've decided ta give ya one more chance. We want ya ta go back and get six horses this time. And we want ta know if'n she's alive or dead."

The three young Cherokee boys looked at each other, then back toward the voice.

"Six? That is a lot of horses to steal," Lives in The Woods said. "She never has more than three in the barn. Do you want us to steal horses from the pasture that have not been ridden or trained yet?"

Again, there was a long silence as the three boys stood there, waiting.

Finally, the man hidden by the trees spoke. "We won't settle fer no less," the gruff voice told them. "Six horses. We'd prefer them ta be ones broke and trained, but in the end it don't matter. We want six of her horses, and if'n ya fail, I reckon things might start ta happen ta yer families – you know, accidents, like trippin' n breakin' their necks - or maybe their tepee catches on fire whilst they're asleep. You get my drift?"

Wolf looked at his companions with a terrified look in his eyes. Both Lives in The Woods and Bullfrog sighed and nodded their heads – the fear of failing and what would happen to their families if they did, filled their chests, making it hard to breathe.

"How long do we have? Wolf asked.

There was more mumbling, then the gruff voice said, "Five days. We'll meet ya right here in five days and you'd better have all six horses. Now turn around and don't turn back til we've inspected the ones ya brought. I'll give ah yell when you can come and pick up yer money."

"We will do our best, but it will take time to find ones that have been broken and trained as you want. We will need at least eight days," Wolf declared.

"Yes, we need at least eight days," Lives in The Woods agreed.

It was close to five long minutes before they heard the gruff voice yell through the trees, "Six days. No more'n six days, so you'd better get ah move on if'n you don't want things ta start happenin' ta yer families."

They could hear the horses being led away, then, in the distance, they heard, "Ya can come and get yer money, now."

The boys walked over and looked at the twenty dollars laying on the tree stump. Lives in The Woods picked up the money and handed it to his two friends, ten dollars each.

"This is not right," Bullfrog said. "We will split the money three ways like we always do."

"Not this time," Lives in The Woods said. "Both of you were injured, so it is you who should have the money. Besides, both of you have families to help take care of. Now go to your homes and get some rest. We need to leave tomorrow morning at first light."

"How will we know if the woman is alive or dead?" Bullfrog asked.

"One of us must go back into the barn and check," Lives in The Woods said. "And we must look and see if there are any horses there, plus we will need rope with which to catch the six horses from the pasture."

"This time it will not be so easy. Do you think we can do it?" Bullfrog asked.

"We have no choice. You heard what he said they would do to our families." Wolf said.

"I wish I knew who the white men are. I would do... do something to put fear in them so they would be afraid to bother our families," Bullfrog said, his words filled with bravado.

"What would you do?" Wolf asked. "Maybe I could help you."

"I don't know," Bullfrog admitted. "But I would do something."

"How could we do something when we do not know who these men are? I for one, wouldn't know where to start. We have never seen their faces and they have never spoken their names. They are like ghosts and I do not know how to find a ghost." Lives in The Woods said, crossing his arms across his chest.

Wolf leaped up onto the back of his pony and looked down at his friends. "First things first, my friends. We have only six days to do what they want. I say we do not wait for morning. I say we leave right now."

Lives in The Woods and Bullfrog looked at each other and Bullfrog said, "I agree with Wolf. We cannot waste even a minute. Plus, we will need money for food and other things," he said holding up his portion of the money they'd just gotten.

After stopping at a small store on the far edge of Ashville, one who would sell to Indians, they bought supplies with some of the money the men had given them.

When they finally made camp for the night, the moon was high in the sky and the lights of Ashville had disappeared behind them several hours ago.

Over a small fire, they ate their meager rations without talking. It had been a very long day and even with their youth, they were tired. They each knew what needed to be done so there was no reason for talk and when they had eaten, Lives in The Woods was the first one to spread his blanket on the ground and lay down.

-

"You think they can do it? Get six horses this time? And do ya think they might 'a killed the Benson gal?" the younger of the two white men asked as they led Loralie's two horses toward a dark shack with a corral next to it, just outside of Ashville.

"Reckon we'll find out in six days," the older of the two said.

CHAPTER SEVEN

-

Several days had passed and Loralie was still in what the doctor called, a coma.

He told them again, that this kind of thing happened sometimes with head injuries and there was nothing they could do but wait for her to wake up, which upset Clay far more than he allowed anyone to see. His real feelings for her lay just under the surface and from time to time felt like they would erupt. He prayed for the day he could get his hands on the ones who did this to her...

The nights were the worst when he had nothing to do but think of all the things that could go wrong. What if she died? He wouldn't allow his mind to even consider that. She had to wake up and be her old self, again. She just had to.

When he was able to think more rationally, he wondered if she had had the forethought to make out a Will? It was what his attorney had told him was the smart thing to do. When he got back, he would go up to Wichita and have one made out.

Clay doubted if she had a Will. But… if she did, who would she leave the ranch to? She had no kinfolks that he knew of. Her parents had been murdered by the Mullins and to the best of his knowledge; she had no relatives. If there was no one to leave the place to, who would take care of the ranch and horses as she would want them taken care of, he wondered. Would the state step in and take it all? And if they did, what could he do about it? Nothing. What was it his attorney had told him when he was telling him why a Will was important? "If you don't have something witnessed by an attorney or judge or someone of authority describing what you want done, all your money and property will wind up in what's called probate and eventually owned by the state to do with whatever they see fit.

If the thought of the state taking everything he owned and had worked hard for hadn't scared him at the time, it did now.

Every time he went to see her it seemed unreal for her to just lay there, unmoving. It was as if she was alive and dead at the same time. With the doctor's help they would roll her over and he would rub her back and legs to help the circulation. The doctor told him this was important to her health and would hopefully help her to wake up sooner.

While he was rubbing her back, Clay realized he missed her smile and laughter. He even missed having to get her out of trouble from time to time. He wasn't much on praying or asking for help but he silently prayed she would come through this and wake up and be the sassy, spitfire Loralie he knew and had come to care a lot for.

There was no visible moon or stars, only the night as Clay sat staring out of the window of his private train car at nothing but blackness. He was trying, once again, to unravel this turn of events. Ol' Son was lying next to him with his chin on Clay's lap. As Clay sat there, scratching Ol' Son's neck and ears, a thought crept into his mind - what if she continued to stay alive, but stayed in this coma state and never woke up? How long could a person exist in a coma, just lying there with no activity? Was that why the doctor insisted on the rubdowns? It didn't seem feasible that a person in her condition could last very long without moving around at least once in a while, but since he had no real knowledge on the subject, he was at a loss over what to do.

Clay suddenly broke out in a cold sweat and his hands began to tremble. Ol' Son looked up at his master and made a low whining noise.

As the sun came inching its way over the top of the mountain, Clay was still staring out of the window; no closer to an answer about what to do than he had been last night. With so many unanswered questions he was becoming more and more restless and irritable. Not only did he worry about Loralie and whether she would survive or not, but also the reason he had come out here in the first place - the rustlers.

On his first trip alone up to Loralie's ranch, Clay rode around looking for recent tracks and only found ones that were old. He tried following them, but just like the sheriff had said, once he got inside the forest, they disappeared. Whoever these rustlers were, they knew their business.

Next, Clay rounded up all of her horses from the pasture and put them in the barn and corrals, hoping they would be safer there. With no idea of how many horses there should be, he took a count of the ones he brought in and had to admit, the rustlers had good taste. Loralie was raising some high-quality stock. He thought the wild horses that he rounded up back in Texas might fit right in. He would talk to her about it when she was on her feet, again.

Each morning, after checking on Loralie, Clay would ride up to her ranch to feed and water the horses and count to make sure none had been stolen during his absence. Once he was sure everything was as it was supposed to be, he hurried back to Cinch Mountain so he could spend the rest of the afternoon sitting with Loralie, hoping the rustlers wouldn't come back while he was gone – but in case they did, he had spent an entire day setting little traps of their passing over a five mile radius from the ranch.

Before going up to Loralie's ranch that first day, Clay had had a conversation with the sheriff who couldn't provide any more information than he already knew. The sheriff told him the tracks led into the forest, then just up and disappeared. At the end of their conversation he admitted he wasn't the best of trackers to begin with. He was from Chicago originally and his time in Dodge was mostly arresting drunks. "I'm just a local sheriff and Loralie's ranch is several miles beyond my jurisdiction," he said. "I was a deputy over in Dodge and know the law pretty well, but I'm a town policeman."

The sheriff apologized for not being able to shed more light on the subject. "Like most everybody in town, I like Loralie. She's a very independent woman who has worked her tail off to make the ranch one of the best in this part of the woods. I feel really bad about what happened to her and I hope you find the ones who did this to her."

Clay nodded his head. "I'll be making that my primary concern."

"And I'll make sure I keep accommodations available to house them when you bring them in," the sheriff said with a grin.

When Clay made no comment, the sheriff looked at him and asked, "You will bring them in, won't you?"

Clay let out a breath of air and said, "I'm sure hoping so, but in the end, I guess that will depend on them. If they show up again, I will track them down."

Clay stood up and shook hands with the sheriff and said, "Thanks," then turned and walked out the door, leaving the sheriff staring at his back.

Keeping the horses pinned up near the ranch house provided Clay an easier way to keep track of the animals, but he wasn't sure whether this was the best plan. Bunched together like this might make it easier to keep an eye on them, than out on the pasture where they could be stolen in small groups without being seen, which might take days or weeks to be discovered. But, if the rustlers came and he wasn't around, they could steal them all at one time without much trouble.

On the other hand, with the horses penned up together near the house, Clay figured it might make the rustlers somewhat more wary – or at least he hoped so.

Clay was having trouble landing his mind on a decent plan. Pro and con thoughts raced through his mind like leaves in a hurricane. It was a quandary.

With the horses penned up all together, the rustlers could scout the place and when they saw no one was there to stop them, they could take them all in one fell swoop. The idea of hiring someone to stay up here and keep an eye out for the rustlers was appealing, but in Loralie's way of thinking, not knowing what kind of men the rustlers were, Clay didn't want to put anyone's life in jeopardy. Risking his own life was one thing, but risking the life of some cowboy just needing some money was altogether different. Although, he knew his own men back in Texas had picked up a gun on more than one occasion; but that was because they rode for the brand. Maybe he would talk to Hank about it.

The biggest problem the rustlers would have, would be covering up their tracks - along with disturbing the small telltale signs he'd set up. That many horses would leave a trail an amateur could follow.

On his way back down the mountain, Clay was no closer to a decision than when he first started thinking about it. He couldn't stay awake twenty-four hours a day, and he couldn't go without some rest any more than he could be in two places at the same time.

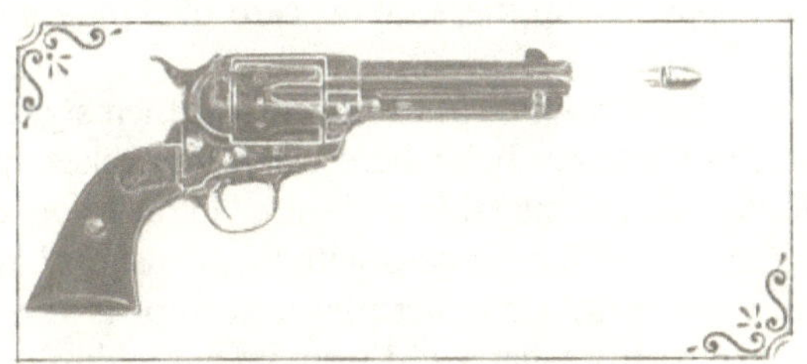

CHAPTER EIGHT

-

On the seventh day, during their breakfast, Clay related his concerns to Hank about Loralie's health. "It's been a week now and I'm really getting worried. I've heard head wounds like that can cause a lot of damage and the longer she stays in that coma, the stronger her chances are of not pulling out of it. I just can't understand why she hasn't woke up yet. I tell you, Hank, this whole thing has me staying awake at night. What if she never wakes up?"

Hank nodded his head in agreement. He too was concerned but at the moment he knew there was nothing he or anyone else could do. "I'm as concerned as you are, but like the doc says, there ain't nuthin' we can do but wait - and I try not ta think too hard on things while I'm eatin'."

"I feel like I should be out at her ranch watching over the place, but I don't want to leave her alone until I know more about how she's doing," Clay said, taking a bite of his egg.

Hank wiped his mouth on the napkin provided, took a drink of coffee, then looked at Clay and said, "I know what you mean. Like I said, I'm worried about her too. But as the doc says, there ain't nothin' we can do until she decides ta wake up. And with that bein' the way things are, I think you should head on back up the mountain and keep an eye on her place. If they come in and steal all her horses while you're down here worrin' about her, she'll be out of business and ah site disappointed with you. If you're not here when she wakes up, she'll be happy yer up there takin' care of things and I'll come up and get ya."

Clay nodded and took a sip of his coffee, then sighed. "I know you're right. I just hate not being here when she wakes up."

Hank looked across the table and said, "Didn't you say she sent you ah telegram askin' for yer help with them rustlers? Well now, it appears ta me, you bein' up ta her place, keepin' it safe from them horse stealers is exactly what she'd want ya ta do, don'tcha think?"

Clay smiled at Hank. For a man who had very little schooling and spoke like a hillbilly, he sure seemed to have a good insight about things. "You're right. That's exactly what she would want me to do. I guess I've been a bit blindsided by her being in that coma."

Hank said, "You go tell her what yer gonna do and I'll see ta gettin' Midnight saddled."

The doctor looked up when Clay entered the office and shook his head. "No change."

Clay told the doctor what he was going to do and asked if he could see her before he left.

"Sure, sure. Go on in," the doctor said, gesturing toward the other room. "I think I'll slip down to the restaurant and get a bite to eat while you're here."

Clay nodded and headed for the room where Loralie had been for the past week.

Just inside the room, Clay stopped and looked at Loralie. In her sleep like state she was beautiful. Her red hair was spread out across the pillow where her head rested and her face had an angelic look to it. Her breathing seemed to be regular and smooth. Laying there like that she was a far different woman from the one who would stand up and shoot it out with outlaws.

Clay walked over and took her hand and began telling her his plans.

From somewhere deep in her brain, Loralie heard that familiar voice again. Who it was, she wasn't sure but somehow she knew something was wrong. Why was the voice telling her to wake up? Suddenly, Loralie could see a bright light, but when she looked around, she was deep underwater – just floating there in limbo. How she got in the water in the first place, she had no idea, but she knew she had to get to the surface somehow, or she would drown. She tried raising her arms but they felt like huge weights and would not move. Frightened, she began trying to kick her feet to push herself upward. At first, it was almost beyond her strength. Frustrated at the slowness, Loralie drew on all of her willpower and strength. Raising her arms, she began to swim harder, her arms aching with the pull against the force that kept trying to drag her back down.

As the light drew nearer, her strength was waning and she wasn't sure she could make it. Her lungs were screaming for air – then with a jerk her head was above the water and she could breathe. Her eyes looked upward and she saw a man holding her hand. He had a sad look on his face as though he was about to cry.

Loralie yanked her hand out of his and sat up – her eyes wide with fright. She looked around the room, then back to the man and asked, "Who are you and where am I?"

"Doc!" Clay yelled, not knowing what else to do.

The doctor had just walked back into his office when he heard Clay yell, and came running into the room.

Loralie looked at the doctor and asked, "And who are you?" Then before the doctor could say anything, she looked at the bed she was sitting on and with a questionable look on her face, she asked, "What is this place and what am I doing here?"

Clay stepped back to allow the doctor to approach her.

"I'm Doctor Roswell. Do you not know who I am?"

Loralie stared at the doctor for a long time, then shook her head. "No. Am I supposed to?" she asked.

"Well, yes. At least I would hope you would. We've been friends for a good many years."

Loralie looked hard at the doctor, trying to recognize him, but finally shook her head. "I'm sorry."

"What about this man?" the doctor said, pointing at Clay. "Do you recognize him?"

Loralie looked at Clay and studied him from head to toe, admitting to herself he was a good-looking man, but then shook her head. "Sorry, no, I don't."

Then with a questioning look in her eyes, she said, "Now that I think about it, I don't even know who I am. How can it be that ah body don't even know who they are?"

"Amnesia," the doctor said. Happens in cases like this sometimes. People with head traumas sometimes lose their memories."

"Head trauma? Amnesia? I ain't got no idea what you're talkin' bout." Loralie said reaching up and finding a sore spot on the top of her head.

"Is this a permanent thing, Doc?" Clay asked the doctor who stood, studying Loralie.

The doctor looked at the floor, then back up to Clay. "Sometimes it is and sometimes it isn't. No way to tell. We just have to wait and see what happens." The doctor shook his head in disgust at his lack of knowledge on the subject of amnesia. "I wish I knew more but I don't. I'm told there are some doctors in the big cities like New York and such that are devoting their time to this amnesia thing, but I don't know if they are any closer to understanding it than us back woods doctors are."

"Are you telling me I might never know who I am?" Loralie asked with a panicked look on her face.

"No, that's not what I'm saying. Not at all," the doctor said, shaking his head again. "What I'm saying is, I don't know enough to give you the answers you're looking for. What I do know is, we can sometimes help people get their memories back by giving you information about yourself to help you remember. They say that helps; at least most of the time. And since everyone around here knows who you are and what your past has been, maybe what we know will be enough to jog your brain enough to restore your memory."

"Isn't there anything else we can do?" Clay asked - the look on his face showing real concern.

"Yeah, Doc. I can't go through the rest of my life not knowin' who, I mean, knowing who I am if this brain joggin', I mean, jogging thing doesn't work."

Loralie got a questioning look on her face. Why had she corrected herself?

The doctor also caught what she was doing and wondered about it. Loralie didn't have much in the way of schooling and as far back as he could remember, she spoke like most of the people around here, so why was she correcting herself? Maybe he would speak to the schoolteacher to see if she knew anything, just as soon as she got back from visiting her mother in Charleston, South Carolina. In the meantime, he needed to answer Loralie's question.

"Yes, there are things we can do. First and foremost, rest seems to help a person's body repair itself. Then, like I said before, talking to you about who you are, along with taking you to familiar places will sometimes jog the memory. There may have been a little brain swelling which might be causing the problem. When that goes down like I think it already has, and is why you woke up, with more rest, I think your memory should come back."

"Are there cases where folks never remember?" Loralie asked.

The doctor thought for a moment, then said, "Yes, but from what little I know about amnesia, those are rare cases. Don't concern yourself with negative thoughts. In my opinion, they are a distraction from what we want to accomplish. Concentrate on positive things like looking at people and places. Try to gain even a small remembrance about anything you can.

"I see," Loralie said, then asked, "What happened to me? Why am I here?"

The doctor smiled and said, "That's a good sign. Yes, that's a good place to start."

Just then, Hank came into the room, saying, "What's wrong? I got Midnight saddled and ready ta..."

Hank stopped dead in his tracks and stared at Loralie, who was staring back at him.

"Loralie, you're finally awake!"

Loralie looked confused and asked, "Is that my name, Loralie? And do I know you?"

Hank looked at her and said, "Of course that's yer name. Loralie Benson. And of course, we know each other. We've been friends since you was just ah young'n. What's the matter, cain't ya remember nuthin'?"

Hank looked at the doctor and said, "What's goin' on, Doc? Why's she lookin' at us like we're strangers err somethin'?"

Before answering Hank's questions, the doctor filled and lit his briar pipe and got it going good, then motioned for Hank to sit down in a nearby chair.

After explaining to Hank about the amnesia, the doctor turned to Loralie and said, "I suppose I should explain what happened to you and we can answer any questions you might have. Hopefully that will trigger a response and help your memory return."

Loralie nodded her head, then said, "As much as I want ta hear, I mean, I do want to hear what happened, do you suppose I could get sometin', I mean, something to eat. Why do I keep correcting myself, Doctor?"

"The doctor chuckled and said, "All in due time, my dear, all in due time. You, my dear, are absolutely right. The first thing we need to do is get something in your stomach, but we need to go slow at first – nothing heavy." He'd been giving her water, but this would be the first food.

Loralie frowned. Right at this moment she was hungry enough to eat a horse. A horse? Something about the word horse triggered a spark in her mind, but she couldn't pin it down.

Hank said, "You tell me what ta get and I'll go down ta the restaurant and get it."

The doctor nodded his head and said, "Oatmeal, milk and coffee, maybe a slice of bread with butter. Thank you, Hank."

Hank said, "I'll be right back," and hurried from the room.

The doctor turned to Loralie and said, "And when he gets back, I'll start filling in all the empty places while you eat, but until then, you need to lay back down and get a little rest."

At first, Loralie started to protest. She wasn't sure how long she'd been asleep but from the way her stomach growled, she guessed it must have been some time. Her mind was whirling with curiosity, but suddenly she felt very tired and did as the doctor said, then bolted back upright and motioned for the doctor to come closer.

When the doctor leaned in close, Loralie whispered, "I need ta use the facility."

Now that Loralie was awake, Clay decided there wasn't much need for him staying here in town. Except for the memory thing, she was all right and he was needed elsewhere. With the doctor's encouragement, Clay decided to go up to Loralie's ranch and make sure everything was as it was supposed to be. Hank could answer any questions she might have, as well as he could - probably better.

The doctor thought that would be a good idea and promised to explain to Loralie who he was and why he was here. If everything was still the same up at her ranch, maybe he could hire someone to keep an eye on the place so he could spend more time helping Loralie get her memory back.

CHAPTER NINE

-

Wolf, Bullfrog and Lives in The Woods, sat staring across the empty pasture where they expected to steal six horses.

"Where are all the horses?" Bullfrog asked, scratching the back of his neck.

"Either she has sold them all so we can steal no more, or she has taken them to the barn and corrals near her house for protection," Wolf declared.

"Does that mean she is not dead and might shoot us if we try to steal her horses from there?" Bullfrog asked, feeling a constriction in his throat.

"Maybe she is dead and someone else brought the horses to the barn and corrals to sell them," Lives in The Woods suggested.

As the three young Cherokee braves sat their ponies, pondering the situation, Wolf spoke up. "We will not know the answer to any of these questions until we go check for ourselves.

Clay was sitting at the kitchen table in Loralie's house, eating bacon, eggs and hardtack biscuits when Ol' Son stood up from where he was laying and began to growl. Clay looked over at him and saw a ridge of hair on Ol' Son's back, standing straight up. Just then, he heard the nickering of the horses in the corrals.

Clay stood up and headed for the door, grabbing the rifle standing there as he passed through.

Someone was attempting to open the back gate but because of the horses moving around, he couldn't get a clear shot at the person, so he fired into the air.

Whoever it was stopped and ran for the woods. Clay raised his rifle to his shoulder, but the sun was in his eyes and, once again, he couldn't get a clear shot, so he fired in the general direction.

Bullfrog heard the rifle shot and thought it was the woman trying to kill him. With the fear of dying welling up inside him, he turned and ran for the trees where his two friends were waiting.

The second shot missed Bullfrog's head by mere inches and lodged itself in the tree he was running past, causing him to swerve and get slapped in the face by a low hanging limb. Undaunted, Bullfrog leaped onto his pony and the three of them raced away as fast as their horses could run back through the dense forest and hopefully, to safety.

In their haste, they had to try and ward off small limbs and got struck on the arms, chest and face, leaving large, stinging welts.

When they finally reached the open place where the horses had been pastured, they raced for the other side where they could hide.

On the far side of the pasture, the three young braves pulled up and looked back to see if anyone was following them, but saw nothing but limbs moving slightly from the steady breeze blowing through the forest.

"That was too close," Bullfrog exclaimed. "I guess she is still alive and able to shoot."

"It was not the woman," Wolf said. "It was a man, and he had a dog with him."

Lives in The Woods looked back across the pasture and said, "And here comes the dog!"

Just then, Ol' Son came running out of the forest on the far side of the pasture and headed their way, barking at the top of his lungs, followed by a man on a black horse. Both the dog and the horse began running full out as soon as they reached the open pasture.

"Ride like the wind!" Wolf yelled.

If there was one thing the three young Cherokee braves were good at, it was riding. They made the most of everything their horses had to give, weaving in and out among the trees until they reached another clearing where they separated and each rode in a different direction.

"We will meet by the gully on the far side of the mountain!" Wolf yelled as he turned his horse off to the left. Lives in The Woods rode to the right and Bullfrog raced off across the clearing in front of him.

When Clay and Ol' Son rode into the clearing, Clay hauled up. "Whoa, big fella', he said to the black stallion, who wanted to keep running.

The black stallion came to a stop and Ol' Son, who was a short distance in front of them, stopped and began sniffing the ground, running first one direction, then another, trying to decide which scent to follow.

Clay whistled and Ol' Son stopped what he was doing, and looked back at Clay, then turned and ran back to where his master sat on the big horse.

"Looks like they split up on us, Ol' Son," Clay said, taking his hat off and wiping his forehead on his shirtsleeve. "Com 'on, let's go back," he said, pulling on the rein, turning the black stallion back in the direction of the ranch.

Far to the left, in amongst the trees, Wolf stood peering from behind a large chestnut tree. He gave a sigh of relief when he saw the white man and dog turn and go back toward the woman's ranch.

Once Wolf was sure they were no longer chasing them, he mounted his horse and headed toward the gully where he hoped his friends would be waiting. As he rode, his mind raced, wondering what they could do next to get the six horses they were supposed to steal. The white men down in Ashville would not listen to excuses. If they did not return with six horses, all stolen from this woman's ranch, and no other, bad things would happen to their families, of that he was sure. And on top of everything else, they had already wasted a lot of time they didn't have to waste.

As Wolf rode to meet with his friends, he tried as hard as he could to come up with a new plan, one that would allow them to steal the horses and save their families, but none of the things that came to mind seemed worth trying. He could only hope that Bullfrog or Lives in The Woods could think of a way.

-

Lives in The Woods came riding out of the trees after using all the skills his father had taught him about losing people who were following you, and smiled.

Bullfrog was sitting on his pony near the gully and when he saw Lives in The Woods, he smiled and waved.

At Lives in The Woods suggestion, they rode back into the forest to wait for Wolf. Neither of them had heard any more gunfire and hoped that Wolf would soon show up.

Bullfrog and Lives in The Woods were sitting on their horses inside the edge of the forest, watching the gully, when they heard a deep voice come from behind them.

"Put your hands in the air or I will shoot you where you sit."

Slowly the two young Cherokee braves raised their hands in the air, then spun their heads around when they heard the uproarious laughter.

"Ha, ha, ha. You should see the look on your faces!" Wolf yelled, riding up next to his friends.

"That was not funny," Bullfrog spat at Wolf. "I almost had a heart attack. I could see my life flashing through my brain."

Wolf slapped his friend on the shoulder and said, "Oh it couldn't have been that bad. Besides, I couldn't help myself. You were both staring so hard at the gully, an army with bells on their horses could have ridden up on you."

Embarrassed, Lives in The Woods shook his head. "If there is a next time, I will be more alert."

They made camp down in the gully where their fire could not be readily seen and made tea from ginseng, they carried with them. Sitting next to the fire, they drank tea and ate pemmican as Wolf told them about the man and the dog, and their returning to the ranch. "I believe we are safe for the time being, but I think we should not stay anywhere for very long. Besides we are already behind our schedule. We need to steal six horses and get back before the white men start hurting our families.

"Do you think the woman is still alive?" Bullfrog asked.

"I do not know if the woman is still alive, but now there is also a man and a dog we will have to deal with," Wolf told him, matter of factly.

Bullfrog nodded his head, then said, "It is the dog that I am worried about. Dogs can sense things long before man does. We must somehow get rid of the dog."

Both Wolf and Lives in The Woods agreed, but neither had any suggestions on how to go about it.

"Maybe we can cause a distraction that will get rid of both the man and the dog long enough for us to steal the horses," Bullfrog said as though he'd just had a revelation.

"What kind of distraction? And who is going to cause this distraction?" Wolf asked.

Bullfrog shrugged his shoulders and said, "I do not have that part worked out yet. It was just a thought."

The moon was directly overhead when Wolf put more fuel on the fire, then rolled up in his blanket hoping he could get some sleep.

A short time later, after tossing and turning, Wolf climbed to his feet, pulling the blanket around his shoulders. He walked a short distance away from the firelight and peered up over the edge of the gully. The forest was dark with no sign of movement except for a small rabbit who hopped from one place to another, nibbling on the grass.

Wolf was awake. His mind was a hurricane of thoughts, wondering how they had gotten themselves into this predicament. It was the need for the white man's money and the men who told them the job would be easy and they would never be in any danger.

Wolf studied the stars and wondered if people lived up there somewhere – people like him and the white people. And if they did, did they have the same kind of problems as he did? Along with those thoughts, Wolf wondered if the man who shot at them had gotten a good look at them? Did he know they were Cherokee braves? And if he did, would he go to the tribal chief?

After more than an hour of pacing around, Wolf still did not have a plan for stealing the six horses the white men wanted, but came to one conclusion that he would need to speak to his friends about come morning.

Satisfied he could do no more, Wolf wrapped himself in his blanket and closed his eyes once again, morning would come soon.

Lives in The Woods gave a sigh when Wolf returned to his blanket. He had also been awake and had watched as his friend left his bed to go wandering around the night.

Tugging his blanket up under his chin, Lives in The Woods grinned and whispered to himself, "I think we will talk in the morning about the plan Wolf has come up with."

Satisfied things would look better in the morning, he closed his eyes for some much-needed rest.

-

The young Indian braves were not the only ones awake late into the night. Clay had also been out wandering around under the same stars, thinking about the situation.

The rustlers had come to the barn to get the rest of the horses in broad daylight, which meant they thought Loralie to be dead or at least wounded to the point where she would be of no threat.

It had all happened so fast – Ol' Son alerting him, rushing to the door, and the sun in his eyes so he could not get a good look at them or get off a decent shot.

By the time the moon was on the far side of midnight, Clay decided wandering around in the dark checking to make sure they hadn't come back was doing him no good. He was tired and having trouble keeping his eyes open. "Whata' 'ya say we sleep in the barn?" he said, reaching down and patting Ol' Son on the head. "That way, if they do come back, we'll be ready for them."

Ol' Son wagged his tail and followed Clay into the barn, where he found some fresh hay to curl up on and was soon sound asleep.

Clay looked at Ol' Son and wished he could go to sleep as easily.

Clay checked his rifle to make sure it was loaded, then leaned it against the wall next to the doorway that was also close to the corral gate. Next, he checked his pistol and laid it down next to his bedroll so that it was within easy reach. He pulled his blanket over himself and closed his eyes, hoping he could get some rest. After taking a deep breath, he vacated his mind of all his worries and like Ol' Son, was soon, sound asleep.

At the sound of his master's snoring Ol' Son opened one eye, then stood up and walked over close to Clay and curled up next to him.

CHAPTER TEN

-

Everyone in the town of Cinch Mountain had gone to bed hours ago – everyone except Loralie Benson. As she stood next to the window in the doctor's office, looking out at the town, she smiled. They had all been so nice, bringing food and coming in to say something to her about how they knew each other and wishing her a speedy recovery.

She'd tried to get some sleep but she was restless and couldn't get her mind to relax. Along with that and the doctor's loud snoring, she decided to get up and walk around. After pacing around the room and staring out of the window, Loralie walked out onto the second-floor staircase landing just outside the doctor's office front door.

Loralie put her hands on the railing and looked up at the same stars Clay and Wolf had looked at. "Who am I and why can't I remember anything?" she said to the night. The moon and stars shined down on her, but gave no answer.

She reached up and gently touched the bump on the top of her head, which by now was only slightly tender. The doctor had taken the stitches out and said it was healing fine. He said there would be a scar, but her hair would cover it.

Once again Loralie looked at the heavens and marveled at the vastness of it all. "They say my name is Loralie Benson and I own a horse ranch up on the side of the mountain. They say I raise a breed of horses called, Tennessee Walkers - whatever that is. They say I've lived here in Tennessee all my life and that fella, Clay Brentwood, and I are... good friends. They say I sent him ah telegram askin', I mean, asking him ta, I mean, to come all the way from Texas out here to Tennessee to help me with some rustlers who've been stealin, I mean, stealing my horses. Why do I keep correcting myself and what kind of friendship does me and that fella have? He shore,, I mean, sure is a good-looking man, I'll give him that, but why would he come all this way if we weren't more than just friends?" A sudden thought raced through her brain like a shooting star. "What if he came because we're kin, she asked herself, hoping that wasn't the case."

Loralie stomped her foot on the landing and gave out with a loud, "Aggugh! Why can't I remember things?"

"Having trouble sleeping are you?" the doctor asked, stepping out onto the landing.

Loralie jumped like she'd been shot and her fists came up, ready to defend herself.

"Whoa, hold on there, missy I didn't mean to scare you."

When Loralie realized who it was, she relaxed. "I'm sorry. I don't know why I reacted the way I did."

The doctor grinned and ran his hand over his face, then said, "Because you're Loralie Benson - that's why. You've always been a strong young woman, a strong young girl who has had to fight for most everything you've ever gotten. How about a cup of coffee? I know I sure would like one."

"Why not," Loralie said. "I can't sleep anyway."

Over coffee and some stale cinnamon rolls left over from yesterday, the doctor filled Loralie in with a few more details about her life.

"Maybe you can remember your folks. Your pa was one of the best horse trainers I ever saw, and you're just as good."

"What were my folks like?" Loralie asked, trying to picture them in her mind, but couldn't seem to conjure up an image.

The doctor thought for a moment, then said, "Your mother was a sweet, kind woman who could drop an Indian at two hundred yards with one shot. She was also one of the most sought-after dance partners at the hoedowns. You look a lot like her you know. She was considered one of the prettiest women in these parts. Why she ever took up with your pa is still a mystery to almost everyone who knew them."

"Was there somethin', I mean, something wrong with my pa?" Loralie asked with a lot of concern in her voice.

The doctor grinned as he filled his pipe and lit it. "Your father was quite a man. He loved those mountains. There wasn't a finer hunter or trapper, or shot, anywhere around these parts that I know of; and he trained you to be just like him. You were the son he never had, along with the finest daughter a man could ever ask for. Your father was a stand-up man. If he told you something, you could be sure it was gospel. And he loved your mother something fierce. But your father also liked his moonshine and a good fight once in a while – while your mother was a god-fearing woman who I'm told, read her bible every day. They were as different as night and day but they somehow made it work."

"Where are they now?" Loralie asked.

The doctor puffed on his pipe for a minute or so while he stared at his feet, blowing smoke toward the floor before he spoke. "Maybe the answer will help you remember, so here it is. They're dead. Silas Mullins and his bunch killed them or so everyone believes. Silas wanted your land for the timber, but your pa said no and one day while you were out hunting, Silas and his bunch raided the place killed your mother and father. When you learned of it, you went to war against him, but there were too many of them for you to fight alone. You tried to get help from the sheriff but as it turned out, he was in cahoots with the Mullins. That's when that ranger, Clay Brentwood, showed up out of the blue and went up to help you. Silas and all but two of his boys were killed in the shootout. Both you and Mister Brentwood were wounded, but nothing serious."

The doctor took a sip of coffee and looked Loralie in the eyes for any kind of response, but saw none. "Does any of what I've just told you stir up any memories? Anything at all?"

Loralie sat there as little pictures of things jumped in and out of her mind. "I don't know. I see fleeting images but none of them are very clear. Tell me more about this Clay fella. If he's from Texas, how did I meet him and why did he suddenly show up here?"

The doctor grinned. "You'd best ask Hank about him. He knows him way better than I do. Or better yet, ask Mister Brentwood."

"Hank. Is that the man who brought me food? The man that owns the livery?" Loralie asked.

"That would be him. Hank runs the livery barn and blacksmith shop down at the edge of town. He's been a good friend of your family for years. Used to go hunting and fishing with your pa. If anyone can tell you about Mister Brentwood, Hank can, but like I said, if it was me, I would go straight to the horse's mouth – Mister Brentwood, himself."

Loralie looked around. "It's too bad it's the middle of the night. I sure would like ta talk to both of them."

As an afterthought, Loralie looked at the doctor and asked, "Where do you think this man Clay Brentwood is right now? Is he still here in town and do you think he'll come around in the morning so I can ask him some questions?"

The doctor shook his head from side to side and began to chuckle, "I don't know for sure exactly where Mister Brentwood is right now, but I think he may be up at your ranch checking to make sure no more horses have been stolen. Maybe he'll come back sometime tomorrow and then you can ask him all the questions you want."

After another minute's worth of thinking, the doctor smiled at Loralie and said, "Maybe you asking questions will work just as well or maybe better than us trying to feed you information that may or may not work."

Loralie looked at the doctor and wondered what he meant by that but decided to wait and see if this Mister Brentwood came back to town.

After taking a deep breath, the doctor said, "I don't know exactly what time he'll be here, but I'm confident Mister Brentwood will come by to check on you. He and Hank are the ones who brought you in. Mister Brentwood hasn't missed a day sitting with you, holding your hand and talking to you to try and get you to wake up. Spent a few nights here as well. Yes, I'm sure he'll be here, especially now that you're awake."

Loralie let this information sink in and roll around in her brain, hoping it would stimulate some jolt to her memory. During the time she was unconscious she sort of remembered someone talking to her and thought at the time she should know who it was, but then she would slip back into the darkness.

The doctor lifted his watch off the table and held it up to the lamp. "Three o'clock. I think we should try and get some rest. We've both had a long day."

Loralie nodded her head in agreement and stood up. "I'm not sure I can get back to sleep since I understand that I slept for several days, but I'll try. You go ahead and get some sleep and we'll see each other again after the sun comes up."

The doctor smiled and patted her on the shoulder and said, "Do try and get some rest. There will plenty of time tomorrow for you to ask all the questions you want, but you'll need to be rested and clear headed." With that, the doctor turned and headed for his bed. He was too old to be up traipsing around in the middle of the night.

CHAPTER ELEVEN

Wolf was already up and rebuilding the cooking fire when the other two rolled out of their blankets. After seeing to their morning necessities, Bullfrog put on some tea to boil, while Lives in The Woods went hunting.

Shortly, Lives in The Woods came walking back into the camp carrying three good-sized rabbits. "I set six traps last night, but only three of them worked," Lives in The Woods said with a grin.

"At least we will have a rabbit apiece to go with our tea," Bullfrog stated as he rubbed his stomach.

Over breakfast, Wolf told his friends his concerns about going back for another try at stealing six of the woman's horses. "We cannot just ride in there and open the gate and drive out the horses we need, not as long as that man and his dog are there."

Both Bullfrog and Lives in The Woods nodded their heads in agreement.

Seeing their heads nod, Wolf continued. "Also, we have no weapons to fight back with and I for one do not want to shoot anyone, nor do I want any of us to get shot. So, if we do go back, we must be very careful. We must use great cunning and we cannot let ourselves be recognized."

When Wolf saw the questionable looks on their faces he said, "Think about what can happen if we are recognized and that man goes to our tribal chief."

Bullfrog was the first one to respond. "We would dishonor not only our families, but the tribe as well and we could be asked to leave."

"And what would happen to our families then?" Bullfrog asked.

"They would not be allowed to speak to us. To them we would be dead," Wolf said matter of factly. "Which leaves us only one option."

"And what option is that?" Bullfrog asked. "We cannot go home empty handed. That would also put our families in danger," Bullfrog stated.

"I agree," Wolf said. "We cannot go back without six of the woman's horses, and we will not. This time we will plan carefully. There will be no mistakes."

As his two friends sat staring at him, Wolf looked at the sky for a moment, then said, "Do either of you have any ideas?"

Lives in The Woods wiped his mouth on the sleeve of his shirt and said, "The only thing I can think of to do is steal them at night so no one can recognize us. I agree, we do not want the man going to the tribal chief."

But what if the man gets more men to help watch the horses, or the dog alerts them we are there, and what if they have guns and are waiting for us to try again?" Bullfrog asked.

Wolf raised his hands and said, "Like I said, we must be smarter than the white man this time," as a sly smile creased his face.

Lives in The Woods looked at Wolf and grinned. "What is running through that cunning mind of yours, my friend?"

-

As the sun came creeping over the horizon, Clay knew he couldn't keep this up much longer. He was having trouble waking up after not much more than an hour's sleep. He needed rest but knew as long as he was here at the ranch that would be impossible. The chance the rustlers would come back was almost a surety. Even though he trusted Midnight and Ol' Son to wake him up if somebody showed up, he still couldn't relax enough to get the rest he so badly needed. Every little noise woke him up instantly and with all the noises coming from the forest, he doubted he would get any sleep at all.

Clay stood up and stretched, then rubbed his tired eyes and stepped out through the door of the barn. He whirled and dove back inside as a bullet tore a hole in the door's framework, just inches from his head, followed by the sound of the rifle shot as it roared through the early morning air.

Ol' Son was standing to one side, growling and staring at the woods.

"Easy boy," Clay said, taking up his rifle and peeking around the lower part of the door frame, searching for someone to shoot at.

"Ya missed 'im," the taller of the two men standing behind trees just inside the forest said with malice in his voice. "All you shot was the doorframe."

"The sun got in my eyes. What about you? You didn't even take ah shot!" the other man hissed.

"I was waitin' ta see if'n you got him. No use wastin' ammunition if'n I don't hav'ta," the taller man said as if that cleared the air.

Both men watched the barn door for any glimpse of the man they were trying to kill, but saw no one. Patience was not one of their better suits.

Clay and Ol' Son had eased back away from the corral door and made their way to a side door on the opposite side of the barn. Without being noticed by the rustlers, they slipped into the forest, and once inside the trees, Clay made his way deeper into the forest, circling around to try and approach the rustlers from behind.

"See anybody?" the taller man asked as they watched the corral door.

"Nary ah soul. I got ah bad feelin' bout this," the shorter of the two men said after watching the barn for several more minutes and seeing no movement.

"Whoever he is, he sure made it convenient for us - him pennin' them horses up like that. We can take all of 'em onc't he's got rid of," the taller man said, spitting a stream of brown tobacco juice onto the ground.

"Yeah, well, we's got ta kill 'm first and I don't see nobody ta kill," the smaller man said staring intently toward the barn, sweat beginning to run down his forehead even though it was still early morning and cool.

The two men heard the low growl of a dog, then the voice of a man coming from their left. The two unmistakable sounds penetrated the morning air and made them freeze where they stood. "Stand real still and drop those rifles and you might live to see another day."

Clay had made his way around through the forest and came at them from the side instead of from behind. He had heard their conversation and knew it was the men who had shot at him.

The two men looked at each other and knew they'd been outsmarted, but being the breed they were, men raised in the mountains on violence, they both whirled and fired three quick shots apiece in the direction the voice had come from, then turned and ran off into the forest where their horses were waiting.

Clay had not expected this and as the two men turned and began firing their rifles, Clay dove to the ground and rolled over behind a tree for protection. When the shooting stopped, he looked for someone to fire at, but the space where they had been was empty.

"Damn," he said and jumped to his feet, following Ol' Son who was already running in the direction the two men had gone, barking loudly.

Even on three legs, Ol' Son quickly out distanced Clay and disappeared into the forest ahead of him.

Dodging tree limbs, Clay followed as best he could, trailing Ol' Son's barking. As he ran, his eyes searched for a glimpse of the two men. He hadn't gone far when he heard someone yell and then a painful yelp from Ol' Son.

Clay increased his speed, running hard toward where the yelling and yelping had come from - hoping Ol' Son hadn't been severely hurt, again.

Shortly, Clay saw Ol' Son laying down on his side. He was obviously in pain and having difficulty breathing.

When Clay got close, he could see the trampled grass where the men's horses had been tethered, but the men and horses were gone. In the distance he thought he heard the sound of horses running hard. Clay stood there, helpless. They were on horseback and he was afoot and by the time he could saddle Midnight and get back, they would be long gone. Besides, he had Ol' Son to worry about.

Clay dropped down on his knees and checked Ol' Son over but found no bloody spots anywhere. However, when he touched Ol' Son on the side, the dog looked up at him and flinched. Clay figured one of the men had kicked him or hit him in the ribs with the butt of his rifle. There was blood on Ol' Son's mouth, which told Clay he must have gotten his teeth into one of them.

After making sure there was no other damage to Ol' Son, Clay scratched his ears and said, "Good boy! You got a piece of one of them." Clay pulled off his shirt and tied it around Ol' Son's ribs to help take the pressure off enough for him to breathe easier. Clay walked back to the ranch house at a slow pace so Ol' Son could keep up. At first, he'd thought about carrying him, but guessed that would put even more pressure against his ribs. Walking would be slow, but easier.

Ol' Son stopped three different times to rest. Each time, Clay stopped with him.

Inside the ranch house, Clay put on a pot of water for coffee and dumped in a handful of grounds. While the coffee was brewing, Clay washed up in the kitchen sink, chuckling. Loralie had had the forethought to drill a well first, then build the house around the well, and placed it where it would be needed the most, next to the sink in the kitchen. The cold water helped wake him up some and he felt his stomach grumble. After looking around and finding a piece of cloth more suitable to wrap around Ol' Son's ribs than his shirt, Clay fixed bacon and eggs for both him and Ol' Son, hoping it would not be too painful for him to eat.

Over breakfast Clay talked to Ol' Son. "That was a good thing you did out there today, but you need to hang back a bit so we can face things together. What if one of them had shot you instead of just kicking you or hitting you? You didn't think about that did you?"

Ol' Son sat looking up at Clay as though he was hanging on every word his master had to say, his tail moving back and forth slowly.

Clay looked at Ol' Son and marveled at the dog's loyalty. They'd been through too much together to lose him now.

Clay reached down and picked up the empty tin plate Ol' Son had eaten his breakfast from and put it in the sink to be washed later, then retied the piece of cloth around Ol' Son's ribs to help relieve the pain and allow him to breathe easier – at least he hoped it would. It had worked for him a time or two, so why not Ol' Son.

While Clay finished his breakfast, Ol' Son stretched out on the opposite side from his bruised ribs and closed his eyes - listening as his master continued to talk. "I figure we run them two gents off at least for the day, so I'm thinking, after we feed and water the stock, we'll have time to go down to town and check on Loralie. Hopefully she'll have her memory back by the time we get there and know who I am. I want her to meet you and I think the two of you will get along just fine. Maybe I can talk to her and Hank about getting some help up here because I'll bet a donut to a biscuit those men will be back and they won't wait too long. For some reason they're anxious to get their hands on her horses."

The only part of Ol' Son that moved was his shallow breathing and the wagging his tail up and down slowly, making thumping noises on the floor.

"On second thought, with those bruised ribs of yours, maybe you should stay here and get some more rest – and maybe keep an eye on the place," Clay said, nodding his head up and down. "But just barking if somebody comes around – no chasing outlaws."

Ol' Son opened one eye and looked at Clay as though he was thinking about what had been said, then climbed to his feet and gave Clay a look that said he wasn't about to be left behind.

Clay studied Ol' Son for a minute then said, "If she does have her memory back, I have a hunch she'll want to come home so she can help protect her horses and this place herself instead of hiring somebody from town who might get hurt or killed."

Ol' Son turned his head slightly and looked at Clay as though he was thinking the same thing.

"So," Clay said as he took his plate, knife, fork and coffee cup over to the sink and pumped water over them then began washing them, "If that is the case, maybe I should take the buggy I saw in the barn. That way both of you can have an easy ride."

Ol' Son's tail wagging increased and Clay would swear he could see a smile on his face.

CHAPTER TWELVE

-

The two rustlers had just topped a small rise and saw the three Indian braves riding in their direction. The older of the two was sure they were well hidden and had not been seen by the young braves.

"You thinkin' what I'm thinkin'?" the tall man asked.

After spitting a stream of brown tobacco juice onto the ground, the shorter man studied the question for a moment, then asked, "Maybe, but just in case I ain't, just what is it yer ah thinkin'?"

The taller of the two men looked down at the approaching braves, then back at his brother. "I'm thinkin' you should go over on the side of the trail and find ah spot where's you cain't be seen. I'll find ah spot on this here other side and when them braves come ridin' past, we can throw a bit more fear into 'm – let 'm know we're ah keepin' an eye on 'm in case they screw up again. Let 'm know we changed our minds and want all her horses this time – the whole herd."

"And do we want all her horses this time? I thought we only wanted six," the shorter man said with a confused look on his face.

The taller man gave a sigh and looked up at the sky and whispered, "If 'n he wern't my flesh and blood..."

"What's that you said?" the shorter man asked.

"Never mind," the taller man said. "And ta answer yer question, yes we want all of her horses this time cause they're all bunched tagether and they'll be easy ta take. If we have all her horses she goes belly up, which is what we're tryin' ta do. She'll be broke and have ta sell the place and we can take the money from the sale of her horses ta buy her place through ah dealer fer practal nothin' thout her knowin' we's the ones who bought it til it's all said and done. Then we gloat cause we got the place all legal like, sorta, if'n ya don't include the horse stealin' part and buyin' the place with money thet was supposed ta be hers. It's brilliant even if'n I do say so, myself."

"But what about that feller and his dog? Are we gonna tell them Injuns bout him? What if he kills 'm?" the shorter man asked.

"If'n he kills them young bucks, so much the better. We can shoot him from inside the trees and they'll get blamed fer it... And when it's all over, we can take the horses at our leisure and nobody'll be the wiser," the tall man said.

-

Wolf pulled his horse to a stop and said, "Hold up."

Lives in The Woods and Bullfrog pulled their mounts to a halt and looked at him to see why he wanted to stop.

Wasting no words, Wolf said, "There are two men up ahead, in among the trees, and they just split up. There is one on each side of the trail and I think they are waiting for us to ride in between them."

Lives in The Woods looked at Bullfrog, then at Wolf. "Why do you think they did that? We're poor Indians and have no money. It would be stupid of them to try and rob us, we have nothing for them to steal."

"What about our horses. They might be planning to steal them," Bullfrog said.

"Or maybe they just don't like Indians and plan to shoot us as we ride by," Wolf said, causing his friends to look at him with fear building in their eyes.

Without waiting for his friends to start asking questions, Wolf said, Bullfrog, you come with me. Lives in The Woods, you go the other way. We will circle around behind them. I would like to get close enough to see what they're up to."

Lives in The Woods nodded his head, then turned his horse and headed in the opposite direction his two friends had just gone.

The shorter of the two men was becoming anxious when some time had gone by and the young Indian braves had not ridden past. He tried to look down the trail but he was hidden back in the trees and couldn't see anything. "Hey, Wilber," he whispered loudly. "See any sign of 'em?"

Wilber Mullins was the larger and older of the two brothers who had escaped the shootout with the Benson woman a few years back. Their pa and brothers had not been so lucky and had been killed. He'd bided his time to seek his revenge and when he learned she had a good paying horse ranch, he decided it was time to seek his just due.

"Samuel, you idiot, will you shut up! And no, I don't see 'm yet! Now jest be quiet and wait. They'll be along," he whispered back just as loudly as his brother had. "I swear you ain't got the patience of ah rattlesnake."

Samuel shrunk back a little from his brother's harsh words. Wilber was always lording it over him and he didn't like it, but there wasn't much he could do about it. Wilber was the oldest and biggest and probably the meanest man he knew, next to his pa, but their pa wasn't around to keep Wilber in line.

A few minutes later, Wilber felt the sweat run down his forehead and drip off the end of his nose. "They shoulda' been here by now," he said to himself. Just as he lifted his pistol from its holster and was about to move out closer to the trail, a voice behind him caused him to pull up.

"I wouldn't do that if I was you, Mister. I have a gun pointed at your back and at this distance I can't miss. Now drop your pistol on the ground very easy like and put your hands on top of your head, then yell across to your partner and tell him to do the same. He is also covered with a gun pointed at his back."

Wilber couldn't see the sweat covering Wolf's face but he could hear the nervousness in his voice and that gave him just the edge he needed. This was one of the young Indian boys, trying to be brave. He doubted if the boy's gun even had any bullets in it. Yes, he had the advantage because he knew who they were, but they didn't know who he was or that he was the one who hired them to steal the horses in the first place.

Without turning around, Wilber said over his shoulder, "I'm sure you don't want to die with an empty pistol in your hand. So, you are the one who will turn your horses around and face the other direction before I kill you and steal the horses myself."

Wolf was taken by surprise; it was the men who hired them. He recognized the man's voice, but what were they doing here? he wondered.

"Yell over to your friend and tell him to do the same, or you'll all die and your family will never hear from you again. Now be quick about it, I'm losing my patience," Wilber said in a commanding voice.

Bullfrog had already turned his horse around and had his hands in the air.

Wolf knew they were defeated and raised his hand to the side of his mouth and called out, "Lives in The Woods, stop and turn your horse around. These are the men who hired us and do not want to be seen. They will kill us if we do not do as they say."

Wilber Mullins turned his horse in their direction and saw they had done as he'd said. He then moved his horse a little deeper into the woods where he couldn't be seen. When he was satisfied, he yelled for his brother to instruct the other Indian boy to come across and join his friends.

In less than a minute, Lives in The Woods came riding slowly across the trail and into the woods on that side, followed by Samuel. Without looking anywhere but straight ahead, Lives in The Woods pulled his horse up next to his two friends and stopped.

When Samuel had joined him, Wilber spoke to the young braves. "I see you ain't got our horses yet. Why? You've had plenty a time."

Wolf sighed and told the men what had happened and that they were headed back with a new plan, which he revealed to them.

Wilber listened and gave their plan some thought. It had merit, but they needed to make a disturbance big enough to keep the man distracted while they stole not just six horses, but the entire herd.

Setting the haystack on fire wouldn't do the trick. They would know it was a diversion and let it burn. Saving the horses would be far more important than a pile of hay. No, the distraction would have to be strong enough to keep them busy while the horses were being stolen.

"You might think we'd jest sit back and wait fer ya ta bring us horses, but as you can see, we've been keepin' an eye on ya from the beginnin'," Wilber said making it sound like this was something they did all the time. "We do it jest in case you get in over yer heads. Whilst I think yer plan has some merit, I got ah better one. Things have changed and now we've decided we want the whole herd."

The three young braves looked at each other. Taking all the horses at one time was both exciting and dangerous. A herd that big would leave a trail a blind man could follow and what would happen if they got caught. Stealing horses was a hanging offense.

On the other hand, at ten dollars apiece, they could take a lot of money home to their families, plus keep a little back for themselves.

"What's the matter, cat got yer tongue?" Wilber yelled at them.

Wolf blew out a breath of air and said, "No sir. We just hadn't planned on stealing more than six horses. That was what you told us to do."

"Yeah, well, like I jest said, the plan has changed, so here's what we're gonna do."

The three young Cherokee braves listened to Wilber as he laid out his plan and gave them instructions on what he wanted them to do.

They looked at each other and wondered if they would still be alive when it was all over. It was clear they weren't given a choice.

"You go on ahead," Wilber instructed them. "We'll foller along behind."

The three young Cherokee horse rustles felt they had no choice but to do as they were instructed and rode out silently in the direction of Loralie's horse ranch.

CHAPTER THIRTEEN

-

Clay Brentwood pulled the buggy up in front of the blacksmith shop and stepped down. The buggy ride down the mountain had taken far too much time, giving him time to think about the rustlers. He wondered if they were watching from the trees and knew the place was deserted? Did they only want the horses or was there more to it than that? There were plenty of other ranches around the area that weren't being raided and he wondered why that was. In his way of thinking these raids weren't just about stealing the horses. To Clay, it meant someone might have a vendetta to settle with Loralie and wanted her out of the horse business - or any other business she might get into as far as that went.

He wondered, could it be another horse dealer? Possibly, he thought, but Clay's gut told him it was much more than that, although at the moment he couldn't see the whole picture - which disturbed him to no end.

And what about this amnesia thing? He was hopeful Loralie had gotten her memory back, but even if she had, would she be in any condition to do anything? Well, yes, he guessed she would be. As it was, she could get up and get around and talk to people. But not being able to remember anything about herself or her past - that had to be one of the most frustrating things he could think of. He suddenly remembered all the times he'd been struck or shot in the head and how lucky he'd been not to be in her condition.

Hank walked out to greet him and take the horse and buggy.

"Mornin'. Everthing alright up ta Loralie's place?" he asked with a grin.

Clay stepped down and handed Hank the reins. "Had a little trouble first off this morning with those rustlers. They shot at me, but only came close. Ol' Son and I ran them off, but in the process, Ol' Son got himself injured, again. When they took off, Ol' Son lit out after them and after sinking his teeth into one of them, somebody either kicked him in the ribs or hit him with the butt of his rifle. Either way, he needs to see a veterinarian. I think he might have some cracked or broken ribs."

Hank walked over and patted Ol' Son on the head. "Sorry ta hear that cause we ain't got no veterinarian here in Cinch Mountain. Closest one's down in Nashville, but now that I think about it, Loralie takes care of all her animals herself. She seems ta know a lot about that kinda stuff... Maybe she can help."

"She get her memory back, yet?" Clay asked, rubbing the back of his neck where he'd gotten a crick in it from sleeping on the barn floor.

"Not the last I heard. There's ah bunch of women has her over ta the restaurant having lunch as they call it and all of 'em talkin' ah mile ah minute tellin' her things they think is supposed ta help her get her memory back," Hank said as he led the horse into the barn and called for Midnight, who was standing at the back of the buggy.

Midnight shook his head up and down as he walked by Clay, and into the barn.

"Mind if I leave Ol' Son here while I go over to the doctor's office and see if he can look at Ol' Son?" Clay asked finally getting the kink rubbed out of his neck.

"Sure. I reckon he'll be just fine layin' there in the buggy," Hank hollered out from inside the barn.

Clay walked over and looked down at Ol' Son and said, "You stay here and I'll be back with the doctor quick as I can."

Clay could tell Ol' Son was in pain because he didn't try to get up. Instead, he just looked up at Clay and licked his hand as though he was saying thank you.

-

Loralie felt like yelling at the ladies and telling them to stop talking. She knew they meant well but enough was enough. Each one of them thought their information would be the kind that would help her regain her memory. But in their eagerness, they were all talking at the same time and Loralie couldn't understand what any of them were saying. All they were accomplishing was to confuse her even more.

Loralie glanced through the window and saw the man they called Clay Brentwood, walking in the direction of the doctor's office. She smiled. He was a good-looking man and she wondered if they were more than acquaintances? Why else would he have come all the way from... where did they say, Texas? Then it jolted her to realize she didn't know where Texas was, either. But from the way the doctor and Hank talked, it must be a long way from here. Hadn't someone said he came here on his own train? If he owned his own train, did that mean he was rich? Was she rich too? And finally, her head was filled with the worse thing she could think – were they related? There were so many blank spaces to fill.

Loralie stomped her foot against the floor in frustration. If she didn't get her memory back soon, she felt like she would go mad.

On an impulse, Loralie stood up and said, "Please excuse me ladies but I have some very important things ta, I mean, to attend to, so if you'll pardon me..."

As she stepped away from the table, she realized no one had heard a word she said. They were each one so wrapped up in what they were saying; none of them would even miss her for some time.

She walked out of the restaurant and looked around, then headed for the doctor's office.

-

Clay explained what happened and the doctor said, "I'm not an animal doctor per se, but since I'm the only doctor this side of Knoxville, I do on occasion treat a few of the animals hereabouts and I'm talking about both, the two and four-legged kind. He chuckled at his little pun as he picked up his medical bag and a roll of muslin, in case he might need it.

Just as they got to the door, Loralie walked in and looked at the bag in the doctor's hand. "Making a house call?" she asked.

Both Clay and the doctor lifted their hats and smiled at her. She is a striking woman, Clay thought to himself, wondering how she would react if she had her memory back. Would she rush over and throw her arms around his neck and kiss him? By the way she looked at him, he could see interest in her eyes and hoped that would be the case.

"Sort of," the doctor explained. "Seems there was a bit of trouble up at your ranch and Mister Brentwood's dog, Ol' Son, got himself injured during the fracas. Clay brought him down in your buggy, which is at Hank's livery. I was just headed that way to see if there was anything I could do to relieve his pain. Clay, here, thinks he may have a broken rib or two. Has there been any change in your situation? Did the ladies say anything that might have helped?" the doctor asked with a hopeful look on his face.

Loralie was shaken for a moment. Trouble at the ranch they said she owned was the last thing she expected to hear, and Mister Brentwood's dog getting hurt. She didn't even know he had a dog.

"No, no change," Loralie said, running her fingers through her hair and glancing at Clay.

"The ladies are trying a bit too hard, I'm afraid." She turned her attention to Clay and asked, "You say your dog was injured at my ranch? What kind of trouble was there?" Suddenly she changed her mind and said, "Oh, that's not important at the moment. We mustn't waste any more time talking about that. We need to go see about your dog."

The doctor and Clay both grinned as Loralie spun on her heel and left the doctor's office in a hurry and headed down the stairs, then turned in the direction of the livery stable.

Even though they were longer legged than Loralie, they had to set a fast pace to keep up with her.

At the livery Loralie climbed into the buggy and knelt down next to Ol' Son and began examining him. "You poor, dear dog. How could anyone be cruel to you," she said as she gently removed the bandage Clay had wrapped around Ol' Son's ribs.

Ol' Son looked up at her with loving eyes as she very lightly ran her fingers over his side and saw the reaction when she came in contact with a sore spot.

"I believe he only has a few bruised ribs, Doctor," Loralie said as the doctor and Clay came up next to the buggy.

"She's probably right," the doctor said, looking up at Clay. "She's more than likely the closest thing we have to having a veterinarian in this area."

The doctor climbed into the buggy to affirm Loralie's diagnosis while Clay stood nearby and watched.

"Yep, they're only bruised. With some rest and inactivity for a few days, he'll be fine," the doctor said. I'll rewrap his ribs with this muslin I brought to help him breathe easier and hopefully heal faster."

"Thanks, Doc. What do I owe you?" Clay asked as Hank walked up.

The doctor looked at Clay and grinned. "Fifty cents for the muslin," he said.

"Put it on my bill if you will, Doctor. After all, he got hurt defindin', I mean, defending my ranch," Loralie said with a deeply concerned look on her face.

Before Clay could object, Loralie looked at him and said, "I insist. Ya'll did say I have money, didn't you?"

"Of course, my dear," the doctor said with a smile.

Clay put two fingers to the brim of his hat as a thank you.

"How you doin, Loralie?" Hank asked, wiping his hands on his apron.

Turning to stare at Hank, she said, "Thanks fer, I mean, thank you for asking. My head is less sore every day, but as far as my memory goes, I still can't remember anything."

Hank turned to the doctor who had just finished wrapping Ol' Son's ribs and was in the process of climbing down from the buggy. "You think if she goes home it might help her memory come back? You know, seein' familiar things."

Before the doctor could answer, Clay said, "I'm not sure that's such a good idea. I do, however, agree that seeing familiar things might speed up the process, but right now it might be too dangerous for her to be up there with the threat of those rustlers coming back."

The doctor scratched an itch on his neck that really wasn't there and said, "I think both of you are right."

Loralie jumped down from the buggy and stepped into the center of the men and looked around at them with her hands firmly planted on her hips. "I'm ah, I mean, I'm thinking the decision should be mine, not any of yours."

She looked up at Clay and said, "As I recall, folks have been sayin', I mean, saying I'm as good a shot as any man. And they also said, I ain't, I mean, I'm not the kind to shy away from trouble. So, if you gentlemen don't mind, I'll be going home as soon as Hank, here, can hook my horse back up to the buggy." With that, Loralie climbed up onto the buggy seat and sat down to wait.

"With your permission, I'll replace a few things I've eaten or used in your absence and ride back up with you," Clay said with a grin.

"Thank you," Loralie said, realizing she wasn't sure which direction she should go to get up to her ranch. Without his help she could only hope the horse would know the way.

Putting two fingers to the brim of his hat, again, Clay said, "If you'll meet me in front of the mercantile store in about ten minutes or so, we can be on our way."

CHAPTER FOURTEEN

Following several yards behind, the Mullins brothers watched as the three young Cherokee boys rode up to the edge of the woods and stopped to survey the ranch to make sure no one was around.

After a few minutes of watching for any movement around the house, the barn, or the corrals, the three young braves gave a sigh, but jumped when the voice behind them asked, "Well?"

Without turning around, Wolf said, "It looks to be deserted, but maybe we should watch awhile longer, just to make sure."

"Quit'cher stallin'. The place is empty and the horses are ours fer the takin'. Now get to it and stop actin' like ah bunch of ninny's," Wilber said in his most commanding voice. He was anxious to get the horses and be on their way. He didn't want to have to deal with that man or the dog, again. His leg was still sore where the dog had taken a chunk out of it.

"Do what Wilber says, and be quick about it. We'll be coverin' ya with our rifles," Samuel told them trying to sound authoritative like his brother.

"No names!" Wilber whispered at his brother.

"Sorry, I fergot," Samuel said, shaking his head.

"Well see thet ya don't fergit again," Wilber said, easing his mount forward so he would have a clear shot in case the place wasn't empty as they suspected.

-

Loralie found driving the buggy and commanding the horse seemed to come natural to her and when they came around the curve in the road and she saw her ranch sprawling out in front of her, she took a deep breath. It was beautiful, she thought. Everything was nice and clean and painted white. It reminded her of something she'd recently seen in a picture book and wondered if that was where she got the idea. Images were flashing in her head - memories she thought she recognized but couldn't quite piece together. The corrals were filled with horses, which brought an excited feeling to her insides. They all looked to be healthy and of good breeding.

How did she know that? There were so many things she didn't understand, yet.

Out of the corner of her eye she saw three men coming out of the trees behind the corrals. They were riding horses toward the corrals at a slow pace and seemed to be looking all around as though they were nervous. "Mister Brentwood," she said in a low voice.

Clay was riding the black stallion and had stopped to look at the tree line just beyond the clearing and saw two men standing there with rifles in their hands. They appeared to be acting as guards for the three men riding toward the penned-up horses. Clay shook his head. So, the rustlers had come back, and even quicker than he thought they might. "Well, so be it," he said to himself.

"Mister Brentwood," Loralie said, again, in a whisper.

He'd already pulled his rifle from the saddle scabbard and stepped down off his horse when he heard Loralie speak his name. "I see them," he whispered. Just stay calm and when the shooting starts, jump off the buggy and head for the ditch."

Without waiting for a reply, Clay lifted his rifle to his shoulder and fired a shot at the largest target inside the tree line and heard a loud yelp, along with a few cuss words thrown in. Swinging his rifle to his right, he fired a second round and heard a second loud yell, then saw the two men turn and run back into the trees. The other rustlers were halfway between the trees and the corral. When the shooting started, they turned their horses and began racing back the way they had come from. Clay fired a third shot and saw the last man in line slump forward on his horse as he disappeared into the forest.

When Clay looked at the ditch where Loralie was supposed to have gone, it was empty. Swinging his head back, he saw her standing next to her horse, hanging onto his bridle to keep him from bolting at the sound of the rifle shots.

"I think you got at least two of them," she said with a smile — maybe three. Are we going after them?"

Clay looked at Loralie and thought she sounded like the Loralie of old, but wasn't sure if her memory had returned. "What do you mean, we?" he asked cautiously.

"Well I can't let you go after them all alone. After all, if what everyone says is true, all of this is mine," she said sweeping her hand all around, "and I'm responsible for it."

Clay looked at Loralie and shook his head in disbelief. "Are you saying none of this looks familiar?" Clay asked, swinging his hand around to include the forest.

Loralie sighed. "I'm getting flashes of things in my head, but I can't seem to put them together, yet. But that won't stop me from going with you. I'm told I'm pretty good with either a rifle or a handgun."

Clay helped Loralie up onto the buggy and they continued toward the barn, with Loralie in awe at the beauty of it all. "All of this is really all mine?" she asked.

Clay pulled his hat off and wiped his forehead. "It is. And it looks a lot better than it did the last time I saw this place. You've done a great job of rebuilding."

"Oh, that's right, they said you and I have been friends fer, I mean, for some time."

Clay had just set his hat back on his head and was about to answer her when a bullet whizzed past his shoulder and embedded itself in the side of the buggy. A second shot followed the first and sent a bullet scorching the left rear haunch of the horse pulling the buggy.

The horse let out a loud whinny and bolted toward the barn, throwing Loralie over the seat and into the back of the buggy next to where Ol' Son lay.

Clay's pistol was in his hand but he saw no one to shoot at as he raced Midnight after the buggy. The rustlers hadn't run away like he'd thought they would. Now they had the advantage of being hidden behind the trees and could shoot at will, while he and Loralie were out in the open and easy targets.

Fortunately, they were moving targets and the men in the trees weren't good shooters.

Clay looked toward the buggy and saw Loralie reach up and grab the back of the buggy seat and haul herself to her feet. She reached across the seat and grabbed the reins, pulling the horse to a stop, yelling, "Whoa!"

The horse came to a stop just in front of the closed door of the barn and out of harms way from the shooters.

Clay shoved his pistol back into its holster, grabbed his rifle and pulled Midnight to an abrupt halt. He jumped from the saddle and using the horses in the corral as a shield, he made his way to the back edge of the barn and dropped down on his stomach to make himself a lesser target. His eyes studied the forest for any hint of movement to shoot at, but saw nothing. In the distance he heard the pounding of horse's hooves against the ground, growing ever lighter as the rustlers rode away.

"Well, we won this round," Clay said as he rounded the front edge of the barn and saw that Loralie had already opened the barn door and had retrieved a rifle from inside.

"Where did you get the rifle?" Clay asked.

"In the office in the barn," she said casually.

"And just how did you know it was in there?" Clay asked.

This stopped her in her tracks. She got a questioning look in her eyes. "I... I don't know, exactly," she said. "When I opened the barn door, I just ran into that room and grabbed up the rifle and headed back to help you."

"Like you knew where it was, all along," Clay said with a grin.

"Yeah, I mean, yes. I guess you're right. Does this mean my memory is comin', I mean, coming back?"

Clay took a deep breath. He was no doctor and didn't know anything about this amnesia stuff, but it did look like a good sign. "Maybe," he said, not wanting to sound like he knew more about it than he did.

"Oh, I wish everything would come back. It's so frustratin', I mean frustrating to not know anything about yourself."

Clay walked over and took her into his arms and held her close. "It'll come. You just have to be patient. I think those pictures in your head you mentioned and doing things by instinct are good signs. Coming up here might be just what you needed."

Loralie leaned against him, feeling the strength of his arms around her. She suddenly felt safe. Something inside her, a heated feeling was beginning to stir. She wanted to put her arms around this Clay Brentwood and hold onto him forever. But instead, she pulled away, trying to catch the breath that was stuck in her throat.

"Thank you. I agree. There's something about this place that seems to agree with me. I like it here," she said, trying to get her feelings back under control.

"I think you should go over to the house and unload the supplies while I tend to the horses," Clay said with a smile, wondering why she had pulled away. Had he mistaken her letters? Was he here only as a friend?"

"Shouldn't we be going after those rustlers?" Loralie asked.

Clay let out a sigh and looked at the ground for a moment before looking back at her. The old Loralie would be hard pressed to be left behind, but he didn't know about this one. He finally decided to try and make it sound reasonable for her to stay behind and not rile her feathers. "One of us has to stay here and protect the horses and this place in case they circle around and come back. Plus, who would watch over Ol' Son if both of us are gone?"

Loralie studied Clay for a long moment, knowing he didn't want her along, then said, "You don't want me along, do you? You think I might panic and get hurt, or worse. Is that about it?"

Clay swallowed. She'd hit the nail on the head, but recovering, he said, "No, nothing like that. This is your place and you're the obvious one to stay here. Didn't you send me a telegram asking for my help? Well here I am and right now the only way I can help is to be the one going after the men who want to steal your horses."

Loralie wanted to refute his statement, wanted to argue that she would not panic and would be an asset, but she wasn't sure how she knew it. Something inside her felt obligated to go after the men who were trying to steal her horses, but when she thought about what Clay had said, she could see the logic in his words. Reluctantly, she said,

"Alright, I'll stay here, but you be careful, you hear?"

Clay turned the buggy horse loose into the corral with the others, then checked his saddlebag for ammunition. Next, he tightened the cinch on his saddle and mounted the black stallion. Midnight danced around, anxious to be gone.

Clay looked at Loralie and said, "You be careful. I don't think they'll be back, but then again; I don't know how desperate they are to get your horses. Feed and water the stock now, while it's daylight, then get inside where you'll have some protection should they come back. I'd get all the weapons you have and place them in convenient places just in case. And if you get bored, maybe there are things inside the house you can look at that might help bring your memory back. Maybe some pictures, if you have any."

For some reason, his words angered her – giving her instructions like she was some adolescent child. "Yes sir," she said, putting her hand to her forehead in a military salute.

Clay looked at her and said, "I didn't mean it like it must have sounded. I meant it merely as a suggestion.

"I'm sorry," Loralie said. "I reckon, I mean, I guess I have a stubborn streak somewhere in me."

Clay grinned and said, "Yes you do. And a few times in the past, it has been a good thing."

"Only a few times?" Loralie asked with a smile.

Clay put two fingers to the brim of his hat and said, "Take care of yourself, Loralie Benson, I hope to be back soon."

Loralie watched as Clay rode off in the direction the outlaws had gone and wondered again what she and this man meant to each other. One part of her wanted to know, while the other part was afraid. What if he didn't feel the same way about her as she thought she felt about him, or God forbid, they were related. But the way he'd just held her wasn't like a relative would do. If only her memory would return so she would know what to do when he came back.

Ironically, as Clay rode into the darkness of the forest, his mind was wondering similar thoughts. If there was something stronger than just friendship going on, and she finally remembered, would she be willing to leave here and relocate her Tennessee Walkers to Texas? They would still be the same horses, only raised and trained in Texas. And what would she do with this property? Clearly the timber was worth a lot of money, but she had made it perfectly clear on several occasions that she didn't want it cut down. She also stated she would never sell it for fear they would strip the mountain for the lumber.

It wasn't as though they needed the money. Maybe they could possibly turn it into a park or reserve of some kind. If things worked out, he would speak to her about it.

CHAPTER FIFTEEN

-

If the horses the young Indian braves were riding could speak, they clearly would have said thank you when they were allowed to stop and allowed to drink from the lake and crop the luscious green grass that grew close to the water.

They were all looking behind them as they had been ever since the man began shooting at them and they raced their horses for the safety of the trees. But once they left the forest and its somewhat protection, the land was much more open with only small clumps of trees growing here and there where they might dart into if they saw evidence of someone following them. Other than that, they were totally unprotected if someone started shooting at them, again. Scared down to the marrow of their bones, they had pushed their horses to the limits and were reluctant to stop near the lake, but they had no choice; the horses were spent and wouldn't make it another mile.

"Is anyone coming?" Lives in The Woods asked, as he scanned their back trail.

"I hope not," Bullfrog said. "Our horses can't go any farther."

Wolf stared long and hard at the area they'd just come from and gave a sigh. "I do not think they could have followed us through the forest with all the leaves on the ground to cover our tracks. He would have to be a tracker as good as Stands Together and there is no one as good as him."

The other two shook their heads in agreement. Stands Together was the best tracker in the entire Cherokee nation. Hadn't the white men said so? When they could not find the tracks of the ones they pursued, didn't they come and say, "We need you, Stands Together."

When they saw no evidence of being chased by the man or his dog, they were at last able to breathe a little easier.

"We will rest here for a while. When it is dark, we will take the road leading down to Ashville. There will be no travelers at night so we won't be noticed. Our tracks will mix in with the other tracks on the road and he will not be able to follow us."

By the time they had eaten some pemmican and the horses were somewhat rested, the sky had turned black with streaks of lightning tearing its way through the clouds striking the ground all around them, and the thunder was almost deafening.

"Maybe we should not try to travel in this," Bullfrog said. "I do not like the lightning."

"And just where do you suppose we go?" Wolf asked. "If we go to the trees will not the lightning find us there? At least out here we can keep moving and hope the storm passes by quickly."

"I agree with Wolf," Lives in The Woods said. "We need to put much distance between us and the man behind us before daylight comes."

Outnumbered, Bullfrog relented and saddled his horse.

Even though there was no evidence of him following them, they knew he would not be far behind.

Less than a mile from the lake, the three Indian braves came upon the road that led down to Ashville and immediately felt better. The road looked to be a well-traveled part of the country and their tracks would mix with others who traveled the road and would make it hard for the man to follow them.

They had gone only a short distance when the storm released its fury – slowly at first, then by the buckets full of wind driven water that soon became a torrential downpour. The wind drove the rain so hard that it felt like pellets shot from a gun when it hit them. They looked around but could see no place to go to for protection, so they continued on, each one feeling pain from the stinging rain and hoped it would end soon. Their only consolation was that the heavy rain would wash their tracks away. As they made their way slowly down the road, each one remembered the words of their chief, Running Dog who said, "As you travel through life, you will be challenged many times and in many ways. When they come, always remember, pain and suffering is only a test of a man's endurance." With those words running through their minds, they continued on.

-

The Mullins brothers made camp in a small ravine where their meager fire could not be readily seen. They drank the last of their coffee and finished off the last of their rations, then pulled out the jug of moonshine and each took several long pulls before rolling up in their bedrolls.

Their horses were standing at the top of the ravine with just the cinches loosened on their saddles and were grazing quietly.

"Get some sleep, little brother, we'll be goin' back come mornin'," Wilber stated.

"You still plannin' on stealin' them horses with thet man still up there?" Samuel asked.

"I do and with the plan I'm thinkin' bout, it shouldn't be too hard. Now shut up and go ta sleep. We got big doin's comin' up."

Both brothers were tired and with the moonshine in them, sleep came easily, but hardly an hour had gone by when the storm arrived with all its wind driven rain.

"What the..." Samuel yelled when he heard the sound of lightning followed by the bellowing thunder. Not realizing the danger they were in, he pulled his blanket up over his head and tried to go back to sleep.

Somewhere in his drunken subconscious, Wilber also heard the lightning and thunder but, in his condition, it took more than a little noise to drag him awake.

Had they gotten up at the first sign of the storm, they would have seen the impending danger along with their horses bolting away, heading for the shelter of the trees some distance to the north. Unfortunately for them, both men decided to ignore the warning of the lightning and thunder and were sound asleep, rolled up in their sleeping blankets, when the wall of floodwater came rushing down the ravine.

The force of the flood water picked them up and carried them along like tree limbs and other debris the water had picked up along the way. Both men were trying to get out of the blankets they were rolled up in. After getting shed of the blankets, they thrashed around, trying to gain some kind of balance and get their heads above water.

Wilber had just gotten his head above water when a broken tree limb slammed into his back and drove him back under the raging floodwater.

Samuel, who couldn't swim any better than a rock, was tossed around like a rag doll and driven down the ravine by the force of the water to finally be deposited against the wall of the ravine close to half a mile from where he'd been sleeping. Why he hadn't drowned he wasn't sure, but instinct told him to get out of the water. Little by little he climbed up the muddy bank and with the last of his strength, pulled himself over the top to safety.

Gasping for air and coughing up water he'd swallowed, Samuel wondered about his brother, Wilber. Between the lightning strikes, the loud thunder and the heavy wind driven rain, Samuel looked around but could see nothing but falling rain and darkness.

Samuel stretched out flat on his stomach, clutching the long grass to keep himself from being blown back into the ravine, thanking the almighty he was still alive.

Farther back down, Wilber had managed to right himself and grab onto the limb that had almost done him in. With the aid of the limb, he was able to slowly navigate himself to the far bank where it made a bend. A tree had been knocked over by the storm with part of its roots still clinging to the ground, but with a large part of it protruding out into the water.

Wilber kicked hard to push himself in the direction of the fallen tree and when the water drove him into the branches, he let go of the limb he'd been holding onto and grabbed a branch and began to pull as hard as he could.

Several minutes later, Wilber climbed out of the water and over onto the backside of the tree and leaned against the trunk to get some protection from the driving wind and rain. His back hurt and his breathing was labored. After a while, he stretched out next to the tree, trying to protect himself from the storm as best he could. Once, he raised his head and tried to see the rushing water and possibly his brother, but the black clouds and heavy rain obstructed his view. In his mind, he envisioned his brother being swept away by the floodwater, never to be seen again, and felt just a twinge of remorse. "Always told him he needed ta learn ta swim," Wilber said just before lowering his head back down on the grass. Trying to regain his strength.

-

In its own way, the angry storm affected everyone.

-

After losing their tracks in the forest, Clay decided to turn back. He'd gone only a short distance when the sky suddenly turned black and overhead, he saw the flash of lightning and heard the rumble of thunder. Living in Texas, he knew about sudden storms and urged the black stallion into a lope, trying to go as fast as they could through the forest and back to the ranch before the storm broke.

By the time he cleared the trees and raced toward the corrals, he could barely see ten feet in front of his horse. When he reached the corral fence, he could see that it was empty and turned Midnight toward the back door of the barn.

Inside the barn, Clay was surprised to see almost every inch of space filled with horses. Leading Midnight he made his way to the front area where he unsaddled and rubbed him down and gave him some oats before leaving to go to the house.

By the time he reached the front porch, he was soaked from head to foot. He knocked on the door and in less than thirty seconds went rigid when a voice from his left said, "Don't make any sudden moves and reach your hands up real slow – like you're tryinn' ta grab the ceiling on this porch."

Clay raised his hands in the air and slowly turned to face the redheaded woman with a rifle against her shoulder. He could see the rifle was pointed at his heart. "Loralie, it's me, Clay Brentwood and I'm not here to hurt you."

Clay watched as realization sunk in and she lowered the rifle. "Well why didn't ya, I mean, why didn't you sing out who you was, I mean, who you are when you come up on the porch. I might ah shot you."

Clay could see she was frightened and confused, so he stepped close to her and looked her in the eyes, then reached out and took the rifle from her hand and stood it against the side of the house before he wrapped his arms around her and drew her in next to him. "It's going to be alright. I'm here. No one is going to hurt you as long as I'm here," he told her softly.

Loralie turned her face upward and saw the strength in his eyes and felt his comfort spreading throughout her body. Being here like this felt right, like this was where she wanted to be.

"I seriously doubt they'll be coming back in this weather," Clay said, nodding his head toward the storm – bringing her back to reality.

For a long time, Loralie stood with her head against Clay's chest, not wanting to lose the feeling of safeness she felt with his arms around her. Reluctantly she admitted to herself that she did feel safer when he was nearby. As she stood there, she wondered what it would feel like to know this feeling each and every day. She wanted to reach up and kiss him, but held herself back in case she was reading everything wrong.

Clay led her into the house and as they entered, he felt the warmth coming from the fireplace in the living room and the heat from the kitchen stove. Mixed with the warm, homey feeling was the smell of fresh coffee.

When they entered, Ol' Son raised his head and looked at them – his tail immediately beginning to wag.

Clay released Loralie and squatted down next to Ol' Son and began scratching his ears. "How you doing?" he asked as if he expected the dog to answer.

His answer came, not in words, but from a lick on Clay's hand and the thumping of Ol' Son's tail against the blanket he was laying on, in front of the fireplace.

"He's been a good dog. He didn't whimper even once when I carried him in from the buggy and he has layed still ever since I put him on the blanket. He drank some water and then ate some meat from my hand. I didn't want him to have to try and stand up. Afterward, he put his head down and went ta, I mean, went to sleep and didn't wake up until the storm hit," Loralie said.

When Clay stood up, Loralie looked at him standing there soaked from head to foot, and said, "We need to get you out of them, I mean, out of those clothes."

Clay looked at her and cocked an eyebrow and grinned. "Get me out of my clothes, you say?"

Loralie's face turned the color of beet juice and she stamped her foot. "You know what I mean. You need to get into dry clothes before you catch a cold. I didn't..."

Clay interrupted her and said, "I know what you meant. I was just teasing you."

"Oh," she said. Once she'd recovered, she pointed, "There's a spare bedroom over on that side of the house. There's some of my pa's old clothes in the closet. They ain't, I mean, they aren't much, but they'll do until your clothes get dry."

"Yes ma'am," Clay said, grinning as he walked by her making his way toward the room she'd indicated.

"I'll fix you something to eat," she called after him, wondering what he would look like, without his clothes on, then blushing, ran toward the kitchen to hide her giggle.

After toweling off with a towel he found on top of the chest of drawers, Clay got dressed in Loralie's father's clothes, which consisted of an old, sun-bleached shirt that had once been bright green. The bib overalls with several patches on them were a little bit long. Her pa must have been a tall man, he thought as he rolled up the pant legs. There were no shoes or boots for him to wear so he decided he would just go barefoot.

He ran his fingers through his hair in some semblance of combing it, then picked up his wet clothes and headed for the kitchen.

"Here, let me have those," Loralie said as he came into the room. "I have ah, I mean, I have a line strung up near the stove. I'll hang them there. There's hot coffee on the table yonder, I mean over there," she said, pointing toward the table.

While Loralie was hanging his clothes on the line, Clay sat down and sipped his coffee. She looked mighty fine standing there and he wondered what she would do if he slipped up behind her and kissed her on the neck, but decided against it. As far as he could tell, she was still trying to come to grips with this memory thing and he didn't want her to think about things that hadn't happened yet.

Turning his head toward the stove, his nose was greeted with the smell of bacon.

"Need some help with the bacon?" Clay asked.

Loralie turned her head and looked at him and said, "Would you mind turning it over and stirring the taters, I mean, potatoes."

Loralie thought it was nice that he'd asked to help. She couldn't remember her father ever asking to help her mother.

"Sure thing," Clay said as he stood up and walked over to the stove and saw a skillet full of potatoes and bacon. "I hope you're planning on eating too. You have enough here for three people."

Loralie looked at him and laughed. "Of course, I'll be eating too. I haven't had anything since mornin', I mean, morning.

Clay walked back over and picked up his coffee, took a sip and then walked up next to Loralie. "Why do you keep correcting yourself?" he asked.

Loralie hung the last piece of his clothing on the line, then looked up at him and said, "I don't know."

Clay could see the confused look in her eyes and nodded his head. "Maybe for... whatever reason, you've been trying to improve your speaking."

Something stirred in her brain as she walked back over to the stove and began putting the potatoes and bacon on a large platter, then began breaking six eggs into the frying pan. Why would she want to speak different than practically all of the people she knew? Looking over her shoulder, she looked at Clay, who was now sitting at the table, sipping his coffee and staring at her. "He don't talk like the folks in town," Loralie mumbled to herself. "He has an accent, but it's different, somehow."

"What was that?" Clay asked.

"Nothing," Loralie answered, turning back to the eggs frying in the skillet.

The meal was eaten in relative silence as the storm's fury continued to rage. Each of them had feelings and questions they wanted answers to but couldn't bring themselves to speak about them just yet.

That night they each went to their separate rooms early. It had been a full day.

In his room, Clay wondered what he would say to her when her memory came back. Would she remember him? Would she be like she used to be or would all of this change the way she felt and thought about things?

As Loralie climbed into bed and pulled the blanket up to her chin, lightning flashed and lit up the room. She stared at the ceiling and wondered how she would feel if and when her memory ever came back. What kind of woman was she? What kind of woman had she been? In her closet she found mostly men's type of clothing and only two dresses. All the women in town wore dresses and smelled like lilac. And if there was something between her and this man from Texas, why would he want a woman like her? Was that the way men down in Texas liked their women?

By midnight the storm had passed and was raising havoc with another part of the state, but neither Loralie nor Clay noticed – they were each tossing and turning – their minds were having a hard time shutting down.

CHAPTER SIXTEEN

The storm had passed and Wilber was standing next to the ravine watching as the receding water rushed past him, wondering if he would see his brother come floating by when a shout made him turn and look north along the bank of the ravine.

"Hey! That you, Wilber?" Samuel yelled when he saw what looked like his brother standing in the distance under a bright, shining moon.

Wilber looked at the sorry looking mess he called his brother coming toward him and felt relief flooding throughout his body and was puzzled. The Mullins were never much into feelings for one another so this emotion he was feeling confused him.

"Little brother, I thought you'd been swallered up by the storm!" Wilber said, trying to cover up the strange feelings he was having as Samuel walked up and stood next to him.

"Was. Thought I was ah gonner fer sure. You know I ain't never been able ta swim ah lick, and thought I'd seen my last day, but somehow, the water picked me up and threw me onta the shore. Soon as I got my wind back, I come on back this way lookin' fer you. And here you are, big as life. How'd you come ta keep from drownin'?"

Wilber thought for a moment then said, "Almost didn't, I reckon. Big tree limb struck me in the back and knocked me under but I grabbed onta a limb and hauled my head out of the water, then hung onto it til I got clost ta the bank and saw ah big tree ta grab onta. I clum up onta the bank and was standin' here lookin' fer you ta come past in the flood water, but instead, you come walkin' down the bank."

Samuel nodded his head in understanding but didn't approach his older brother – even though he wanted to hug him, that wasn't the Mullins way.

"What do we do now?" Samuel asked.

Wilber gave out with a sigh and rubbed his chin whiskers. "I reckon we start walkin' toward Ashville. We can get fresh horses and supplies there, then come back and do the job right this time."

"So, yer still plannin' on takin' everthin' away from that Benson woman?" Samuel asked.

"Course I am. You don't think ah little rain storm is gonna cause me ta tuck my tail and run away, do ya?"

Samuel grinned and said, "Reckon not."

-

The storm had passed – the moon and stars once again filled the sky as three, cold, wet young Cherokee braves rode slowly down the road in the direction of Ashville, where they hoped to get something to eat and hopefully, get dry and warm, again.

"I wonder what happened to the white men?" Bullfrog asked no one in particular.

Lives in The Woods shook his head and said, "With whites, you never know. Some are smart while others are..."

The other two looked at him and nodded their heads in understanding.

A few minutes later, Bullfrog who was riding just behind his two friends, heard a noise and looked back over his shoulder.

Turning his horse around, Bullfrog called over his shoulder, "Brothers, look what I have found."

Wolf and Lives in The Woods pulled their horses to a stop and looked back over their shoulders.

Coming down the road were the white men's horses.

Touching the sides of their mounts with the heels of their feet, they went back down the road to join Bullfrog who had the horse's reins in his hands and was speaking to them with a soft tone to his voice.

"These are the horses of the white men, I recognize the brands on their hips," Bullfrog said as his friends rode up and stopped their horses.

"Like our horses, they look tired. What do you suppose happened?" Wolf asked.

"Maybe they were not staked down and the storm scared them away," Lives in The Woods stated.

"Yes, that sounds like what could have happened," Wolf said.

The three young braves looked at each other for a moment before Bullfrog asked, "What do we do now? Do we go back and try to find the white men, or do we take their horses back with us and leave them in the trees where we always meet with them?"

Wolf looked at his two friends and said, "I think we should go look for the white men and return their horses. If they are not dead, maybe they will give us money for returning them."

"What if we cannot find them?" Bullfrog asked.

Lives in The Woods grinned and said, "Then we have two new horses that we can keep for our own, or sell."

Bullfrog was confused. "How long do we wait to see if the white men return on their own before we sell them? And who will we sell them to? An Indian with horses to sell, especially ones with saddles, will cause great suspicion, will it not?"

Lives in The Woods and Wolf both considered this bit of information for some time before Wolf said, "Bullfrog has spoken the truth. There will be much suspicion if we try to sell the horses to the whites – but if we sell them to one of our own, who will question us?"

Lives in The Woods looked at his friends and said, "Yes, that would work, but first we must try and find the white men and return their property if we can."

With feet heavily caked with mud, the two Mullins brothers trudged their way down the road – their heads bent down. They were having a hard time of it. Neither of them was used to walking very far and between what the storm did to them and the miles they had had to walk today, they were all in and did not see the three young Indian braves riding toward them until they were right upon them.

Startled, both the Mullins brothers looked up and immediately turned their backs on the young Indians not wanting them to see their faces. So far, they had kept their identity a secret and saw no reason to change now.

"We found your horses and brought them back to you, but if you do not want them..." Wolf said with a sly smile. They had already seen their faces and now knew who they were. They had a bad reputation around Ashville as bullies and crooks.

"No!" Wilber said. "Yes, we want our horses back and thank you." This last part choked in his throat. He was not in the habit of being obliged to anyone.

"Then turn around and take them," Wolf said, winking at his two friends.

"Just leave'um and ride away like always," Wilber said.

"And if we do, will you be leaving ten dollars apiece like always?" Wolf asked, trying hard not to laugh, although both Bullfrog and Lives in The Woods were already holding their hands over their mouths, shaking with silent laughter.

"What?" Wilber shouted. "You want money fer givin' us our own horses? Why you young..." He was so flustered he couldn't finish the sentence and whirled around ready to pull his pistol and take their horses back by force if necessary, but when he grabbed for his gun, the holster was empty."

Looking up at the three young Cherokee braves he realized they had backed off far enough that he couldn't charge them and grab the reins of their horses.

"It is alright, Mister Mullins. You do not need to hide from us anymore. We know who you are and we will not charge you for returning your horses to you."

To prove his bravery, Wolf slipped off his horse and taking the reins of the two Mullins horses in his hands, he walked up to Wilber and handed the animals over to him.

Wilber took the horses, then looked down at his feet, not knowing exactly what to say.

"Will you still be going back to steal the woman's horses?" Wolf asked, bluntly.

Wilber's head came up and he stared at Wolf and realized for the first time that the three young Cherokee braves he thought were mere boys, were actually young men.

"Reckon I will," Wilber said with authority. "If'n the three of ya er still interested in makin' some money I reckon we can use yer help."

Wolf turned and looked at Bullfrog and Lives in The Woods and winked at them.

"I do not know," he said, lowering his head and looking at the ground. "With the man and the dog there, it is very dangerous. The man will not hesitate to shoot us and as you already know, the dog is also very mean," Wolf said, stifling a chuckle. "It is not like it was before. You are now asking us to risk being killed."

Wilber looked at him and said, "You tryin' ta shake me down fer more money?"

Wolf shrugged his shoulders and said, "I am only saying that it is more dangerous now with the man and the dog there and if you want us to risk our lives..." Wolf let the sentence hang in the air for Wilber to think about.

"It is for you to decide how bad you want the horses," Wolf said and then shut up.

Wilber walked back and pretended to talk with his brother but in reality, he was talking to himself.

"How bad do I want ta see the Benson woman broke and in the poor house, is what he should be askin'. We'll make some money sellin' the horses, but thet ain't the real reason, no sir, not by ah long shot. I want ta see thet Benson woman destroyed fer what she did ta pa and our brothers."

The fact that his father had murdered her parents and was trying to steal their land played no part in the way he felt about things.

Finally, Wilber turned around and said, "Alright... Alright, I'll give ya fifteen dollars fer ever horse ya bring back to us, but it has ta be all of'em or you don't get ah dime and this time I call the shots."

Wolf felt the exhilaration well up inside him. He had just negotiated with the white man and made himself and his friends half again more money. With a sober face, he stuck out his hand.

CHAPTER SEVENTEEN

-

After breakfast, as Loralie was cleaning up the kitchen, Clay announced that since the storm had passed, he saw no need to keep the horses penned up inside the barn.

"I'll move them back out into the corrals for the time being. I think it's a mite too soon to take them back out to the pasture. We may have run them rustlers off, again. My gut tells me they'll be back. For some reason they seem to want only your horses. Why none from any of your neighbors? Can you think of any reason why that might be?" Clay asked, hoping to jog her memory.

Loralie turned and stared at Clay for a long time, her mind searching for any sign of memory, but at last she blew out a long breath of air and said, "Sorry, I can't."

Clay had just turned the last of the horses out into the corrals and was reaching to close the door to the barn when a bullet whizzed past his head and slammed into the side of the barn.

On instinct, Clay dropped to his knee and pulled his pistol out of its holster, looking for the shooter, but after seeing no one, he began to inch his way toward the barn door opening. He'd barely began to move when a bullet tore up the dirt in front of him, causing him to move to his side and fire at where he thought the shot had come from, then dove into the interior of the barn and came to his feet sprinting to the side.

Wilber looked up in the tree where Samuel was standing on a limb with his rifle laying across another limb to steady his shot. "Ya missed both times. You blind, er what?"

"It's hard, shootin' from this angle," Samuel said, trying to explain why he missed such an easy shot, both times.

Disgusted that his plan wasn't going as he'd thought it would, Wilber said, "Well come on down and we'll try again from ah different angle."

The three young Cherokee braves sat on their ponies, patiently waiting for the signal to go let the horses out of the corral and drive them into the forest and head them in the direction of Ashville.

"That one, Samuel, he is not a very good shot, I think," Bullfrog announced as if this was something the others didn't know.

"I doubt either one of them can hit the side of the barn without being very close to it, Wolf declared, which made the other two laugh with their hands over their mouths.

"Yer makin' us look bad if front of them young redskins," Wilber said as Samuel dropped down to the ground.

"Then maybe you should let them do the shootin', er do it yerself," Samuel said squaring his shoulders in defiance of his brothers criticizing.

Wilber thought for a minute then grinned. "Ya know, little brother, sometimes you say somethin' that actual makes sense."

Samuel scratched his neck, wondering what he'd said. "I did?" he asked.

"If we let them redskins do the shootin' and either kill that feller or pin him down ta where we can turn them horses loose, then we can get outta here with the horses and be long gone whilst them boys over there are still here, shootin' it out with that man in there," Wilber stated.

"Well now, if that ain't the galldarndist idea you've come up with lately," Samuel said, not realizing he was the one who came up with it in the first place.

Turning toward the three Cherokee boys, Wilber pointed to a spot farther back inside the woods, indicating they should meet him there, and then headed in that direction.

-

Loralie heard shots that sounded like they were coming from the woods and yelled, "Oh my god, the rustlers are back!" She dropped the pan and towel she was holding and ran to the window and looked out, but by then Clay had escaped to the inside of the barn and she couldn't see anyone near the corrals or in the area between the barn and the forest.

She let her eyes scan the ground inside the corral, looking in between the horses stomping around – jumping and kicking. She gave out a sigh of relief when she could not see Clay's body anywhere. She hoped he had escaped into the barn, but was he all right? He could be wounded and bleeding.

She ran back into the kitchen and grabbed some towels and the rifle standing next to the door, then very carefully opened the door just wide enough for her to see out.

Everything was quiet. She looked at the barn door closest to the house to see if Clay might be trying to make a break for the house, but it was as though the place was deserted except for the horses in the corrals. They were still agitated from the shooting.

-

The boys listened to Wilber's new plan and did not like it one bit, but when Wilber told them he would add a hundred dollars to their fee if they could keep the woman and man pinned down long enough for him and his brother to sneak in and open the gate and drive the horses out, this caught their attention.

"As soon as we're in the clear, you can foller us," Wilber said with great sincerity.

"Why are you doing this, giving us so much money?" Wolf asked, suspicious of anything Wilber had to say.

Wilber looked at the ground and scuffed his toe in the dirt. "I ain't likin' ta admit it, but you boys are probably better shots than me or my brother. Thing is, somebody needs ta keep'm pinned down whilst the others turn the horses loose and run'em off – and well, I reckon me and Samuel is the ones thet need ta risk our necks goin' in there an turnin'm loose."

Wolf looked at Wilber and tried to make up his mind whether Wilber was lying to them or not. He did not like Wilber and trusted him about as much as he would, an angry bear. "And you'll give us an extra hundred dollars just for keeping the man and woman pinned down long enough for you to steal the horses and we don't have to kill them."

Wilber looked at the sky and nodded his head. "Yes sir, thet's what I said and thet's what I mean – my word as ah gentleman." And with that, he stuck out his hand.

Wolf looked over his shoulder at his two friends who were standing nearby, listening to what Wilber said. All of them doubted if Wilber was a gentleman, but in the end, they grinned and nodded their heads in approval.

Wolf turned his head back and looked at Wilber, then reached out and for the first time in his young life, shook the hand of a white man.

Wilber's handshake didn't convey much strength, it was as soft as a snake's belly, and to an Indian, strength meant honor and he knew that was something Wilber had very little of. But they would soon be taking more money home than they had ever seen before and that was enough for now. Once this was over, they never had to see them again.

Since there were only two rifles, it was decided that Wolf and Lives in The Woods would do the shooting. Bullfrog did not mind. He hated shooting at anyone or anything. To the best of his knowledge he had never killed anyone or anything except a fish, and then only because he was hungry and needed something to eat – and he liked fish.

From his place behind the tree, Wolf lifted the rifle to his shoulder and took aim when he saw the woman come sneaking out of her house. He did not want to kill her. Maybe if he only came close and frightened her, she would go running back into the house.

Taking careful aim, he drew in a deep breath, sighted down the barrel and as he let his breath out, he squeezed the trigger.

Loralie had taken only two steps out of the door, watching the forest for any movement when the bullet passed by her head so close, she could almost see it before it tore its way into the side of her house.

Instead of running back into the house like Wolf thought she would, Loralie dove off the porch and rolled over, coming up on one knee with the rifle against her shoulder. As fast as you could blink your eyes, Loralie sent three pieces of lead into the forest, then leaped to her feet and ran for the barn.

Without her realizing it, Loralie's bullets came close and tore chunks of wood from the trees the rustlers were hiding behind, causing all of them to drop to the ground for their safety.

Once she was past the corner of the barn, neither Wolf nor Lives in The Woods had a clear shot at her.

Climbing to his feet, Wilber spat a stream of tobacco juice into the dirt and cursed under his breath, "Damn."

Inside the barn, Loralie called out, "Mister Brentwood, are you in here? Are you all right?"

From the far end of the barn, she heard his reply. "Yes, but what are you doing out here?"

"I heard shots," she said as she ran down the length of the barn, and when she got close, she said, "I didn't know if you'd been killed or wounded or what."

She could see he had been looking through various cracks in the wall and apparently didn't see anyone sneaking up on the barn or the corral, or the one who shot at her, either.

"How many are there?" she asked.

"No idea." Clay said. "I heard a shot but I wasn't looking through a crack in the wall, yet. Did they shoot at you?"

"Yes, but I don't think whoever it was wanted ta, I mean, wanted to kill me. Although I will admit the bullet came mighty close to my head. I jumped off the porch and took three shots att'em, then ran to the barn. I wonder what they'll do next? Why did they stop shooting?"

"They're waiting for us to show ourselves," Clay said.

"So, do you have a plan? Are we going to show ourselves?" Loralie asked.

Clay grinned and said, "I wasn't planning on making targets of either of us." He thought for a moment then looked at her and said,

"Do you think you can watch through these cracks and if any of them come toward the barn, maybe you could take a shot at them through that knothole there?" he asked pointing at a large knothole about shoulder high to Loralie.

"Of course," she said. "I would love to get one or two of them in my sights. They sure wouldn't feel so high and mighty if I put some lead in 'm, I mean, in them, but where will you be?"

"I'm going out that side window over there" he said, pointing to the window on the far side of the barn, "and try to sneak around behind them."

-

After what happened the last time, Wilber was suspicious of the quiet and climbed on his horse and rode it over to where he could see the far side of the barn and shortly, he saw the man climb out of the window and hunker down.

Wilber stepped down from his horse and handed the reins to Samuel, saying, "Hold my horse whilst I tend ta some business."

Samuel took the reins of his brother's horse without a word.

Wilber watched as the man made his way into the woods and got a lot closer to them before he made his move.

As Clay stepped out from behind the tree he'd been hiding behind, Wilber stepped out in front of him no more than thirty feet away. Wilber had his pistol in his hand and it was aimed directly at Clay's chest.

With lightning speed Clay pulled his own pistol from its resting place and as it came up, Clay was already squeezing the trigger and diving to his right.

Wilber hadn't expected the man to pull iron and especially be so fast. Both pistols went off at exactly the same time and both had the same results.

Like Clay, Wilber moved to the side as he took his shot, only he dove to the left.

Both men felt a stinging sensation on the upper part of their shoulders where the bullets

ripped against the skin on each man's arm, but otherwise did no real harm.

Clay fired two more shots in rapid succession then ran back and dove head first through the open window, rolling over in a forward roll and coming to his feet, then returned to the window to make sure he wasn't followed.

For the next few minutes there was no noise except for the sound of the wind and the chattering of the birds.

While Clay looked through the crack in the wall, Loralie wrapped a piece of clean rag around Clay's shoulder to stop the bleeding. She was just tying the knot when the birds stopped complaining about the intrusion into their domain.

After final instructions from Wilber, Wolf and Lives in The Woods, from strategic places behind trees, began firing at the barn to distract the man and woman inside, leaving Wilber free to put the next part of his plan into action.

Clay was about to look through one of the cracks when several pieces of lead slammed against the side of the barn. Several of the rustler's bullets penetrated the wall close to where he and Loralie were standing causing them to move away. Fortunately, the lumber was thick enough that the bullets had lost their momentum by the time they entered the barn and fell harmlessly to the floor. Clay's biggest concern was if a bullet happened to hit one of the wide cracks...

Clay grabbed Loralie by the arm and propelled her back deeper into the barn and safely away from any bullets that might find their way through.

-

Wilber was about to send Samuel in to open the corral gate and start the horses through when he spied the bows and quivers of arrows hanging from the Indian horses.

He grabbed Bullfrog by the arm and asked, "Can you shoot one of them bows with any accuracy?"

Bullfrog swelled up his chest and said, "Yes, I am very good with my bow and arrows. I have won several competitions."

"Well now, thet's jest fine, yes sir, jest fine indeed. Now here's what I want ya ta do."

-

Clay and Loralie were standing near the corral door while Clay peaked through the narrow crack made by opening the door ever so slightly. He was expecting to see one of them trying to sneak in and open the corral gate, but saw no one, which confused him slightly.

He was sure the covering fire was meant to allow someone to sneak in and let the horses loose. He was about to close the door when he heard the thump, thump, thump on the roof of the barn.

"What was that?" Loralie asked, fear shining clearly in her eyes.

Clay heard the crackle and then the smell of smoke. "Fire! They've fired the roof!

The fire raced across the dry roof and down into the barn like a racehorse headed for the finish line.

"We have to get out of here!" Clay yelled as he pulled her toward the front door of the barn. "We have to make a run for the house," he said. "Think you can do it?"

As he pushed the front door of the barn open and shoved Loralie through it, Clay could feel the heat of the fire that had already found its way to the hay stored in the loft. "You go first. I'll be right behind you trying to distract them."

Loralie leaped out of the doorway and ran for all she was worth toward the house, with Clay only a few steps behind her. He ran sideways, firing his pistol over his shoulder into the forest. Unless he was very lucky, he doubted he would hit anyone, but maybe he would come close enough to make them flinch and give him and Loralie time to reach the house.

Wilber saw them running toward the house and directed the boys to change their targets from the back of the barn to the man and woman running toward the house while both he and Samuel also fired their pistols at them.

Loralie was about to leap onto the porch when she felt the sting in her leg as a bullet drove its way through the meat on her right leg, causing her to lose her balance and fall headlong into the top step of the porch, knocking her unconscious.

Clay heard her yelp and saw her lose her balance and begin to fall. He shoved his pistol back into his holster and grabbed for her, but was too late.

She dropped onto the porch steps like a rag doll and was very still.

With bullets peppering the porch, Clay lifted Loralie into his arms and ran up the steps and over to the door, and without slowing down, he drove his shoulder against it. The door gave way and with another step, he and Loralie were inside the house.

Kicking the door closed with his foot, he deposited Loralie on the couch then pulled his pistol and ran to the window, looking for somebody to put lead into, but again, saw no one. As soon as he and Loralie entered the house, the shooting stopped, but the barn was ablaze.

When Clay looked over his shoulder and saw Loralie laying on the couch; her face pale and drawn, he felt the anger beginning to grow inside him.

"Who the hell are these people? And how could this happen again?" Clay asked of no one.

Another quick look out of the window revealed the wind had come up, sending large flames into the air. The horses were becoming more and more agitated – jumping and kicking up their heels. There was nothing he could do about it. If he tried to go out and turn the horses loose, he would more than likely be shot and no help to Loralie, so he moved over next to the couch to check on her.

She was still unconscious, which was obvious. He moved down to where he could inspect her leg and saw two holes in her jeans. With his knife, he cut away the area where she'd been shot and found that it was not life threatening. The bullet had gone all the way through without hitting anything vital, but she was losing blood. He ran into the kitchen and got a clean piece of cloth, then ran back into the living room. He tore off two small pieces to place over the enter and exit wounds, then tied what was left of the cloth around Loralie's leg to stop the bleeding until he could put a proper bandage on it.

When he finished, he made his way back over to the window just in time to see what appeared to be three Indians and two white men coming out of the forest. They were still too far away for a pistol shot, so that was out of the question. He looked around, searching for a rifle, then realized it was laying on the ground just beyond the porch where Loralie dropped it when she'd been shot. He remembered his rifle was still in the bedroom and he sprinted to the bedroom and found it standing next to the bed.

By the time he got back to the window and looked out he saw the three Indians firing burning arrows toward the house and heard the thumping of the arrows hitting the front side. A bullet tore through the windowpane, barely missing his head.

Pieces of broken glass embedded themselves in his face and chest, followed by more fire arrows being fired onto the roof of the house. Smoke was already beginning to fill the room.

After picking the glass from his face and neck as best he could, Clay grabbed his rifle and made his way back over to the couch and lifted Loralie into his arms and headed for the back door. He had to get her out while he still could.

Deep into the forest, Clay laid Loralie down on a pile of leaves and brushed the hair away from her face. Even in her unconscious state, she was beautiful.

"Hang in there, Loralie Benson. Don't you let'em beat you," he whispered.

Taking off his coat, Clay laid it over the upper part of Loralie's body and was just standing up when he heard the sound of running horses. They had won.

Clay walked to where he could see the house and barn, or what was left of it. The fire had already taken its toll, leaving only black smoke bellowing into the air. Everything she owned was gone. The horses she'd asked him to save were gone – the barn and house burned to the ground – Loralie was wounded and unconscious, again. He had accomplished absolutely nothing. It reminded him of the time the Beeler gang raided his ranch and burned it to the ground, only this time, he wasn't near deaths door and there was no dead wife.

Clay walked back and stared down at Loralie. "They may have won this round, but it isn't over. I will track them down, I promise. I've got a double reason now - Midnight was in the corral with your herd of horses."

Suddenly, he remembered Ol' Son and tried to remember seeing him lying in front of the fireplace but couldn't, there had been too much going on. Clay checked to see that Loralie was all right, then turned and headed back toward where the house had been, calling Ol' Son's name. He was close to the edge of the forest and all he saw was ruin. His heart sank and he leaned against a tree, feeling empty inside. Ol' Son couldn't have survived a fire like that. His mind returned once again to the scene when the Beeler gang raped his wife and left her inside the burning house. There hadn't been much to find then, either, and he knew there wouldn't be much to find now.

As he stood looking at the rubble that used to be Loralie's house, from somewhere behind him, he heard a soft whimpering noise and looked back over his shoulder.

Ol' Son was crouched down next to Loralie, licking her face, his wagging tail scattering fallen leaves in two directions.

Something inside Clay filled him with relief. The house, barn and outbuildings, along with the horses were gone, but both Ol' Son and Loralie were alive and that, to him, was enough – at least, for now.

Hank was just leaving the livery barn and was headed for the restaurant to get a bite to eat when he saw the black smoke rising into the sky. Shielding his eyes, he could see that it was coming from up on the side of the mountain. "That looks like it's comin' from Loralie Benson's place," he said to himself as he turned and ran toward the doctor's office.

"Doc," Hank yelled when he got close to his office.

CHAPTER EIGHTEEN

-

Wolf, Bullfrog and Lives in The Woods moved the small herd of horses through the forest to an area several miles away from the burning buildings – a place they'd seen on one of their earlier trips and thought it would make a good hiding place if they ever needed one.

Coming along behind, at a slower pace, Wilber and Samuel watched their back trail in case the man was following them. To their relief, he was not, and when it was evident they were not being followed, they continued on, following Wolf's instructions on where to find them and the horses.

When Wilber rode into the small clearing that was well hidden until you were right up on it, he whistled. It was not a large valley, but big enough to hold the thirty odd horses they had. There was an abundance of grass and a small lake where the horses could drink. It was the perfect place to hold the horses for a day or two until things quieted down. If you didn't know where this valley was, you would probably never find it unless you accidentally rode into it. Wilber hoped the man didn't know about it.

For a good half mile behind them, Wolf and Lives in The Woods were already busy erasing the trail the horses made by dragging brush over the tracks - while Bullfrog made sure the horses were settled in and calmed down from all the running and excitement.

"I sure would 'a never found this place," Samuel said when he rode up and stopped next to his brother. "It's like it was just dropped right outta the sky and plopped down here in the middle of the forest, jest waitin' fer us ta come along. Wonder how them redskins knowed it was here? They're plumb ah wonder, sometimes."

Wilber looked at Samuel, then back to the valley and the horses grazing near the lake. He decided there might be a little more to these three young Cherokee braves than he'd originally thought. "They say the Indians know these mountains better'n anybody else. Reckon thet's why they can disappear inta the hills and vanish inta places like this so easy like."

Samuel pondered that for a moment, then nodded his head in agreement. Samuel was not stupid, but he'd never had to think many deep thoughts – his pa and now Wilber did most of the serious thinking for him and his brothers.

Bullfrog rode up next to them and said, "We can stay here for a couple of days to let things settle down. It will hard for them to find us here."

Wilber was skeptical. "I know they're coverin' over the trail fer ah ways back so's the horses tracks caint be follered – I can understand thet – but what about thet dog? Cain't he foller our scent – you know smell our trail?"

Bullfrog grinned. "The dog will not be able to follow us here. In fact, he will not even come close. Wolf found some stink cabbage down by the far end of the lake and when he and Lives in The Woods finish erasing our tracks, they will spread the juices from the cabbage over our trail. When the dog comes sniffing along the ground and comes to the cabbage juice, he will pull back and begin digging his nose in the dirt to try to get rid of the smell. To him and the ones who follow us, they will think a skunk has been there. No, Mister Mullins, we are safe here for a few days."

Wilber mulled this over for a minute or so, thinking again, that these boys were a lot smarter than he had given them credit for. "Maybe I need to rethink my plan for getting out of this without paying them anything," he mumbled to himself. He'd thought them to be mere boys, like the ones he's seen in town, but realized they were nothing like them. Would they be angry enough or brave enough to come after him if he stiffed them out of the money they had coming? He would need to think on it some more.

"They're comin' back," Samuel said, tapping his brother on the shoulder.

Wilber looked in the direction they were coming from and saw Wolf and Lives in The Woods, both, dragging something behind them, and letting go of it just before entering the camp.

"Stink Cabbage," Bullfrog said with a wide grin.

Later, after his friends and the two white men were asleep, Bullfrog stood looking over the lake, silently praying the man and woman, and the dog had not been burned up in the fire. He'd only gone along with shooting the fire arrows at the barn and house because he was afraid Wilber Mullins would do bad things to his family, if he didn't cooperate.

CHAPTER NINETEEN

-

Clay squatted down next to Ol' Son and rubbed his back. "Glad to see you got out. I was worried you'd been trapped in the house."

Ol' Son looked up at Clay, then turned his head back at Loralie.

"I know, she's unconscious again, just like the first time we found her. Let's just hope no further damage was done," Clay said as he reached down and lifted her into his arms and with a shove of his leg, he grunted and stood up.

"Let's get her back down to the house, or where it used to be," Clay said to Ol' Son, who was already headed in that direction, walking slowly.

Clay found a shady spot under a tree near where the house had been and laid Loralie down. It had a few scorched limbs, but fortunately, it had not caught on fire.

The wind had been short lived when the barn and the house was fired by the young Cherokee brave shooting fire arrows at them, so the nearby trees and the edge of the forest were spared catching on fire. If that had happened there would have been no stopping it. Most, if not all of the forest, would have been destroyed.

Clay stood up and looked around at the devastation, then rolled and lit a cigarette. What was he was going to do? He had no way to take Loralie back down to Cinch Mountain except in his arms or over his shoulder, which left a lot to be desired. How long it would take, he had no idea, but he knew if he couldn't find a horse it might be his only option.

Ol' Son turned and looked down the road, then began to bark.

Clay turned to see what Ol' Son was barking at and saw a buggy coming hell bent for election toward him. He stood motionless, his hand near his pistol, until he saw who it was, then began waving and shouting, "Over here!"

The doctor and Hank were riding on the buggy seat and four heavily armed men were trailing behind them as they came to a stop next to Clay, creating a large cloud of dust.

The doctor climbed down and immediately went over to Loralie and hunkered down. When he saw she was unconscious, again, he gave a sigh and said, "Oh Lord, not again."

"Looks like the rustlers came back," Hank said as he walked up next to Clay.

Clay looked up at the sky, took a deep breath and said, "Yeah, they came back. I thought I'd scared them off, but I figured wrong and they caught me unawares. I was in the corral when they started shooting at me. I made it into the barn without taking any lead but then Loralie, who was in the house at the time, came out to the barn to see if I had been shot. That's when they torched the barn with fire arrows. When Loralie and I ran for the house, she took a bullet in the leg, which caused her to fall forward and hit her head on the porch step."

Clay took a breath, then continued. "I got her into the house and began shooting back at them. There were five of them – two white men and three Indians. It was one of the Indians that shot the fire arrows into the barn and the house."

"Indians?" Hank said in astonishment. "All the Indians around here are real peaceful. We get along with 'm just fine. Fact is, they come inta the livery ta get their horses tended to and trade skins and such fer my labor. Hell, ole Atsila himself likes ta come in and sit an jaw whilst we drink coffee. He's the chief and he surely does like coffee – the stronger the better. The womenfolk take things they grow in their gardens over ta the mercantile and trade 'um fer cloth and such. They grow some really good, maize, beans, squash and tobbacie.

"The barber is married ta one of 'm. Her name is...? Oh yeah, it's, Ankita – which means, marked. That's on account of ah strawberry lookin' mark on her shoulder. Don't reckon the barber minds; they been hitched close ta six or seven years, now. She's gonna be takin' over as the new school marm just after Christmas. Miss Whitehouse, the current school marm is goin' out ta St. Louis ta marry some fella who's been courtin' her by mail fer some time now."

Clay had listened patiently, then asked. "What tribe are they from?"

"Who? You mean the Indians thet live close by?" Hank asked.

"Yes. The ones that live nearby," Clay answered.

"Why, the Chiaha, of course. Most of the Cherokee moved off down ta North Carolina – near Ashville, close as I can recall."

Clay thought for a moment, then said, "Yes, now that I think about it, I believe they might be Cherokee. That's what was so familiar about them. I have three Cherokee working for me on my ranch back in Texas who have the same look as the three who stole Loralie's horses."

Hank looked surprised. "You got Indians working fer ya back in Texas? We always heard the Indians out west was all blood thirsty heathens."

Clay laughed. "Yeah, I heard that too, but it isn't true. Some of them, like the ones who work for me, have more education than I do, and speak better English to boot."

"Well, I'll be hog-swallered," Hank said, scratching his head, then looked at Clay and asked, "You think they come all the way up from Ashville just ta steal her horses?"

Before Clay could answer, the doctor called out, "Boys!"

Clay and Hank ran over in time to see Loralie open her eyes and look around. "What happened?" she asked sitting up and looking toward the house and barn that were now nothing more than two, large piles of ashes. "Oh no!" she cried when she saw her barn and house had been burned to the ground.

"Just take it easy for a moment and let everything come back to you," the doctor said, hoping her memory had returned.

Still a bit confused, Loralie looked all around, then reached up and touched the bump on her head.

"Do you know who you are and where you are?" the doctor asked.

Loralie thought for a moment, then said, "I think somebody told me my name is Loralie Benson and that I own a horse ranch." She seemed to be struggling to remember and finally said, "And there was something about horse rustlers. Is that right?"

Clay squatted down next to Loralie and took her hand. "Yes, that's correct. I'm your friend, Clay Brentwood from Texas. You sent me a telegram asking for my help with the rustlers and I came out a week or so ago, but I was a little too late. From what we've been able to piece together, the rustlers hit you in the head and when you woke up you couldn't remember anything about who you are or your past. We've been trying to help you get your memory back. I brought you up here to see if being here would help, but the rustlers came back and..."

Before he could continue, Loralie said, "And set the barn on fire. We were runnin', I mean, we were running from the barn toward the house when I got a sharp pain in my leg and felt it givin' away under me – and then everything went black."

"You fell forward and hit your head on the porch step. You were knocked unconscious," Clay told her.

"How... How long have I been unconscious?" Loralie asked with concern in her voice.

Clay looked at the sky and said, "Two, maybe three hours; long enough for Hank and the doctor to get up here with help."

She looked toward the buggy where four riders stood, waiting for instructions on what to do.

"Were they able to save my horses?" Loralie asked, looking back at Clay.

Clay looked her in the eyes, not wanting to lie to her. "Sorry, the doctor, Hank and those men just got here. The rustlers got away with all the horses, several hours ago."

Loralie looked at Clay and her eyes got a sad look in them. "They got away because you took time to take care of me. That's the truth of it, right?"

Clay gave a slight grin and said, "I do believe you're a site more important than a few horses. Besides, the doctor is here now and I can turn you over to him, which leaves me free to go after them, that is if I can borrow a horse from someone?"

Loralie's head jerked up. "They stole your horse, too?"

"He was in the corral with the others," Clay said, shrugging his shoulders.

"I'm so sorry," Loralie said, placing her hand on Clay's arm.

"I've got ah couple of good mountain horses you can use," Hank offered.

"Enough of this chit-chat," the doctor said. "We need to get this young lady back down to town so I can tend to her properly, then you can decide what you want to do."

"Guess you won't be needing us fer now," the tallest of the four riders by the name of Sam Little, spoke up.

Clay stood up and walked over to them and looked up at the four men who volunteered to come with Hank. "Thanks for coming up. I guess the dance is over for now. How much do I owe you?" he asked reaching into his pocket.

Sam Little looked at the other three, then back down to Clay. "Nothin'. Didn't do any shootin' or use up any of my lead. Maybe if'n you need help later on gettin' her horses back and if'n we got the time..." he said, letting the sentence trail off.

"Much obliged then," Clay said, offering his hand to each of them. "I'll keep you in mind."

Loralie rode on the seat next to the doctor, with Ol' Son sitting next to her while Clay and Hank rode in the back of the buggy. The men who had volunteered to come up to help, rode along behind as they headed down the mountain.

CHAPTER TWENTY

-

Wilber was getting anxious to move on. The Indian boys had told them they would be safe here in this hidden valley, but he wasn't so sure. It was true that he and his brother had been raised not too far from here and had never seen this valley, but he knew there were men who lived in these parts that knew every square inch of this mountain – and if the man hired any of the locals to help him, there was a good chance he would get one who knew about this valley.

"I say we move out at first light," Wilber told the three young Indian braves over the evening meal.

"But why? We are safe here." Wolf said.

"Thet might be but if he hires any of the locals, there's ah good chance they know where this valley is and would figure like you, it'd be ah good place ta hide out," Wilber stated.

"We will keep a watch and if we see anyone coming, we can leave before they get here," Lives in The Woods said.

Wilber shook his head. "If'n they's thet close, we couldn't out runin 'm with this many horses. They'd come down on us afore we got a mile down the trail."

The three braves thought about this and decided the white man might be right.

Wilber broke into their thinking. "Sides, you know what month it is?"

The three young braves looked at each other, then back to Wilber, shaking their heads, no.

"It's December, and why this mountain ain't covered with snow is beyond me," Wilber said, breaking into their thoughts. "Usual, they's at least two feet by now. Now what if it comes ah heavy snowstorm and we wake up with ah foot er two on the ground, we'd be hard put ta get the horses outta here thout leavin' tracks ah blind man could foller."

Wolf looked around, envisioning what the white man said. Yes, snow would make it hard to travel without leaving tracks. "We will do as you say, Mister Mullins," Wolf told him.

"Good. We'll leave at first light," Wilber told them.

-

Down in Cinch Mountain, the doctor had finished his examination and declared Loralie to be in sound condition. His only concern was that her amnesia hadn't changed much. Oh, she would remember little things – like things since she first woke up, but nothing yet about her past.

Clay got her a room at the hotel and Loralie purchased clothes from the mercantile with money loaned to her by Clay. After a long bath and soak in the tub provided by the hotel, Loralie walked into the restaurant and looked around, noticing that every male head was staring at her with a smile on his face.

Mrs. Evans, the mercantile owner's wife had taken Loralie under her wing and helped her pick out her wardrobe – and now, here she stood, wearing an emerald green dress that enhanced her eyes and fiery red hair. Mrs. Evans had also gone over to the hotel and did up Loralie's hair with a green ribbon, tied in a bow at the back, then presented her with a gold chain with a round pendant that had a horse engraved on it. Mrs. Evans told her Mister Brentwood had purchased it. "He said he thought it would look good on you... and it does.

Clay looked toward the doorway of the hotel restaurant and got a lump in his throat. The light coming through the windows seemed to form a halo around Loralie. Along with every other man in town, Clay thought Loralie Benson had to be the most beautiful woman in Cinch Mountain. Clay took several deep breaths, trying to get his heart to slow down.

Loralie was having mixed feelings. Somewhere in her brain, it was telling her this isn't the way she normally dressed, which made her feel somewhat self-conscious – but another part of her brain was reveling in the attention she was getting. As her eyes roamed around the room, she spotted the man called Clay Brentwood and their eyes locked onto each other.

What she saw in his eyes made her blush. She felt heat rushing up to her face and she was suddenly short of breath. Was he feeling the same way? she wondered?

Everyone at the table, Doc, Hank and Clay stood up. Clay stepped over and pulled out a chair for Loralie as she approached.

"Whooie!" Hank declared. "If you ain't the purtiest thing I've ever laid eyes on! Why I'd marry you today if'n I thought you'd say yes."

Sitting down in the chair, Loralie smiled and said, "Thank you, Mister Collins. You don't think this dress makes me look, too...."

"Nothing of the sort," the doctor said, jumping in. "You look like you could be a queen. I swear, that dress was made for you."

Loralie could feel her face getting hot and looked over at Clay, who was just sitting there staring. "Thank you very much for this beautiful necklace," she said, fingering the pendant.

Clay swallowed, took in a deep breath and said, "I...," he stammered, "I just thought it would look good on you and maybe help you remember the horses you raise and how that came to be."

Clay nodded his head up and down and continued, "The doctor was right, that dress was made for you and you for it."

Loralie sat there, staring at the man who had come all the way from Texas to help her, experiencing difficulty finding the words she would like to say to him.

She looked around, and after taking a deep breath, she said, "What's good to eat? I'm starving, and I'm sure Ol' Son is too."

Ol' Son had moved over and was sitting next to her chair and when she spoke his name his tail began to wag. Normally, dogs weren't allowed in the dining room, but the owner had made an exception, this time.

"I think he should have a steak," Loralie declared, relieving the tension, along with changing the subject from her to Ol' Son.

After their meal, the doctor headed back to his office to do some paperwork and Hank suggested Clay come by first thing in the morning so they could put an outfit together for him.

Still early in the evening, Clay suggested he and Loralie take a walk and she readily agreed. She wanted to spend some time with him and try to find out more about him and how they had become such good friends.

There wasn't much to see in Cinch Mountain, a few stores, a bank and the livery, the sheriff's office and that was about it. The sun was just sneaking over the horizon when they ended up down at the train station. Loralie was amazed that someone could own their own train.

Clay offered to show her his private car and Loralie jumped at the chance to see the inside.

"Why, this is just like a home," she said as she wandered though the car, examining everything, lingering a moment longer as she stared at the bed. "Better'n most of any in Cinch Mountain," she said, hurrying back to the living area, a little uncomfortable with the feeling she was getting.

Clay looked around and said, "I guess it is. I never gave it much thought before. It is a very comfortable way to travel. Do you like champagne?"

Loralie thought for a moment, then said, "I'm not sure I even know what it is. Do you think I might have had some in my past?"

After studying the question for a moment or so, Clay said, "Knowing your background, you may not have. It's a beverage served in most all of the better restaurants. I think you might like it. May I pour you a glass to try?"

"Sure, why not," Loralie answered. "And maybe you can fill me in on what you know about us. Maybe something you say will turn my brain back on."

"It would be my pleasure," Clay said as he poured two glasses of champagne and offered one to Loralie.

"Oh," Loralie giggled. "The bubbles make my nose feel funny."

Clay took some time as he related what he knew about her and how they'd met, refilling her glass from time to time.

By the time Clay opened a second bottle, Loralie was feeling very relaxed. Sitting next to him on the sofa, she suddenly wanted to touch him and have him touch her. She wondered what it would be like to kiss him, not like a brother or father kiss, but a long passionate kiss, like those men and women she'd read about.

At these thoughts, she felt herself flush. She looked down at the fresh glass of the bubbly liquid and smiled. She liked the way it made her feel.

Clay leaned back against the couch and raised his glass. "To you," he said, noticing the effect the champagne was having on her.

Loralie looked into his eyes and saw something she couldn't explain. It was as if he was staring straight into her soul and she felt her heart beating a little faster. Her reverie was shortened by Clay's next statement.

"I just want you to know how sorry I am for the way things have turned out. I feel a part of it is my fault, and come morning I'll hit the trail. I promise to do everything I can to get your horses back."

"Thank you," she said, placing her hand on his arm and feeling the electricity between them. "I don't know how I'll ever be able to repay you for all your kindness."

Clay set his glass on the small table in front of the sofa, then took both of her hands in his. "I'd like to think after all we've been through, we are more than just good friends. In fact, I was planning on coming out here to see you just before I got your telegram."

"You were?" Loralie asked. She was suddenly feeling swallowed up by the look in his eyes.

"I was," Clay said as he leaned in close and kissed her gently on the lips.

As Clay leaned his head toward her, Loralie's first instinct was to draw away, but when their lips touched, it was as though she had been struck by lightning. His lips started a fire inside her she couldn't rightly understand, and when he put his arms around her and drew her close, she didn't try to resist. In fact, she scooted closer to him and put her arms around his neck, never wanting to let go.

-

The morning sun came creeping under the window shade of Clay's private train car bedroom and shone on Loralie like a spotlight. Her hair was spread out across the pillow and her face had a look of contentment.

Clay looked down at her and felt his heart beat a little faster. Something about the way the light shone on her seemed to give her an angelic glow. He bent over and kissed her on the top of her head, then eased out of bed, got dressed and left his private train car.

Clay headed for the livery stable with Ol' Son trotting along beside him, his bandage was gone and he seemed happy to be up and moving around. Clay decided he was well enough to come along if he wanted to.

Hank had been up for some time and had two horses ready for Clay when he and Ol' Son came walking up. One was a buckskin mare he'd purchased from Loralie when she was just getting started. She had captured it running wild up above her ranch and had broke and gentled it to ride, but had never broken its spirit. He figured of all the horses he had in his stable, this one had sand and would suit Clay's needs best. The other one was a dapple-gray mare that he'd come into possession of because the owner had been killed in a gunfight with money still owing on the horses keep.

"Mornin'," Hank said, raising his hand in greeting.

"Morning," Clay responded as he walked up and inspected the two horses. "You've made good choices my friend, but what have you got on that packhorse? Looks like everything but the kitchen sink."

"You et, yet?" Hank asked, changing the subject.

Clay grinned and said, "Guess I just plumb forgot."

"Excited about gettin' on the trail, I reckon," Hank said with a grin.

Clay rubbed the tip of his nose and said, "Sure, let's go with that."

Hank was puzzled by Clay's response, but said nothing, not wanting to pry into the man's personal affairs, which might involve a certain redhead.

In the restaurant they drank black coffee while waiting on their food. "You want to tell me about what's on that packhorse or am I going to have to unload it to find out?"

Hank grinned and set his cup on the table. "Course there's the usual - food and coffee and other vitals, along with an extra box of ammunition – forty-four, right?"

Clay nodded his head, appreciative of Hank's thoroughness. "And what else?" he asked, raising one eyebrow.

"Well sir, it's like this. It's December, and normally we'd already have two feet or more of snow on the ground, and colder than ah polar bear's feet. But this year we seem ta be havin' ah late winter. But don't let that fool ya – ah blizzard could come waltzin' in at any time – maybe even today," Hank said as he took another sip of coffee, then continued.

"When I got up this mornin' it was ah site colder than it has been in some time. So, I got ta thinkin' bout you up there on the trail and what would happen to ya if'n ah storm hits. Folks have been knowed ta die up there durin' storms and figured you might need a place ta crawl inta. But if'n there weren't no cave close by, er shelter of some kind... Well sir, I reckon ah good strong tent would come in mighty handy, so thet's what's up on top – ah good, strong tent. Took it in trade some time back but ain't had no occasion ta use it til now."

Clay thanked Hank and asked what all of this had cost, but Hank waved it off and said, "This is fer Loralie. It's the least I can do."

Clay nodded and thought it was a good gesture. He was glad the people of Cinch Mountain thought so highly of her. It helped his own feelings. He would figure a way to repay Hank without making him mad.

The horses and tent he already had, but Clay knew Hank couldn't afford the food and other things. He was a good man and Clay didn't want to embarrass him by forcing money on him so while they sat, drinking their coffee and making small talk, he decided to leave some money someplace that would be safe, yet easy to find. Clay knew that like many men, Hank was proud and if he happened onto the money without having to face Clay, maybe he would accept it in the way it was meant.

Breakfast was delivered by the lady who owned the restaurant – a widow woman of around forty who still had her looks and gave

Hank that special smile women save for someone they have an interest in.

Clay noticed it, but said nothing. He also didn't fail to see the smile and wink Hank gave her in return.

Sometimes answers come from places we least expect. Leaving the money he wanted to give to Hank with the woman would be perfect, he decided as he watched the silent communication between them. "She'll see he gets it after I'm gone," Clay whispered to himself.

When the waitress had gone on to take care of other costumers, Clay dove into his breakfast, finding he was hungrier than normal this morning.

"Seen Loralie this mornin' - you know, ta tell her you're leaving?" Hank asked as he attacked his breakfast of steak, eggs and fried potatoes.

Clay filled his mouth and mumbled, "She's probably still asleep. These last few days has been rough on her. I didn't want to disturb her."

His words implied she was still in her hotel room, but his mind was filled with the memories of last night and the way she looked this morning with the sun shining on her. He hoped she'd understand when she woke up and found he was gone. Maybe he should have left a note, but it was too late now.

"Uh huh," Hank said, noticing the redness in Clay's cheeks that hadn't been there before his asking about Loralie.

Before Hank could ask any more questions, the waitress came by and filled their coffee cups, giving Hank another smile that would melt ice.

CHAPTER TWENTY-ONE

-

Wolf, Lives in The Woods and Bullfrog pushed the horses at a reasonable pace toward the top of the mountain and the trail down the backside that would lead them to Ashville.

Wilber would rather have run them hard to get as far away as they could before the sun reached its peak, but even as nervous as he was and always looking back over his shoulder for signs of someone following them, he told them, "Hold them to an even pace, maybe a lope at the fastest, but no hard running. I don't want them wore out in case he shows up and we half 'ta make ah run fer it."

As they came into a wide area where the trees had been cut down, they could see the top of the mountain in the far distance and breathed a sigh of relief.

Lives in The Woods looked around, then rode up next to Wolf and said, "We should be looking for a place to get in out of the storm."

Wolf looked at the sky and saw only blue, with a few puffy clouds drifting lazily across the sky. "What storm?" he asked.

"You will see," Lives in The Woods said as he turned his horse and rode back to his position in the drive.

Wolf looked at the sky again and debated on Lives in The Woods advice. He was known to have instincts about things, but there was no sign of a storm coming – no wind or dark clouds – nothing but sunshine. Maybe this time he was mistaken.

Less than two hours later a blistering wind came roaring through the trees and out into the clearing and slammed into them like a herd of buffalo escaping from captivity.

The horses immediately stopped and formed a tight group, turning their backs to the cold wind.

The Mullins brothers were caught unawares with no warm clothing to put on and were feeling the sting of the icy wind chilling them to the bone.

"We need ta find ah place ta hole up," Samuel yelled over the wind.

"If'n you know ah place, lead the way, little brother," Wilber yelled back.

Samuel just shrugged his shoulders and wrapped his arms around his body, slapping himself on the back, trying to stave off the cold wind.

"Yeehaw, get moving," Wolf yelled as he tried to get the herd to move on by slapping the rumps of several of them, but they refused to budge.

Wolf looked over at Lives in The Woods, wondering how he knew a storm was coming and why he hadn't paid attention to his advice.

Even as cold as they were, the Mullins brothers joined in, trying to move the horses forward. Finally, Wilber pulled his pistol and pointed it up in the air and pulled the trigger three times as fast as he could.

Startled by the gunshots, the horses broke into a run, leaving the rustlers behind.

Once the horses broke over the top of the mountain and headed down the backside, the black stallion raced to the front of the herd and took command. He led them to a place just off the trail. It wasn't a cave, but a large indention in the mountain, surrounded by large boulders and scrub trees. There was grass here for them to eat, and sheltered them from the icy wind. How he knew where to lead them, only he would ever know.

Wolf, Lives in The Woods and Bullfrog were the first to catch up with the horses and for the first time, noticed the black stallion.

"That is a fine horse. One with a great spirit," Wolf said as they drew up next to one of the large boulders that helped shelter the place.

Lives in The Woods watched as the big horse circled the herd making sure all the horses were where he wanted them to be. "This one is not one of the horses that belongs to the woman. I think we would have noticed him a long time ago. I think this one belongs to the man with the dog."

"I agree," Bullfrog said. Shaking his head, he said, "And if that is so, I think the man and his dog will come searching for our trail. He will not want to lose a horse like that."

The three young Cherokee braves sat their horses and watched as the two Mullins brothers rode in and stepped down from their mounts.

"Why'er ya jest sittin' there like ah lump on ah log? Get down here and get a fire started so's we can have some hot coffee, or are ya plannin' on freezin' us ta death?"

Wilber and Samuel squatted next to a boulder, out of the wind as the boys jumped down from their horses and turned them loose to graze while they gathered firewood.

Approximately thirty minutes later, they were all huddled near the back wall of the indention where a blazing fire had been made. They were squatted on their haunches with cups of hot coffee in their hands - watching as the horses stood quietly grazing, glad to be out of the freezing wind.

"Thet big black 'n sure is somethin', ain't he," Samuel said as more of a statement, than a question. "Wouldn't mind havin' him fer my own."

"Don't remember seein' him afore," Wilber said, taking a sip of his coffee. "Sides, you couldn't handle ah horse like thet."

Samuel scowled. He didn't always like the way his brother spoke to him but said nothing about the rebuff. Instead, he asked, "You suppose he belongs ta thet feller who's been hangin' round the Benson place?"

"I reckon thet jest might be," Wilber said, staring at the black stallion. "They's somethin' familiar bout that man, but I cain't seem ta put my finger on it."

Samuel suddenly got a gleam in his eyes as a memory came to him. He said, "You don't suppose he's thet Texas Ranger thet fit against pa and was trapped in the cave with thet Loralie gal, do ya? You remember - the one pa took his whip ta."

Suddenly Wilber went rigid. He began to swallow repeatedly and his hands began to shake. His breathing became labored and Samuel could see the anger rising in his face.

"You all right, Wilber?" Samuel asked, afraid his brother was about to have a heart attack.

"I want thet man dead," Wilber said with venom in his voice. "I want ta walk on his dead body! Yer right, he's the one helped kill our kin. I want ta burn him at the stake whilst he's still alive!"

All three of the young braves, along with Samuel, sat motionless, afraid if they moved, Wilber, in the state he was in, might draw his pistol and shoot them.

Samuel had never seen his brother this angry and it worried him some. "I wouldn't want ta be thet ranger," he said to himself.

Wilber glared at his brother and asked, "What was thet?"

Samuel was ready to jump and run, but calmed hisself and said, "I was jest sayin' thet when we catch thet ranger we should do all them things you was ah talkin' bout."

"And we will, little brother, and we will," Wilber said, calming down a little.

As they rolled up in their meager blankets to try and get some rest, the wind died down and was replaced by large snowflakes, drifting lazily to the ground.

CHAPTER TWENTY-TWO

-

Loralie Benson woke up late and looked around, expecting to see Clay but she was alone. She wasn't ready to get out of bed, not just yet. She wanted to savor the memories of last night. She was still a bit shocked and embarrassed about what she'd done, but not sorry she had done it. After all, they were going to get married, weren't they? He'd kissed her and made love to her. He wouldn't have done those things if he didn't intend to marry her, would he? Suddenly she became worried, her mind filling with stories she'd heard about how a man would take advantage of a woman then move on.

At last, she swung her legs over the side of the bed and stood up, calling out Clay's name. She wanted to know his intentions, but the answer she got was one she didn't expect.

Harold, the engineer spoke to her through the door. "Good morning, Miss Benson. Coffee has been made if you would like some, and breakfast will be prepared when you're ready."

Loralie sat back down on the bed and stared at the door. Did he know why she was here instead of at the hotel and did he know what they'd done? How could she ever face him? She didn't want to feel shame for what she'd done, but now she wasn't so sure.

After a moment, she said to herself, "Just brazen it out. Pretend that he's going to do the right thing and you're already Mrs. Clay Brentwood. What would she do?"

"Thank you, Harold, just some coffee for now. Black, please. Is there a place where I can wash?"

"There's a room at the back with full facilities, ma'am. I've taken the liberty to heat some water for a bath if you desire."

"Oh," she said, not expecting anything that elaborate. "In that case, hold off on the coffee, please.

"Will Mister Brentwood be joining me for breakfast?" she asked as she stood up and headed for the hot bath she was looking forward to.

"Sorry, ma'am, but Mister Brentwood rode off early this morning and instructed me to tell you to check out of the hotel and make yourself at home here on the train. He said to tell you he hoped to be back with your horses very soon and not to worry. He also left some money in case you need anything. He said for you not to worry about anything but getting your memory back."

"Did he go alone?" Loralie asked.

"That is my understanding, yes ma'am," Harold told her.

As Loralie soaked in the hot water, she felt some of the tension that was built up inside her finally begin to ease down. He had invited her to move onto his train and had left money for her and instructions for Harold to look after her. He wouldn't do that if he didn't plan on marrying her, would he? She still felt he should have taken someone with him, but it was too late to do anything about it now.

She reached out with her index finger and popped a bubble made by the soap on her bath water and wondered if she would ever get her memory back. It was so frustrating not knowing anything about your past; important things like, had she and Clay ever spent the night together before? Had they ever talked about marriage? And where would they live? She couldn't imagine leaving her beautiful mountain with its forest and all the animals that lived there - to live in a flat, windy place like Texas.

Suddenly she sat up in the tub. How did she know Texas was flat and windy? Had she ever been to his ranch? It was one of the many mysteries floating around in her head. Surely, she would remember if she had, wouldn't she?

What kind of a person had she been? Was she a loose woman who slept with men, or was Clay the first and only? She hoped the latter was true.

Along with her other thoughts, she wondered if she had enough money to rebuild her house and barn and other things she would need – and if she did, where was it – in the bank here in Cinch Mountain, or stashed somewhere?

Dressed and feeling ready to meet the day, Loralie walked into the dining car of Clay's private train and sat down at the table like it was an everyday occurrence.

Harold smiled as he poured coffee for her. "As always, you're looking very lovely Miss Benson. What would you like for breakfast?"

Somewhere inside her, Loralie knew this was not the kind of life she normally lived, not with a horse ranch to run, but at the moment she felt very much like a lady. "Whatever you think," she replied.

Harold chuckled and bowed at the waist. "Very well, madam, but don't expect too much. I'm not a Kansas City chef. How about ham and eggs and fried potatoes?"

"Sounds delicious!" Loralie replied. "I can hardly wait, I'm famished."

Harold said nothing but had a sly grin on his face as he approached the cook stove.

As Harold was sitting Loralie's breakfast on the table, a blast of wind slammed against the dining car, causing it to rock. Both Harold and Loralie looked out the window and saw dirt being thrown into the air, along with some wooden crates that must have blown off the station platform.

"Oh my god," Loralie exclaimed. "I hope Clay, I mean, Mister Brentwood, isn't caught out in this!"

"I'm sure he'll be just fine, ma'am," Harold said with more assurance than he felt.

After breakfast, which was less appetizing than before the wind came ripping across the land, Loralie, struggled against the heavy wind as she made her way to the mercantile store and purchased a pair of jeans, a heavy shirt, boots and socks, a winter coat, a hat, gloves and a wool scarf.

Next, she went to the hotel and checked out, then fought her way back to the train, where she changed into her new clothes. She looked into the full-length mirror and sighed. Was this the same woman she'd admired earlier, wearing her store-bought dress, looking very much like a lady?

When she walked into the dining area, Harold was sitting at the table with Andy, his coal stoker. They were having coffee and both men looked up as she came near.

Harold's eyes lit up and he whistled. "This is quite an unexpected change," he said. "And if I might ask, why are you dressed this way? I hope it's not what I think it is."

"I can't let Mister Brentwood go after my horses alone and since they are my horses, I'm the one to help get them back," Loralie said with all the strength she could muster. Truth be told, she was afraid she might not be able to find him. The heavy wind would have obliterated any tracks he might have left. Plus, she wasn't sure she knew anything about tracking someone. What if she got up on the mountain somewhere and got lost? Would she be able to find her way back? She wasn't sure. The only thing she was sure of was that she was going to give it a try. Someone had to. He was up there alone, against how many she wasn't sure, but thought she remembered him saying he'd seen five of them.

"I don't think that's such a good idea, ma'am. If he'd have wanted you to go, he would have awakened you. He'll be all right, I'm sure. He's been in some pretty tight places in the past and has always come back," Harold told her, hoping she would change her mind.

"Besides," Andy added, "I doubt you could find him in this storm. And what if it gets worse, what'll you do then?"

Loralie had those same thoughts but she was not to be deterred. She would get a couple of horses from Hank and some supplies at the mercantile store, and head out. Besides, in all likelihood, the storm might be over by the time she was ready to leave.

"Thank you for your kind advice gentlemen. I know you're just thinkin', I mean, thinking of my safety – but my mind is made up. If

Mister Brentwood should happen to get back without me finding him, tell him if I don't find him soon, I'll return."

And with that, she donned her new coat and hat and headed out the door.

The wind was now blowing so hard she had thoughts of changing her mind, but deep down inside her there was a stubbornness that wouldn't be denied.

She found that if she stayed close to the buildings, she was able to make her way a little bit easier and when she came up in front of the gun shop, she stopped and stared in the window and saw the gunsmith, Horace Billingsley working on a rifle.

As she entered the shop, Loralie had to grab the side of the door to keep it from being torn off its hinges.

"Miss Benson, it's nice to see you up and around and dressed like your old self. Has your memory returned?" Horace asked as he lifted his head from his work and pushed his glasses farther back up on his nose.

He was a frail little man who mostly kept to himself, but was considered by many, herself included, to be the finest gunsmith within a hundred miles of Cinch Mountain.

Now how did she come by that knowledge? she wondered. But like every other thing she couldn't remember except for little snips and pieces like this one, she pushed it aside until later when her memory would come back and she could understand all the things she couldn't understand now.

Smiling at the gunsmith, she said, "Only bits and pieces so far, but I'm still trying."

"Glad to hear it. Yes ma'am, glad to hear it. Now what can I do for you on such a blistery day like this?" Horace asked, standing up from the stool he'd been sitting on.

Loralie fished in her pocket and pulled out a wad of bills — money she had from what Clay had left her and saw that she had more than enough to buy a gun or maybe two. "I need a good shooting, low priced rifle and pistol," she told him.

Remembering the old Loralie, he knew she would haggle if the price was too high and decided to give her his fairest price right off the bat. "Have just the thing," Horace said, moving over to a spot on the wall where several rifles hung and lifted one off its pegs. "It isn't much to look at, but it shoots true," Horace said with a smile. "And I can let you have it for, well, let's say, a very reasonable price. I took it in on a trade and to be honest, because of its looks, I gave very little for it."

Loralie had to admit it didn't look like much. The stock was scarred and the rifle itself looked as though it had been left out in the weather for some time. "But you say it shoots true?"

"As true as any rifle I have in the store," Horace said with a grin. "I went through it as I do all my weapons and I would put it up against any thing here," he said, sweeping his arm around the store.

"Thirty caliber," Loralie said, moving the lever to open the breech. She then lifted it to her shoulder and sighted down the barrel. "Okay then. Now about a pistol..."

Horace reached under the counter and came out with a pistol that looked to Loralie like it would fit her hand.

"This here is an 1877 double action Colt that shoots .30 caliber ammunition. It only weighs two pounds fully loaded with six rounds. I can let you have it very reasonable also, because most of the men around here want a 44 caliber," Horace told her.

Loralie left the gun shop with a pistol strapped around her waist and carrying her rifle in her hand. She was feeling anxious to be on her way but she still needed a couple of horses and some supplies. Plus, she planned to stop by the bank and see if she had any money deposited there.

Luckily, the bank was on the same side of the street as the gun shop, and only a few doors down.

The teller, an overweight man of around fifty, with mutton chop sideburns, bright blue eyes and a wide, toothy smile, looked up when Loralie came in, followed by a huge gust of wind.

"Miss Benson, how nice to see you. How can I be of service to you today?" he asked.

Loralie looked at the bank teller and knew his face looked familiar, but for the life of her, she couldn't recall his name. Brazing it out, she stepped up to the window and said, "I don't know if you've heard, but some rustlers burned my place down and stole all my horses. All of my records were burned up in the fire, and so, I was just wonderin', I mean, wondering if you can tell me if I have any money here in the bank and if I do, how much?"

"Why of course. First, let me say, yes, you have an account with us. Now, let me get the ledger book so we can see how much there is in your account."

Loralie stood there, shifting from foot to foot while the bank teller walked over to the back of the room and retrieved a large book from a table standing next to the vault door.

Taking his time, he walked back, carrying the ledger book like it was heavy and laid it on the counter in front of his teller window. "Now, let's see, Loralie Benson," he said, opening the ledger book and running his finger down the page. "Ahh, here it is," he said, giving a low whistle. "You should be able to rebuild quite nicely," he said, looking up at her.

Loralie swallowed and said, "Really? Do you suppose you could write the amount on a piece of paper so I won't forget?"

"I would be glad to. And do you need any cash today?" he asked as he wrote down the amount.

Loralie hadn't thought about that and asked, "Could I get a hundred dollars?"

"Of course," he said as he pushed the piece of paper over to Loralie's side of the counter. "Will a hundred be enough?"

Loralie picked up the piece of paper and gave a gasp. The amount written on the paper read, twenty-seven thousand six hundred and fifty-one dollars. She was rich!

The teller asked again if one hundred dollars would be enough, bringing Loralie out of her shock. Looking up at him she said, "Yes, Carlton, one hundred dollars will be just fine for now."

As he opened the cash drawer, Loralie realized she'd remembered his name was, Carlton!" Even that bit of remembering filled her with hope.

"Here you are Miss Benson," he said as he counted out the money. "And I think I speak for all of us here at the bank when I say we're all pulling for you."

A little bit embarrassed, Loralie said, "Thank you," then took her money and left the bank before she began to cry. Everyone was being so nice to her - if she could only remember why?

Hank looked up from the horseshoe he was working on when he heard loud pounding on the front door of the livery barn.

"Now who in blazes could thet be on such ah day as this?" he asked himself.

Lifting the bar that held the doors closed, he opened one side just wide enough to let Loralie slip through.

All bundled up in her coat and hat, and a scarf around her face, Hank wasn't sure who had come in – but after replacing the bar across the doors to hold them shut, he turned around and to his surprise, saw Loralie removing the scarf.

"Loralie! What in blue blazes are you doin' out in weather like this?"

"I understand Mister Brentwood left earlier this morning to go after my horses."

"Yes," Hank replied, wondering why she needed that information confirmed.

"And I suppose you supplied the horses for him?" Loralie asked.

"I did. Now what's this all about?" Hank asked and immediately knew the answer. "Now wait just ah gall-darned minute! You ain't plannin' on doin' what I'm thinkin' you are, are ya?"

"If you think I'll be goin', I mean, going after him, you would be correct. Now, I'll need two horses – one for riddin', I mean, riding, and one to pack the supplies I'll be takin', I mean, taking."

Hank looked at her in disbelief. She couldn't possibly be thinking of trying to find Clay in weather like this. Every track would have been blown away and the only thing she could possibly know was that he started his search up at her ranch. In weather like this, he was probably holed up somewhere trying to wait out the storm, and even then, it would be like looking for a needle in a haystack.

"Sorry, but I ain't got no horses available right now," Hank told her, crossing his arms across his chest.

Loralie looked down through the barn and saw at least a dozen horses in various stalls and felt the anger rising in her. He was trying to keep her from following after Clay and she guessed for good reason – it was because of the storm. Even she had had second thoughts, but once again her stubborn streak took control. "I ain't lookin' ta rent no nags," she told Hank, reverting to her old way of speaking because of her anger. "I'm here ta buy two horses and I've got cash money. So, now Mister Livery Man, do you have any horses for sale or do I go elsewhere?"

Hank looked at the floor, admiring her tenacity, but not overlooking the absurdity of the whole thing. "Loralie, I know you're worried about Clay and I have to admit, with some reason, but goin' out there huntin' fer him in this weather makes absolutely no sense atall. At least wait til this storm blows over and when it does, I'll go along with ya."

Loralie swallowed and felt a little relief from Hank's words. "But how do we know how long the storm will last? What if he's layin' out there somewhere with ah bullet in him and needs help now?"

"And what if he's just holed up somewhere, waitin' fer the storm ta pass. In case I didn't mention it, I sent ah good tent along with him just in case somethin' like this might happen."

"So, you don't think he's caught up to the rustlers yet?" She asked, trying to speak correctly.

"Shoot, he jest left ah few hours ago. Don't reckon he's got any further than your place, and if he got hit by this storm, he's more'n likely doin' jest like I said, sittin' inside his tent with ah cup of hot coffee in his hand, waitin' fer the storm ta blow over."

Loralie sighed. Maybe she had gotten a little carried away, but she was worried about him. She didn't like it that he had gone off alone like that.

Seeing her shoulders slump slightly, Hank knew he'd penetrated that thick skull of hers and said, "Just think about it and you'll half'ta agree thet I'm right. Goin' out in this storm will be nothin' but trouble."

He watched as his words took effect, which gave him hope and he said, "Look, why don't we see about packin' up the supplies we'll need and when the storm lets up, we'll be ready. And like I said, I'll go with ya."

Loralie looked at Hank and said, "Alright. What you say makes sense. I can only hope the storm doesn't last much longer, and that we're not too late."

Hank let out a long breath of air and said, "Think you can make it over ta the mercantile and see about food and ammunition and such, whilst I get the horses and pack animals ready. I'm sorry but I don't think I have another tent... I..."

"Don't worry about it. I'll get one while I'm over at the mercantile. What else don't you have?" Loralie asked.

CHAPTER TWENTY-THREE

It was true, Clay had just reached the burned down ruins of Loralie's ranch when the wind hit. He immediately rode in among the trees and found a spot where he could make a hasty wind break for the horses. He then pitched his tent with its back to the storm so he could make a small fire just in front for both cooking and heat. Before climbing inside his tent, he fed the horses and made sure they were all right. While the wind shook the tent, threatening to rip out the pegs holding it down, Clay sat inside, drinking coffee; thinking about things.

First on his mind was Loralie. Had he done the wrong thing by taking advantage of the situation? She was vulnerable right now and needed someone to tell her everything was going to be all right. He hadn't planned on things going as far as they had, but one thing led to another and before he knew it, they had both lost control.

He smiled as he remembered her exuberance, her eagerness. She was quite a woman. But he somehow knew he couldn't face her come morning and that was why he'd left when he did. What could he have said to her?

"You were a coward, is what you were," he said out loud, the words disappearing into the wind.

He wondered what she'd done when she woke up and found him gone. And had Harold been able to smooth things over? "I guess it's too late to worry about it now, huh?" he said to Ol' Son who was lying next to him.

Ol' Son raised his head and began wagging his tail.

"We can't waste our time thinking about what has already been done can we? We need to think about what needs to be done to get her horses back, don't we." Clay said, rubbing Ol' Son's neck.

Ol' Son moved his head and laid it on Clay's leg, his eyes looking up at him.

Clay tossed the remains of his coffee out the front opening of the tent, then layed down, pulling his arm under the back of his head. "We might as well get some rest while we can. As soon as this storm lets up, we'll need to be hunting for tracks if there is any to be found. You can bet those rustlers aren't going to be waiting around for us to catch up to them."

Ol' Son wagged his tail like he'd understood every word and agreed.

Clay made himself comfortable and did what he always did in situations like this – close his eyes, let his mind go blank, knowing no one would come sneaking up on him in this weather – and shortly, drifted off to sleep.

-

The storm raged on all day and through most of the night. Somewhere along the way, depending what part of the mountain you were on, the wind and rain was replaced by large white flakes of snow drifting slowly to the ground where they began to pile up and cling to everything, creating a deep blanket of snow, covering any tracks that had once been available to see.

Clay hadn't gotten much rest before leaving on his quest to find the rustlers and the herd of horses and slept the sleep of the dead through the day and all night. During the early morning hours, he was dreaming about a giant weight pushing him down and opened his eyes. The inside of the tent was caving in on him from the heavy layer of snow piled on top of it, which inadvertently caused his dream.

Pushing up with both his hands and his legs, he shoved the canvas upward and felt the load lighten as the snow slid off the tent and onto the ground. He then turned and did the same thing to the other side and when he was able, he opened the tent flap and saw at least two feet of snow covering the ground. "Well, now ain't that just great," he said to Ol' Son who was whimpering like he needed to get outside the tent.

"You and me both, partner," Clay said as he began to dig his way out and stand up. He'd no more than gotten himself upright when Ol' Son dashed passed him and began to make his way deeper into the woods. Clay grinned and stomped off, following him.

Clay had a quick meal of potatoes, with a few slices of bacon thrown in for good measure and was in the throes of packing the last of his supplies on the packhorse when the icy wind arrived, again – this time driving the snow in front of it.

Clay looked at the sky and said, "You do realize you're not making this easy for me, don't you?"

Clay finished breaking camp and had just put a foot in the stirrup so he could step aboard his horse, when he heard Ol' Son whimpering. He looked over his shoulder and saw Ol' Son was trying to make his way on three legs through snow deeper than he was tall, and was having a hard time of it.

Clay stepped back down from his horse and made his way over to Ol' Son and lifted him into his arms, then walked over and set him on top of the packhorse's load. As he turned to go back to his horse, he would swear on a stack of bibles, Ol' Son was grinning.

CHAPTER TWENTY-FOUR

Wilber had everyone up and moving by the time the sun came over the horizon. "We need ta put some miles between us and thet ranger," he said, trying to get them to move faster, but the braves insisted on building a huge, blazing fire to warm up and have something to eat before starting out. Having only a blanket between them and the storm, they were chilled to the bone and their stomachs were growling.

Over coffee, Samuel said, "Shouldn't we jest wait fer him here and ambush him when he rides up. If we leave now, he'll fer sure be able ta follow us through all this snow."

Wilber thought about this and said, "You jest might ah come up with ah good idea fer onct, Samuel... Yes sir. We can kill him right here when he rides by, and by the time somebody finds his carcass there won't be nuthin' left ceptin bones. Now, here's what we'll do," Wilber said, laying out his plan to ambush Clay.

-

Loralie and Hank left Cinch Mountain before first light. The storm had stopped and she was anxious to be on the trail. Half way to her ranch, the new frigid air hit them and later as she and Hank rode into the area where her ranch house and barn used to be, they could see where the cold wind had blown away any tracks they may have followed. The storm was making it difficult for everyone.

"We'll never find him now," Hank declared, shaking his head at their bad luck.

"Don't be so sure," Loralie said as she rode over to where Clay had made his camp in among the trees. These tracks ain't covered up yet and we can see the general direction he is headed."

"And what happens when those tracks run out?" Hank asked.

"We follow our gut feeling," Loralie responded.

"Well that may not be the best suggestion I've ever heard," Hank mumbled.

"What was that?" Loralie asked not fully hearing what Hank had said, due to the howling wind.

"I was jest sayin' we maybe should get ah move on afore what tracks there is gets all covered over with this wind driven snow."

"Good idea," Loralie said as she nudged her horse in the ribs turning him to follow Clay's tracks that were quickly fading away under the falling snow.

-

Clay was following his gut instinct as he topped over the mountain and headed down the backside. From what he'd learned back in Cinch Mountain, he was guessing the rustlers were taking the horses over in to North Carolina. His guess would be they were heading for somewhere in the neighborhood of Ashville, where the horses could be sold with phony bills of sale and no one asking any questions.

He had ridden no more than two hours when the few tracks, he could still follow, veered off to the right. The cold wind was pushing against Clay's back driving him forward.

Whirlwinds of snow were everywhere as the icy wind picked it up and twirled the fallen snow in the air, then sent it flying across the ground in front of him. He was cold and his hope of finding shelter for a few hours was waning. Only his strong desire of finding the rustlers and Loralie's horses kept him from returning to Cinch Mountain and the warmth of his train car.

The first shot tore Clay's hat off his head and sent it flying in the wind. Clay grabbed his rifle and carried it with him as he drove himself from the saddle and landed on a roll in the soft snow.

He quickly buried himself in a pile of deep snow and lay still, his eyes scanning the area in front of him, searching for the shooter. But with the snow swirling in his front of his eyes, he could see no one.

While trying to scan the area, off to his left, he saw a small herd of horses and surmised they must be Loralie's, but he could see no one tending to them. He felt Ol' Son crawl up next to him and stop. "Good boy," he said, never taking his eyes off the area where the shot had come from.

"Oh great," Clay said when he saw his horses racing toward where Loralie's horses stood with their backs to the storm.

Out of his peripheral vision, Clay saw movement on his right side and shifted to see better, and when he did, a shot rang out. The bullet tore up the snow just inches from his face.

Clay rolled over to his left several times and came up behind a fallen tree as bullets followed him, tearing up the snow where he'd just been and slammed into the tree trunk with a thunk, thunk, thunk. While the tree trunk was getting peppered with lead, Clay inched himself farther along until he was at the root end of the tree and could get a look in the direction of the woods without being seen.

From time to time he saw the smoke puff of a rifle being fired and took his time sighting in just to the left of the smoke, where the shooter should be. He took a deep breath of the cold air and let it out slowly as he squeezed the trigger and felt the jar against his shoulder.

He was rewarded by a yelp as someone cried out, "I'm hit! I'm hit!" The words were slightly garbled by the time he heard them.

Clay rolled back behind the tree as bullets filled the area he'd just left.

-

Samuel was in tears, but was unable to talk without mumbling and spitting blood. Clay's bullet had driven its way through the right cheek of Samuel's face, missed his teeth and went out through the left cheek. His mouth was quickly filling with blood and he was continually trying to spit it out.

"Am I ganna doie?" Samuel mumbled through a bloody mouth when Lives in The Woods eased over next to him and inspected his wound.

"Are you asking me if you are going to die?" Lives in The Woods, asked, not fully understanding what Samuel was saying.

When Samuel nodded his head, Lives in The Woods said, "I do not think so, but we do need to stop the bleeding."

"Do what'cha gotta do, Indian," Wilber said in a hushed whisper, then turned to Wolf, "You take up his rifle and do what ya can. I want thet man dead."

Reluctantly, Wolf eased over and picked up Samuel's rifle, vowing not to be as stupid as Samuel and stay in the same place after he'd taken a shot.

While all of this was going on, Clay belly crawled to a new position, closer to the horses and in a shallow ditch he had accidentally stumbled, or slipped into. The snow covered it and when he put his arm out to pull himself father along, it went down into the ditch. Clay glanced over his shoulder and saw that everything was still quiet as he inched his way down into the depression, which turned out to be only about three feet deep. But that was enough to at least allow him to move toward the horses, and hopefully without detection.

Clay was at the end of the ditch and looking toward the trees, trying to see a movement, when Ol' Son began to growl. "What is it, boy?" he asked, turning his head to look in the direction Ol' Son was looking.

"Easy," Clay whispered as he laid his hand on the dog's shoulder and took a hand full of fur to keep him from bolting toward the mountain lion that had just walked over to the tree where Clay had recently been, and began sniffing around.

He had a good shot at the big cat, but he knew he couldn't take it without exposing his position. But... if the mountain lion turned and followed his smell, he would have no choice.

As luck would have it, the mountain lion hopped up onto the trunk of the tree to look around and instantly felt a bullet slam into his hip, knocking him off the fallen tree.

The big cat let out a scream that would curdle blood, then ran into the forest in the direction of the rustlers, but didn't get far when the second shot rang out and the big mountain lion tumbled headfirst into a snow bank - turning the snow red with his blood.

Clay held his position, waiting to see what was going to happen next, but no one came out to check on the big cat. It didn't matter, because now, he had a fix on their location and any movement they made, they would make them an easy target.

"What are you doin'?" Wilber hissed at Wolf. "Cain't ya tell the difference between ah mountain lion and ah man?"

"I'm sorry. I am nervous. I saw movement and then he came running toward us. What was I to do, let him come in and attack us?" Wolf limply explained.

"Well get over it and don't be so quick ta shoot at anything thet moves. At least the one thing we do know is thet he ain't by that tree trunk no more. The mountain lion done scared him off. Keep a sharp eye out, he likes ta sneak up on people."

"If I was him," Lives in The Woods said, "I would try to get next to the horses. After all, one of them is his."

"Jest what I was ah thinkin'," Wilber said, not wanting the young Indian brave thinking he'd outsmarted him. "You stay here and tend ta my brother whilst me an Wolf slip back inta the woods and circle around ta where the horses are. And no shootin' at shadders," he said over his shoulder.

And with that, Wilber nodded for Wolf to follow him, then eased his way back, deeper into the woods.

Clay watched the place where the shot had come from and saw what looked like two of them moving back into the woods. Whoever it was moved too quickly for him to get a shot at.

Clay looked at the horses, then into the nearby forest and knew what they were up to. Instead of going to the spot he'd originally planned, he belly crawled further down to his left to get on the lower side of the herd where he wouldn't be seen when he put his plan into action.

CHAPTER TWENTY-FIVE

-

The tracks had long disappeared and Hank and Loralie were doing what Loralie had suggested back down at her ranch – they were following their gut instinct – actually, Loralie's instinct.

Hank had just given Loralie his opinion about what he thought they were doing. "I know you mean well and all, but we ain't seen no tracks now fer several miles. What in blazes makes you think this is the way they come? We could be wastin' our time out here in this freezin' cold fer nuthin'. We could be goin' the wrong direction and not know it."

"Maybe," Loralie said, "but I don't think so. I know this mountain like the back of my hand and I say they're headed for Ashville. It's the only place that makes sense."

"To you, maybe. Ain't you cold?" Hank asked, blowing warm air into his folded hands.

Loralie looked back over her shoulder and said, "Course I am, but so is them rustlers and Clay."

Hank couldn't dispute that, but continued his argument. "But what if they didn't come this way? What if they went north or west?"

Loralie was about to give her opinion on that when they heard the gunfire in the far distance.

"It's them!" she called over her shoulder just before she set her heels against her horse's sides, urging her into a dead run, or as much as the horse could in the deep snow.

"Slow down," Hank hollered. "She could slip on the ice or step in a hole! Plus, she'll get winded real quick like tryin' ta run in the deep snow."

The voice of reason was a hard pill to swallow, but she knew Hank was right. If her horse went down or got too winded to run, she would be afoot, which would not be good.

Loralie hauled back on the reins and pulled her horse to a fast walk, gritting her teeth at the thought of Clay being shot or killed by the rustlers and her not being there to help him.

Hank rode up beside her and said, "We'll get there. The shots sound closer now."

A few minutes later they topped over the mountain and in the far distance they could see a wide, treeless clearing.

"The shooting had stopped, but something inside Loralie knew it wasn't over, yet. She urged her horse forward, touching her rifle in the scabbard attached to the saddle.

As she and Hank rode slowly down the mountain, they looked for movement of any kind but it wasn't until they had gone close to a mile that they saw the horses off to their right.

Loralie pulled up and stopped her horse, with Hank doing the same. They sat there, waiting for something to happen so they could determine what to do.

The wind was blowing and snow whirled in the air, sometimes making it hard to see very far.

"What 'ya think?" Hank asked, turning his head so he could see Loralie's face through the whirling snow.

"I think we..." Which is as far as she got when she heard the pistol fire over the wind and saw the horses turn and run toward the trees.

"One of'em is stampeedin', I mean, one of them is stampeding the horses toward the other one, but which one is which?" Loralie asked, as the horses suddenly came to a halt when whoever was in the trees also began firing in the air.

She and Hank watched as the horses headed back down the mountain at a dead run, followed by two men and three Indian braves, riding like their tails were on fire.

Loralie pulled her nasty looking rifle from its scabbard and pushed the butt against her shoulder and took aim at the man in the rear. Taking her time, she sighted in on his back and squeezed the trigger.

Evidently, the mare Loralie was riding had never been shot off of before because the sound of the rifle roaring in her ear caused her to rear up in the air and come down with her head between her front legs and began to buck for all she was worth, Loralie's shot missed its target by a mile.

The men and horses continued on down the mountain as fast as they could go.

When her horse began to buck unexpectedly, Loralie's rifle went one way and she went the other, landing on her back in the snow with a loud, "oomph."

Hank jumped off his horse and grabbed the reins of Loralie's horse and yelled, "Whoa! Easy girl... Easy now," pulling her to him and when she was still, he rubbed her on her forehead and said, "Good girl."

Once he had the horse settled down, Hank turned and looked at Loralie, who was trying to get to her feet, but every time she tried to stand up on the slick ground, she would lose her balance and fall back down. Hank walked over and stuck out his hand, giving Loralie a hand to her feet.

"You all right?" he asked with a grin.

"My faith in shooting off the back of a horse has been altered somewhat. I thought everbody trained their horses to be shot off of. Guess I was wrong. They got away, didn't they?"

"Yes, they got away. I just recently got that horse so I didn't know you couldn't shoot off of her. Plus, I didn't know you were gonna try."

Loralie was about to say something when she and Hank heard a shrill whistle, and looked in the direction the sound came from.

Loralie's heart began to beat a little faster when she saw Clay come crawling out of the ditch he'd been in and put his hands to his mouth and whistled, again.

Hank touched Loralie on the shoulder and said, "Look! It's Clay!"

Loralie turned and looked in the direction Hank was pointing and saw the black stallion turn and make his way out of the racing herd and begin running back toward Clay, its head held high, his tail arched and his mane blowing in the wind.

Wilber saw the black stallion leave the herd but wasn't about to go after him. His first priority was to get as far away as he could before the man came after them, again.

"Oh, isn't he beautiful!" Loralie said as she watched the big horse come to a sliding stop just in front of Clay and lay his chin over Clay's shoulder.

"He sure is somethin', alright," Hank said, grinning from ear to ear.

Clay put his arms around the black stallion's neck and hugged him. "I don't reckon I've ever been so glad to see you, boy. I wish I had an apple or something to give you, but I don't."

Midnight just stood there, enjoying his master's touch.

Clay lowered his arms and turned toward the sound of his name being called...

"Clay! Clay Brentwood!"

Clay couldn't believe his eyes. Hank and Loralie were riding toward him with big smiles on their faces.

"Now where in blazes did you come from?" Clay asked as Hank and Loralie came to a stop in front of him.

"Oh, we was jest out fer ah mornin' ride and saw you got yourself in trouble again and decided ta come ta yer rescue. You are in trouble, ain't cha'?" Hank asked with a wide grin on his face.

Clay looked up at Loralie and said, "Your friend has quite a sense of humor. How are you? And maybe you can tell me why the two of you are here?" he asked, waving his hand around.

Loralie glanced over at Hank, wondering how far back this morning she should go, when Hank butted in.

"She came by the livery this mornin', wantin' ta get ah couple of horses so's she could come lookin' fer ya, and, well... I, I tried ta talk her out of it, but you know how stubborn she can be..."

This time Loralie interrupted. "You do know I'm right here next to you."

"Well, it's true. Once you set yer mind ta somethin'..."

"That's enough arguing for today. Now, the fact is, you are both here and I probably can't talk you into going back. So, if you're going to come with me, it will be under my rules. We clear on that?" Clay told them. Secretly, he was glad they were here.

Loralie began to grit her teeth and said, "Depends on what them rules are. Those are my horses and I got ever right ta go after the men who stole 'm, usin' my own rules ta do so."

Clay gave out with a long breath of air and scratched the back of his neck. "You are right, those are your horses and you have a right to go after the rustlers. But if you think you can get them back, alone... Why did you send for me?"

Loralie puckered her lips and looked at the sky. "If'n I could get all my rememberin' back I might could answer thet question, but you know I cain't, don't 'cha, Mister Texas Ranger.

At this point, Loralie was so frustrated she didn't realize she'd slipped back into her old way of talking.

Suddenly, the wind calmed down and the snow stopped falling. The dark clouds separated and allowed the sun to brighten the day.

"I don't mean to come down hard on you. It's just that I'm concerned for your safety. I know you're good with both of your weapons, but you've also got a lot of emotional attachment to the situation and that might mean trouble," Clay told her.

"What I'm asking is for you to let me call the shots. You have to admit, I do have a little more experience with rustlers and such than either of you."

"Well, since you're asking and not demanding..." Loralie said, looking down at the ground, not wanting him to see he had won the debate.

Loralie had calmed down about a hundred degrees and her new way of speaking was returning.

"Thank you," Clay said, glancing at the packhorse. "Are you carrying supplies?"

"We sure are," Loralie said with pride.

Clay nodded his head and grinned. "Do you suppose we could have some coffee before we strike out?"

"But... but what about those rustlers? They're getting away!" Loralie protested.

"They won't get far, running those horses like they are in conditions like this," he said, kicking the snow. "Not only will they wear out their own horses, but your horses will get tired as well and they'll just stop and rest. Let's get over there close to the trees where we can find some wood for the fire," Clay suggested.

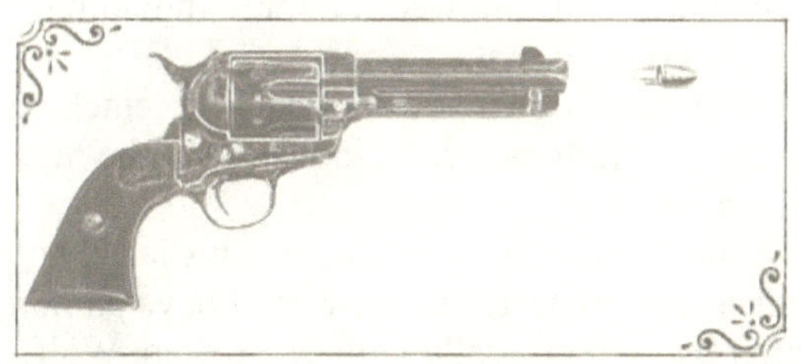

CHAPTER TWENTY-SIX

-

Exactly as Clay said it would happen, Wilber's horse stumbled and almost went down from trying to run in the deep snow. Wolf, Lives in The Woods and Bullfrog had already slowed their horses down to a walk.

"I stay wie tak ah brek," Samuel said in his garbled way of speaking. Mi ceeks ar ah killun me.

Lives in The Woods had plugged both holes with pieces of Samuel's shirttail to stop the bleeding, but it didn't stop the pain, of which Samuel continually reminded everyone.

Wilber's horse finally stopped and just stood there, drawing air into its lungs. He was so worn down he was shaking and Wilber could feel it. In the near distance, up ahead of them, Loralie's horses had stopped and were all standing with their heads drooping.

Looking back over his shoulder, Wilber could see no one coming after them and gave a sigh. "Alright, we'll take ah break here. The horses need some rest and I could use ah cup of coffee."

Wilber looked at the three Indian boys and said, "You boys get ah fire goin' whilst I get the coffee. We can fill the pot wit snow ta get water. Now get ah move on, we ain't got all day. As soon as the horses are rested ah mite, we'll move on."

"All da, wuld be arigt wid me," Samuel mumbled as he climbed down from his horse and followed the three Indian boys to the spot where they were going to make camp.

As Wilber stepped down and loosened the cinch on the saddle so his horse could breath easier, he looked over the herd and got an angry look on his face.

"We lost the black when the ranger whistled!" he blared loud enough for everyone to hear. "So now he'll have ah horse and he'll be comin' after us, so don't dally with that coffee. Wolf, keep an eye on them horses and let me know as soon as they can move, even if 'n it's jest at ah walk."

As one, the others all turned and looked at the herd. Finally, Bullfrog said, "As we were riding away, I thought I heard a whistle. Maybe the man whistled for his horse. I have heard you can train your horse to come to you when you whistle. I have never done this, but it is what I have heard."

Wilber looked over at the herd once again and saw Clay's saddle horse and his pack horse standing in the middle of Loralie's horses. If Samuel's suggestion was true, the ranger would be riding bareback, Injun style, which to his mind wouldn't be very comfortable.

Wilber grinned and led his horse over to where Lives in The Woods was building a fire. As he got near, he called out to Wolf, "See if 'n you can get thet ranger's horses and bring 'um back over here. He might have somethin' in his pack we can use."

Wolf looked the herd over and decided it would not be difficult. The horses were tired and probably wouldn't bolt at the smell of an Indian, as some did.

Without saying anything, Wolf walked slowly as he circled the horses and came at them from downwind so they wouldn't get his scent too early.

Speaking softly, Wolf walked among the herd until he reached Clay's horses. First, Wolf drew the reins of the packhorse over its head, then led the packhorse over to where the saddle horse was standing.

Speaking softly Wolf patted the horse's neck, then put his foot in the stirrup and stepped up onto the saddle. Satisfied, when the horse didn't buck, he turned the horse and made his way out of the herd and then rode back to the camp, leading the packhorse.

When Wolf stepped down, Wilber walked up to him and said, "Ya did good. Seems you got ah way with animals."

Wolf didn't respond as he handed the reins to Wilber, then walked over and squatted down next to Lives in The Woods and began talking to him.

Wilber gave the two Indian boys a stern look, then led Clay's horses away to a spot where he could find out what was in the pack.

"Don't reckon I'll ever understand Indians," Wilber muttered to himself.

Squatting down next to Lives in The Woods, Wolf played with a stick in the fire and after a moment, he said, "I have been doing some thinking."

Lives in The Woods looked up, knowing Wolf had some kind of scheme rolling around inside his head. He rubbed both his eyes with the heels of his hands, to ease the sting from the smoke, then asked, "And how deep into trouble is that thinking going to get us?"

Wolf studied his friend for a long moment before he said anything. "You may be right, there could be trouble, but hear me out before you say anything or try to object."

"Shouldn't Bullfrog be here to hear what you have to say? He is - after all, an equal partner."

"Of course. I didn't mean to leave him out. I was just going to run the idea by you first, but you are right – Bullfrog should be here.

Wolf gave out with a low whistle and Bullfrog, who was gathering more firewood, turned and looked toward his friends.

Wolf made a motion with his hand for Bullfrog to return.

Samuel had gone off into the woods to do his business and Wilber was rummaging through Clay's pack, leaving the three boys alone to discuss Wolf's idea in low voices without the white men realizing something was afoot.

"Like I said, I have been thinking. As you know, the Mullins brothers only pay ten dollars a head for stealing horses for them, and have reluctantly agreed to pay us fifteen dollars a head for these horses."

Both Bullfrog and Lives in The Woods nodded their heads in agreement, wondering where Wolf was going with this.

Bullfrog added a piece of wood to the fire and waited. Whatever Wolf's new scheme was, he knew he would go along if Lives in The Woods did.

Lives in The Woods also waited for his friend to unveil his latest thinking. Trying to second-guess Wolf would be like trying to run down a scared rabbit.

Wolf scratched behind his left ear, then said, "I am beginning to get the feeling that once we get the horses back down to North Carolina, Wilber will shoot us because he will no longer need us. Plus, that will save him paying us the money he will owe us. Thirty-one horses at fifteen dollars each is a lot of money. Plus, we can't forget the extra hundred dollars apiece he promised us. And we know how he hates to part with his money."

Both Bullfrog and Lives in The Woods let this information roll around inside their heads before Bullfrog said, "What you say makes sense, but what can we do about it?"

"I agree. Wilber Mullins will want to get rid of us when he no longer needs us. But even if we can somehow figure a way to steal the horses from them, how do we get rid of them? Who will we sell them to? No one will buy that many horses from three young Cherokee braves – especially ones our age," Lives in The Woods said.

Wolf gave his two friends a sheepish grin. "But what if we do have a buyer? One who is willing to pay more than fifteen dollars a head?"

Bullfrog and Lives in The Woods looked at each other, then back at Wolf. "And who is this mysterious person who will pay three enterprising young braves such as ourselves that kind of money? And how did you come to know such a person? Have you spoken to him about this?" Lives in The Woods asked. "Did he say he would buy the horses?"

Wolf jabbed the fire with the stick, sending sparks flying into the air. "I have never spoken to the person I'm speaking about and it is not a he, it is a she. I'm talking about the woman we have been stealing horses from. Do you not think she will pay whatever we ask to get her horses back?"

Wolf grinned as he looked at his two friends staring at him with stunned looks on their faces - their mouths open and their chins hanging down close to their chests.

"It is a good plan, yes?" Wolf asked.

After recovering from their shock at the idea of selling the woman's horses back to her, they both nodded their heads in agreement.

"But now, we must come up with a plan on how we can steal the horses from the Mullins and get away with it. If we just take them during the night, they will know it was us. Wilber Mullins will be very angry and we will be dead as soon as he finds us. Then he will do harmful things to our families."

Lost in the idea, Lives in The Woods was thinking only about the money and not the possible consequences if the Mullins brothers caught them. "We could give most of the money to our families, then go west. I hear there is great adventure out there," Lives in The Woods said, lost in the dream of what might be.

"I have heard the same thing," Bullfrog said with a big smile. "I say we do it."

"That sounds like a good plan except knowing Wilber Mullins, he will figure out what we have done and even if we get away with it, he will give our families much grief. He will tell the authorities lies and take the money away from them," Wolf stated.

About that time, Samuel came back to the fire and said, "Wiber aunts ta kno when da coppe is ganna be redy?"

"It is ready now. Would you mind taking him a cup?" Wolf asked, hoping to get him away so they could continue their talk.

"I shur vood mind. My ja urts too ad. oou do it," Samuel muttered.

"I will do it," Bullfrog said, standing up and going to the fire.

After pouring coffee into a tin cup to take to Wilber, Bullfrog looked around to make sure no one was watching, and hacked a glob of phlegm and spit it into Wilber's coffee, then with a stick, mixed it into the hot brew.

Wilber took the cup from Bullfrog and lifted the cup to his lips and took a long drink of the hot liquid. Smacking his lips, he said, "Now thet's ah good cup o coffee."

Bullfrog grinned as he turned and walked back toward the fire.

Shortly after Bullfrog returned to the fire, the three young braves were laughing hysterically, causing Wilber to wonder what was so funny. "Probably talkin' bout the women they're gonna spend their money on," Wilber said to himself. "But the jokes gonna be on them if'n I have anythin' ta say about it."

-

Clay, Loralie and Hank were just finishing up their coffee and slices of bacon Loralie cooked while the coffee was brewing when Hank asked, "So, what's the plan?"

Clay finished the last of his coffee and admitted, "Don't have one, yet. First, we need to catch up with them, and hopefully without them knowing we're close by. Then we follow them and wait for an opportunity to get the horses back. At that time, we'll make a plan on how to do it."

"Sounds like a good plan ta me," Hank said with a chuckle.

"If we're finished, I suggest we clean up and get going. I'm getting anxious to find that opportunity that leads to the plan for getting my horses back," Loralie said with an ice melting smile.

Clay almost laughed out loud. This was something the old Loralie would say and hoped it was a sign that her memory was beginning to come back.

Loralie was on her saddle and Clay was about to swing up on Midnight when Hank spoke up. "Hold on."

Clay turned and looked over at Hank, who had a painful look on his face. "Something wrong?"

Hank took off his hat and twirled it in his hands. "The thing is," he said, finding it difficult to speak. "As much as I want ta, I can't go with ya."

Clay was about to say something when Hank held up his hand. "I truly would like to go along and help get yer horses back, Loralie, I surely would. But when we left I thought we'd only be gone ah day er two, but now who knows how long it will take. Jeb, the young man

I left ta take care of the place... well, he can clean up and feed n water the stock, but he don't know nuthin' bout shoein' ah horse er pricin' er any of the things ah fella needs ta know about runnin' the place. They's people thet count on me bein' there and I hope you understand. I truly am sorry."

Loralie stepped down from her horse and ran over to Hank and hugged him. "You don't need to apologize. You've already been more help than you realize. You're a good man, Hank Collins, you truly are and I thank you for all you've done. Now, you go on back to Cinch Mountain and no more of this, I'm sorry talk." And with that, Loralie kissed Hank on the cheek and said, "We'll see you when we get back."

Once again, Clay was about to swing up onto Midnight's back when Hank said, "Clay."

When Clay looked at Hank, he was unsaddling his horse. "What are you doing?"

"I'm givin' you my saddle. Where you're goin' you'll need this saddle ah site more'n I will," Hank said with a grin and nod of his head.

Clay was surprised at Hank's generosity but happy about it. If it came to riding and shooting at the same time, having a saddle under him could make a world of difference and he guessed Hank realized that. "Are you sure about this?"

"You know I'm right. I'll jest be ridin' home, but who knows what you'll be doin' and how long it's gonna take ta get them horses back."

Clay walked over and shook Hank's hand and said, "Thank you, my friend," then lifted the saddle off Hank's horse and set it on the ground while he rubbed down Midnight's back a little before putting the blanket on. "Some folks don't realize it but it's best not to throw a cold blanket on your horse's cold back. They can get a might testy about it."

Once he had Midnight saddled, Clay stepped onto the saddle and put two fingers to the brim of his hat. "Much obliged," he said to Hank.

"Jest get back safe with all her horses, and my saddle," Hank said before waving and riding off.

Clay and Loralie rode out, riding side by side, neither saying anything about the night on the train, even though both were thinking about it.

Clay wondered if that was the reason Loralie had come looking for him, while Loralie wondered if that was the reason he left.

As Hank disappeared into the thick forest, he began to chuckle. He was remembering the looks between Loralie and Clay, and had come to the conclusion that there was something going on between them. What it was, exactly, he wasn't sure but he guessed it had something to do with her sending that telegram asking him to come out here. He might be guessing but he thought her inviting Clay to come out had more to do with the real reason she had for wanting him here, than because of those rustlers.

CHAPTER TWENTY-SEVEN

-

As they started the horses moving south, in the direction of Ashville, the three young Cherokee braves were each looking at their surroundings and a place they might be able to steal the horses from the Mullins brothers and not make it look like it was them who did it. Wolf was wishing they had some help to make it look like an ambush.

Ashville, North Carolina was still a good-ways off, and depending on the weather and the trail, the man could easily catch up with them.

Ashville was located in what was called, the French Broad River Valley at an altitude of somewhere in the neighborhood of twenty-two hundred feet – deep in the southern Appalachian Mountains.

Between where they were and Ashville there were a lot of hills and valleys to follow – some steep and rocky and others following a stream or creek, while other trails that had been hatched through thick vegetation where the going would be single file.

Most of the ridge tops would be dry and rocky. The truth was, all the trails would be rocky, making the drive slower that the Mullins brothers wanted, causing them to watch their back trail with a lot of anxiety. Everyone knew the man would not be far behind.

Along the way there would be fern, tall hemlocks and rosebay rhododendron - that at this time of year would be bearing no flowers – with of course, lots of mountain laurel thrown into the mixture.

Where or how they would steal the horses was still just an idea, but one each hoped they could pull off. Selling the horses back to the woman was a much better idea than taking a chance with the Mullins brothers who would rather kill them than pay them the money they owed. Both Bullfrog and Lives in The Woods would be trying to come up with a plan, but would ultimately look to Wolf to put a plan together. He was the one who always came up with good ideas.

The snow was a good two feet deep and the panicked horses left a trail a two-year-old child could follow, so there was no use in trying to hide their progress, which was slow going. Wilber was agitated by this and did a lot of yelling and swearing at them.

Clay allowed the horses to set their own pace, not worried as much about catching up to the men who had stolen the horses as he was about how to get them back. There were five of them and only Loralie and himself. The odds weren't good, but he'd seen worse.

Clay was deep in thought about what to do when they did finally catch up to the rustlers, when out of the blue, Loralie said, "I'm sorry about last night."

Clay pulled Midnight to a halt and stared at Loralie. "Why are you sorry?" he asked cautiously. In his mind there was no reason to be sorry unless them being together that way had never crossed her mind. Did women think about those things he wondered? She had been so eager and responsive he'd just assumed...

Loralie stopped her horse and turned to look squarely at Clay. Why had he asked if she was sorry? Was she sorry? She didn't think so. She had enjoyed being with him more than she wanted to admit. In fact, over the past few years she had dreamed about being with him and what it would be like – and last night had been even better than her dreams.

Loralie took a deep breath and said, "I didn't actually mean I'm sorry. What I meant was, I… I think the champagne caused me to do what I did before I was supposed to. After all we aren't married and I don't want you to think I'm some sort of harlot or a loose woman who goes to bed with any man who comes along."

Clay sat there for a full minute trying to decide how to approach the subject without making himself sound like someone who preyed on drunken women.

Finally, he said, "I guess with your memory loss you don't remember the letters we've been writing to each other."

"Letters? We've been writing letters to each other?" Loralie asked, angry that she hadn't remembered writing any letters to him or receiving any from him. Had they been frank about their feelings and desires? She couldn't imagine putting something like that down on paper. Who was the real Loralie Benson? Apparently, a woman who spoke her mind.

"Yes, we have and as I said before, if you hadn't sent that telegram, I was planning on coming out to see you on a completely different matter."

"And what might that matter be?" Loralie asked, her heart beginning to beat a bit faster.

"According to our letters, it was apparent we have feelings for each other and both of us are tired of living alone. I know there would be problems to work out, but I felt confident we could talk about them and work them out. That's part of what I was going to talk to you about and didn't want to do it in a letter. I wanted to talk to you face to face."

"But I thought you said you didn't live alone. You said you have your housekeeper and a lot of people who work for you," Loralie said, trying to lighten the moment and figure out how she knew this. And was he talking about proposing marriage? Had she indicated in her letters that she wanted to marry him? And he was right… there would be problems. Where would they live, in Texas or in Tennessee? They couldn't live in both places, could they? Oh, if she could only remember, then she would know what to say to him.

"I see you're struggling with this," Clay said, reaching out and laying his hand on her arm, "so I suggest we wait until your memory comes back fully so that it won't be a one-sided conversation. And by the way, don't be sorry about last night. I'm not."

And with that, Clay touched Midnight in the sides with his boots and rode on down the trail wondering if he should move Loralie back into the hotel until she was back to normal, or just let things stay as they were. What he knew about courting a woman wouldn't even half fill one of those tiny teacups they liked to drink from. He pulled his hat down a little tighter and tried to concentrate on the problem at hand.

For what seemed an eternity, Loralie sat there, staring at his back as he rode away, excitement rippling throughout her body. He wasn't sorry about last night! And now she admitted to herself, neither was she!

CHAPTER TWENTY-EIGHT

-

For some reason he couldn't explain, Wolf felt like Wilber was keeping a closer eye on him and his friends. Did he suspect something or was it just his imagination? The man surely couldn't know anything about their plans, could he? Had Lives in The Woods or Bullfrog let something slip? He knew he hadn't, and hoped they hadn't.

Wolf rode over next to Lives in The Woods, who like him, was riding drag to make sure none of the horses tried to turn back or take the others in a direction they didn't want them to go.

"Do you think Wilber is watching us closer than he normally does?" Wolf asked.

Before Lives in The Woods could answer, Wolf continued, "Do you think he suspects something?"

Lives in The Woods tapped the sides of his horse with his feet and chased after a roan stallion who wanted to pull away from the herd.

Wolf stayed where he was and helped keep the rest of the horses headed down the trail. He smiled when he saw Bullfrog pull away from the herd to go help Lives in The Woods who was having trouble with the headstrong young stallion.

Fifteen minutes later, Lives in The Woods rode up next to Wolf and said, "No, I don't think he has any idea that we are thinking about stealing the horses from him. I think he has never trusted us and now with this many horses and the man who will soon be upon us, he is being overly cautious."

"I hope you are right," Wolf said, feeling a little better.

"Have you come up with an idea?" Lives in The Woods asked. "I have thought about many ways to do it, but none of them were worth the effort."

"I too, have thought about several ways to do it, but like you said, none of the ideas were worth considering."

"Something will come. I have faith in you," Lives in The Woods said, galloping away to chase another stray back into the herd.

Wolf watched him go and wondered why it was left up to him to come up with a plan?

-

The entire day had slipped away without Wolf coming up with a decent idea. He was riding along, for the moment, not thinking about anything, when Wilber rode up next to him and said, "It's gettin' late. Where are we gonna make camp?"

Startled at not hearing him approach, Wolf jumped when he heard Wilber's gravelly voice so close to him.

"What'cha so jumpy about? I jest asked ah simple question," Wilber said, giving Wolf a stern look.

"Nothing. I just had something on my mind. You just startled me, that's all."

"Startled ya? I thought you redskins was supposed ta have super hearin' and smell and sight and all that other stuff," Wilber said. "You know somethin' you ain't tellin'?" Wilber asked, suspiciously.

Gathering himself together, Wolf sat up a little straighter and said, "I don't know what you are talking about. We are people just like you. Well... maybe not like you, but we have no special powers. We are just taught at an early age to be aware of things, like our surroundings, or a movement that shouldn't be there - things like that. I was thinking about my mother and hoping she his all right. She wasn't feeling well when we left," Wolf lied.

"Well, keep yer mind on the business at hand. Now ride on up ahead and find us ah place ta spend the night."

Without another word, Wolf slapped his feet against the sides of his horse and galloped away – glad to be away from Wilber's prying.

As he rode along, scouting for a place to spend the night, an idea began to creep into his brain and take root.

A little less than a mile down the trail, Wolf found a place they could stop for the night. It had good grass and water for the animals from a creek that spurred off from the river a little farther to the west. The area was off the trail less than a quarter of a mile. It was a place he remembered them using before.

As he sat on the trail waiting for the others to catch up, he more and more liked the idea that had popped into his brain. "It just might work. Yes, it just might work. I will talk to Lives in The Woods and Bullfrog when it is time to sleep," he said to himself.

CHAPTER TWENTY-NINE

-

Loralie rode up next to Clay and asked straight out, "Have we ever done that before – what we did last night?"

Clay was startled by her bluntness, but the truth was, that is exactly the way the old Loralie would have approached it – direct and to the point.

"No. That was the first time and I'm sorry if I made you feel compromised in any way, or uncomfortable. When we began to kiss... well... I guess I sorta got carried away. I mean, it wasn't like you pushed me away or seemed to object or anything."

Loralie felt the heat in her face and knew she was blushing. She wanted to refute his words but knew she couldn't. She had wanted him to kiss her and the other things, too. She was nothing more than a shameless hussy. She started to pull her horse away but Clay reached out and grabbed her horse's rein and kept him from bolting away.

"Whoa. You started this, now don't run away until we've cleared the air," Clay said as he looked directly into her eyes.

Loralie swallowed. Her throat was dry and it was hard to speak. "Please let go of my horse. I don't think we have anything more to talk about. I already know what you must think of me and I don't need to be reminded of my lustful way."

And with that, she slapped her heels against her horse's ribs and sent her flying down the trail as fast as the deep snow would let her.

Clay watched her go and said, "That sure is one mixed up woman."

As if understanding what Clay had said, Ol' Son leaped onto the trail and began chasing Loralie, barking as he ran as best he could on three legs in deep snow.

Clay pulled off his hat and swatted Midnight on the rump, while at the same time digging his heels into the big horse's ribs. The race was on.

They were in deep snow so neither of the horses could run full out, but being taller, and with longer legs; Midnight quickly passed Ol' Son and closed in on Loralie's horse.

As the two horses came abreast, Clay reached out and grabbed the reins of Loralie's horse once again, but this time he didn't let go and brought both horses to a halt – then reached over and grabbed Loralie and lifted her off her saddle and sat her down across his legs and before she could protest, he kissed her hard on the mouth.

At first Loralie tried to struggle. She tried to pull herself away but his kiss sent streams of excitement racing all through her and in the end, she threw her arms around his neck and returned the kiss with as much desire and passion as Clay was giving her.

When at last they came up for air, Clay looked at her and said, "Now, isn't that a lot better than fighting."

Loralie started to say something but Clay put his finger to his lips indicating she should be quiet and when she just sat there, staring into his eyes, he reached up and brushed a strand of hair away from her face and said, "You're very beautiful you know – and a bit hard headed, but in spite of all of that, I kind ah think I've fallen in love with you."

At first, she resented the part about being hard headed, but when she saw the grin on his face and the twinkle in his eyes, she had to swallow and fight back the tears that were welling up in her eyes. He'd said he loved her. She tried again to say something but her throat was dry and when Clay put his finger to her lips, again, and continued speaking, she was glad.

"I know there will be things to get worked out, like where do we live and a whole bunch of other stuff, but if you feel about me the way I feel about you, we'll figure it out."

Loralie looked at him for a long time, taking in every line in his face and the deep blue of his eyes, then, without a word, reached up and kissed him, again, giving Clay the answer he was looking for.

-

The moon was high in a sky, and filled with bright twinkling stars. The heavens were beautiful but down on the ground the temperature was below freezing when Wolf eased himself out from under his blanket.

As he stood there looking over the camp, loud snoring was coming from both Mullins brothers, along with lighter snoring coming from his two friends. Wolf wrapped the blanket around his shoulders and eased his way out to the trail and looked back to the north where the man would be coming from. He was hoping to see the glow of his camp fire, but saw nothing, which didn't surprise him. The man was smart and if he was back there somewhere, he would build his fire in a place that would be hard to see by anyone until they were right up on it.

A breeze had come up that had an icy bite to it and Wolf was anxious to get back near the fire if he couldn't do what he hoped to. Without hesitation, Wolf trotted over to a tall tree and after laying his blanket on one of the lower limbs, he began to climb.

Near the top, he stopped and concentrated on the trail and off to each side. After maybe a half a minute, he thought he saw just a small flicker of light in the far north reaches of his eyesight. He turned his head away for a few seconds, then looked back and sure enough, there it was, a very small glow no bigger than a lightning bug's tail.

Wolf nodded his head and smiled. The man was there and would be coming after them but for now he could not implement his plan, the man was too far away. The man would need to be close enough for him to walk to. Judging the distance to the man's fire, Wolf figured if he tried to walk, he would freeze to death long before he reached the man's camp.

Wolf climbed down and eased back into their camp and sat down next to the fire and added more wood, pulling the thin blanket tighter around his shoulders.

Wolf hadn't been there very long when Lives in The Woods eased up next to him and sat down. He had his blanket wrapped around him to stave off the cold wind that was picking up in intensity. "Did you see his fire?" he asked.

Wolf looked at his friend and realized he also had been awake and had been watching him. "Yes. He is there, but still a long way off – too far to walk to in this weather. We will wait until he gets closer and hope we can reach him before the fighting starts."

Lives in The Woods nodded his head. "Yes, it would be better to speak with him before he tries to reclaim the horses. He does not know we want to return them and even if we try to help him, he might shoot us, thinking we are still trying to steal them."

"Yes, we must find a way to speak to the man soon," Wolf said, "and without the Mullins brothers knowing what we are doing or they, will shoot us."

Wolf put more wood on the fire, then looked at his friend. "We must get as much rest as we can – there may not be much time later."

The two young Cherokee braves layed down next to the fire and closed their eyes.

On the other side of the fire, Wilber Mullins had been watching Wolf and Lives in The Woods through squinted eyes so they wouldn't notice him through the flames. He hadn't been able to hear what they were talking about but he knew in his gut they were up to something. It was a known fact; you couldn't trust a redskin any farther than you could throw a horse. What he did know, they wouldn't be trying anything before morning. With that knowledge, he closed his eyes and tried to go back to sleep. He would need to be awake and alert when they tried to do whatever it was they were planning to do.

CHAPTER THIRTY

Loralie Benson's eyes popped wide open and she stared at the star filled heaven with its round shining moon lighting up the night. It took her a moment to realize where she was and when she did, she smiled. She was a happy woman. They had made love again and she was lying next to the man she'd had dreams about making love to. He was lying next to her with one arm across her side and she could feel his body warmth against her back, along with his light snoring close to her ear. If this is what contentment felt like, she wanted to stay this way forever. She stared at the glow of the fire, feeling more happiness than she could ever remember. She was having a hard time believing this was happening. Happiness wasn't something she was used to. Her life had been filled with hardship, with very few happy times that were only memories of when her folks were alive. But now that was all over. He said he would take care of her and her life could be happy, again. Could it be true? She looked at the sky and prayed it was. After a while, Loralie snuggled a little closer to the man she hoped to be with forever and let herself drift off to sleep, her mind at peace with the world.

Clay woke up, needing to go relieve himself but was afraid to move in case he might awaken her. Their lovemaking had been much more than he'd ever hoped for and knew it had been the same for her. He leaned a little closer and allowed his nostrils to inhale her sweet scent. Even the smell of her was intoxicating.

The need to go into the woods was overpowering and he eased himself from beneath the blanket and outer covering that helped keep out the cold.

With teeth chattering he hurried into the woods to do his business and as he stood there in the moonlight, naked as the day he was born, other thoughts began to fill his head. Had he done the right thing coming here? What would Martha say? Would she approve of Loralie? Was he just feeling this way because of his long absence of being close to a woman and was his need only from lust?

Climbing back into the warmth of their bed, Clay dared not touch her until he was warm again for fear of shocking her awake. She stirred and rolled over, throwing her arm across his chest. She flinched at the coldness, but didn't pull her arm away, instead, she snuggled even closer, throwing her leg over his and settled herself against him.

Desire in him felt like a rushing tide but he let out a long breath of air and tried to control the eagerness he felt. Her hand drifted down across his stomach and he knew going back to sleep would not be an option.

CHAPTER THIRTY-ONE

-

Over hot coffee, flapjacks and bacon, Clay and Loralie talked about the future in loose terms. "We've got plenty of time to make our decisions," Clay finally told her. "Our first duty is to get those horses back and make the men who did it, pay for what they've done."

-

Wilber woke up with plans of his own. First thing after a quick breakfast, he told Samuel and the boys to start pushing the horses south. "I got some business ta attend to and I'll catch up to ya as soon as I can."

Wilber sat his horse for some time, watching the small herd of horses disappear over the hill before he turned his horse and headed for a nearby stand of trees.

Inside the trees and off to the side of the trail, he found a spot where he had a clear view and a tree with a limb sticking out at shoulder height. He was beginning to shake from the cold and knew he wouldn't be able to get off a good shot trying to hold the rifle in his hands, but laying the barrel on the limb would allow him to hold the rifle steady, giving him a much better chance at hitting his target. He blew into his hands to try and warm them up - then stuck his right hand into his pocket to warm his trigger finger. It would do no good if he couldn't pull the trigger when the time came to kill the ranger.

-

Lives in The Woods rode over next to Wolf and asked, "What is he up to?"

"If you mean Wilber, I think he is going to find a place in the woods and wait for the man to come by and shoot him from ambush," Wolf said with a sigh.

"But that will ruin all our plans!" Lives in The Woods declared with a lot of anxiety.

"I know," Wolf said. "I have been thinking and I have come up with a plan. It is not much of a plan, but at least it is something. We cannot let Wilber kill the man."

Lives in The Woods rode a little closer to hear what Wolf had in mind.

After a short conversation, Wolf pulled his mount to a halt and climbed to the ground and lifted his horses left back hoof and began inspecting it.

As he was doing so, Samuel rode up and looked down at Wolf. With his cheeks swollen, he was still having trouble speaking so you could understand him. "Wha's goin' on? Wha's rong wit yer horst?"

Wolf dropped the horse's hoof and looked up at Samuel. "I think he picked up a stone somewhere and has a bruised foot. I need to dig the stone out and maybe allow him to rest for a few minutes."

Samuel shook his head, perplexed. Wilber wouldn't want them to wait on a lame horse. His instructions were to get the horses down the trail as far and fast as they could before the man came looking for them. Wilber hadn't told him what he was going to do or why he was hanging back, but it didn't matter - he had his instructions.

"We cain't vate on ya. Vee gots ta mov on. Vilber sad no stoppin'," Samuel told him and then motioned for Lives in The Woods to move out.

"You will be alright, brother?" Lives in The Woods asked.

"You go ahead, I will catch up as soon as I can," Wolf replied, then watched them ride away in the direction of the herd, a grin spreading across his face.

-

Clay and Loralie rode out of camp and headed south, following the trail of the horse herd.

"If there's any shooting, you get behind something," Clay told Loralie as they rode at a lope down the trail left by the horses, which made following them, easier.

"And what will you be doing, Mister Texas Ranger?" Loralie asked in a smug sort of manner.

"Not having to worry about you," Clay replied with a grin.

Loralie clinched her teeth to keep herself from saying something trite in return. After all, he was just worried about her safety. Even so, she couldn't just ride along quiet like – like most of the women in town would have done. Seething with anger at being treated like the weaker sex, her mouth got the better of her good senses

"I guess you must have forgotten – these are my horses we're goin' after and you're just someone kind enough to help me get them back. And since they are my horses, I'll decide what I'll do, or not do."

Clay hauled back on Midnight's reins and came to a stop, his own anger flaring up, and when Loralie swung her horse around to look at him, he said, "I guess you're right. They are your horses and you have the right to do as you please, but I'm not on your payroll so I don't have to take orders from you. You want to do as you please, go right ahead, but you'll be on your own."

Clay could see the shocked look in Loralie's eyes and immediately wished he could take back what he'd said, but it was too late, he couldn't back down now.

"You... You... You tellin' me you're gonna leave me all alone out here to go up against five men all by myself?"

Clay just sat there, unable to answer her without looking foolish. Of course, he would never leave her out here alone, but he couldn't find it in himself to tell her that. How he was going to get out of this predicament he didn't know, but he needed to think of something, quick.

Taking off his hat and wiping the sweat band, giving himself time to think, he looked at Loralie, so beautiful sitting there on her horse, ready to do battle, her face, red from the icy wind and her eyes blazing daggers.

A grin spread out across his mouth as he asked, "Is this our first pre-marital spat?"

Loralie was shocked at Clay's question and just sat there, staring at him.

After a moment, Clay rode over next to her and laid his hand on hers where it sat on her saddle horn. "May I suggest we start over and solve this problem, together?"

Loralie looked at his smiling face and felt her anger fade. "Well," she finally said, "if we can each voice our opinions, I guess that would be all right."

Clay leaned over and gave her a quick kiss and said, "Then it's settled. We're partners. Now what is your plan?"

Loralie felt her face redden. She didn't have a plan; she just didn't like being spoken to like a child. "I don't have a plan," she admitted. "I just don't like being ordered around like a child and when you said what you did, it sent my temper soaring sky high."

While Loralie was speaking, Clay rolled and lit a cigarette, and when she finished, he asked, "If it comes to a shootout, what do you want to do?"

"Well, shoot back of course, but from a place of cover," she admitted.

Clay nodded and said, "That was what I meant to say, but I guess it didn't come out like that, did it?"

"No, it didn't," Loralie said with a chuckle.

As they turned their horses and started down the trail once more, Ol' Son looked up at them and barked as he loped along beside them.

-

In his hiding place, in among the trees, Wilber was getting restless and colder by the minute. He'd expected the man to come riding down the trail some time ago. He'd been here close to an hour and was about to give up when he heard the dog barking.

The bark didn't sound like an angry bark or a growl, more like a happy bark. Leaning forward, Wilber scanned his back trail and in the far distance he made out two people riding side by side. The three-legged dog was running along beside them, jumping up and down like someone had just given him a T-bone steak.

Wilber stretched his neck a little farther to try and see who the second rider was, but they were still too far away. Whoever it was, they were talking and laughing like they were two people on a Sunday afternoon ride, which made no sense at all to Wilber.

Wilber stamped his feet to get some feeling back into them, then turned and checked to make sure his horse was securely tethered to the tree behind him. If there was to be much shooting, he didn't want the horse running off and leaving him afoot.

Satisfied, Wilber levered a shell into firing position on his rifle and laid the barrel across the limb and waited.

As they rode closer to where Wilber was waiting in among the trees, Clay noticed both horse's ears go forward. He looked down at Ol' Son and saw that he was staring at the trees on their right and a low growl was coming from between his bared teeth.

"Easy boy," Clay whispered. "Easy."

With a grin on his face, Clay looked at Loralie and spoke as if he was saying something funny for the benefit of whoever was hiding in the trees. "Grin or laugh if you want to, but be ready to find a place to shoot from. There is someone in the trees to our right. Don't look!" Clay hissed as Loralie involuntarily started to look to her right. "Hold up," Clay whispered, still grinning.

When they came to a stop, Clay and Loralie both stepped down, keeping their horses between them and the trees on their right.

"How do you know there is someone over there?" Loralie asked.

"I'll explain later, but right now I need you to get behind that fallen tree over by the ditch and cover me."

"What are you going to do?" Loralie asked with a bit of panic in her voice.

"Not sure, but we can't just stand here and let someone ambush us. Now, please, do as I say."

"You think it's the rustlers?" Loralie asked in a jovial tone.

"Who else could it be?" Clay asked, nodding his head. "Now please, do as I ask."

Loralie walked her horse over close to the fallen tree, pulling her rifle from its scabbard, then slapped the mare on her hindquarters and yelled... "Hiiiiiya!

At the same time, Clay swung onto his saddle and sent Midnight flying down the trail with Clay leaning over, Injun style, and firing his pistol under the big horse's neck in the direction of the trees.

-

The action caught Wilber off guard and when the bullets came whizzing through the trees, barely missing him, he had to drop down on his belly to keep from being shot.

"Damn!" he yelled as he scooted backward to where his horse was between him and the ranger, wondering where the ranger had disappeared to.

Looking over the horse's back, Wilber saw the dog coming straight toward him. Shaking his head at his bad luck, he raised his rifle and laid the barrel on the saddle and was about to take aim when a voice came to him from his backside. "I wouldn't do that if I was you, that is, unless you want a bullet to the back of your no-good head."

Wilber stood there, anger welling up inside him. This ranger had more lives than three cats. Should he take a chance and turn and try and get off a shot or throw up his hands and wait for a better opportunity?

Ol' Son ran up to just a few feet from him and stood facing him with his teeth bared and a low growl rumbling from his chest.

Wilber looked down at the dog, then tossed his rifle on the ground and turned around.

Clay stood looking at Wilber, thinking he'd seen him somewhere, but where, he wasn't sure. "Do you know who I am?" Clay asked.

Wilber looked down at the ground, shaking his head from side to side, then back up to Clay. "Yeah, I reckon I do. You're thet Texas Ranger."

"And how do you know that? And am I supposed to know you?"

Before Wilber could respond, Loralie and a young Indian boy came walking up. "Oh, I think you'll recall this feller when I tell you who he is. Hello, Wilber."

Wilber Mullins just stared at Loralie with a snarl on his lips.

"This is Wilber Mullins. You remember the Mullins, don't you?" she asked Clay. "They are the ones who killed my folks and tried to steal my land. I believe you still have the scars on your back from his pa's blacksnake whip."

Clay's mind went straight back to the time when old man Mullins hung him from a tree and cut his back open with his whip, with Wilber and the other brothers egging him on.

"Yes, I do recall him and his family," Clay said. "And now it all makes sense. He's at it again. He figures if he steals all your horses, you'll go belly-up and he can get your land for a song. That's about it in a nutshell, isn't it, Wilber."

It was a statement rather than a question. Wilber looked at Clay, then over to Loralie, and then at Wolf. "I'll deal with you later, redskin," he said, then turned to Loralie and Clay. "You'uns killed my pa and brothers and I ain't fergot! You owe me fer thet and I aim ta collect my due!" he spat out at them.

"As I recall, you had another brother that sneaked off with you when the fighting started. Both of you were low down stinking cowards when it came to face to face lead tossing and ran scared, leaving your father and brothers to deal with the consequences," Clay said, staring Wilber in the eyes.

"I ain't no coward and I ain't afraid of you, ranger!" Wilber yelled, his temper getting the best of him.

"Well now, that's real good to hear," Clay said with a smile on his face. "Because you had me fooled by hiding here in the trees, planning on ambushing us as we rode by like some coward would do."

Shaking his head, Clay continued. "Don't you agree, that sounds like something a coward would do? A brave man would have stepped out onto the trail and challenged the person he wanted to kill in a face to face shootout."

Clay looked at Loralie and gave her a look that meant, stay out of this, then turned back to Wilber. "You say you're not a coward and you're not afraid of me, which is good for what I have in mind. Now, just so you'll know, I'm not here as a ranger, just a friend who is trying to help. So... it will be just you and me, and let's just say, out of the goodness of my heart, I'm going to give you a chance to prove you don't have a yellow streak down your back a mile wide."

Clay stepped to the side, leaving Loralie and the young Indian boy out of the line of fire, then looked at Wilber and said. "You're still wearing your handgun and I'm standing right here in front of you, no more than five feet away, so I'll be a sure thing target. What do you say, Wilber, just you and me? Let's settle this thing right here and now."

Even in the bitter cold, Clay could see the sweat breaking out on Wilber's face and saw his hands begin to tremble. In his condition, Wilber would do one of two things, crumble, like the coward he believed Wilber to be, or, in his nervous condition, go for his gun.

Clay gave Wilber a wink and said, "Tell you what I'm going to do – I'm going to let you draw first. Now a man can't be fairer than that. Whata' ya say, you man enough to face me straight up?" Clay raised his hands in the air, saying, "I'm ready any time you are."

The next thirty seconds seemed like hours for Wilber, who stood facing a man he hated and feared. He couldn't out draw or out shoot this ranger and he knew it, which made him even angrier. He'd let his temper get the best of him and now he was going to die because of it. He felt the warm liquid running down his leg as tears began to run down his cheeks.

Swallowing, Wilber found his voice and said, "I ain't gonna fight you ranger. Yer jest tryin' ta egg me on so's you can shoot me down." And with that, he lifted his pistol from his holster with just two fingers and dropped it on the ground.

Clay looked at Loralie and said, "Keep an eye on him while I get something to tie him up with."

Loralie drew her handgun and pointed it at Wilber and said, "Please, do something to give me an excuse ta shoot you and save the authorities the time and money ta hang ya."

Wilber was suddenly filled with bravado and said, "I'll not see ah hangman's noose – no sir. And you won't shoot me in cold blood. I know your kind. You're too weak fer cold blooded killin' – an so is thet ranger friend of your'n."

Clay was rummaging through the saddlebags from Hank's borrowed saddle and came up with several pieces of pigging string used to hobble a horse and decided they would do. He had just laid them across the saddle and was tying the clasp on the saddlebag when Ol' Son began to growl.

Clay looked around and saw a man standing next to a tree some fifteen feet or so away.

"Verbody jest sta eal quit ike if ya vant ta eep on reathin'," the man said, pointing a rifle at Clay's chest.

Loralie looked over and saw Samuel, Wilber's younger brother standing there with a blood-soaked piece of cloth wrapped around his cheeks.

"Gib yer istol ta mi rother, issy, er I ill yer oyriend," Samuel said with a lot of effort.

Loralie looked at Clay, then back at Samuel, whose eyes had suddenly turned ugly.

"Ow!" Samuel yelled.

Loralie sighed and reluctantly handed her pistol to Wilber.

Wilber took Loralie's pistol with one hand and slapped Loralie across the face with the other, knocking her to the ground.

Ol' Son started to move, but stopped when Clay yelled, "No! Down boy!"

Ol' Son looked up at his master and after a moment, dropped down on his stomach, the hair on his back still standing on end.

"You made the right call, pilgrim," Wilber said as he reached down and picked up his own pistol.

He stuck Loralie's pistol in the waist of his pants and walked over and backhanded Clay across the face with the barrel of his pistol, which got an immediate response from Ol' Son, who leaped at Wilber's throat with bared teeth.

Wilber grabbed Ol' Son by the throat and was choking him when Clay smashed his fist against the side of Wilber's head, staggering him to the side and releasing his grip on Ol' Son.

Clay stepped in and was about to deliver another blow to Wilber's head when a bullet singed his ear.

"Tet's nough, anger! Da ext 'un ill be ded enter of yer cest," Samuel said pointing his rifle at Clay.

After recovering from the blow to his head, Wilber put his pistol in his holster and took the pigging strings and jerked Clay's hands behind him and tied them securely, then did the same thing to Loralie.

When they were both tied securely, he reached out and grabbed Wolf by the shirtfront and yanked him off the ground. "Whata' ya tell'm? And don't lie ta me if'n you know what's good fer ya."

Thinking quickly, Wolf said, "I didn't tell them anything. I thought you might need some help but when I came sneaking up from over there," he said, pointing to the area where Loralie had been laying in the ditch, "I did not see the woman and she got the drop on me. And then she brought me here."

Wilber looked at Wolf for a moment then said, "Ok, well then, ahhh, take the woman's pistol and rifle and keep an eye on her and thet dog. If either of'em moves, shoot'em."

Wilber then looked over to Samuel who had walked over and was standing nearby.

"Where's the horses and the other two injuns?" Wilber asked.

Grinning, Samuel said, "Yu'll be roud o me. I ot'em hid in ah atch ah trees ah ittle sout of ere. I ot da oter two injun oys atch ober'm. Told'em if'n nythin' appened toa da orses, they vould be buzzar ait. Hen I come ah ightailin' it ack ere ta chec on you – an ah ood thin I did, too. Uh?"

Wilber studied his brother for a moment and finally figured out what he'd said, and hoped Samuel had done the right thing by leaving the two Indians alone with the horses. He'd felt uneasy about the three Indian boys for some time now, but on the other hand, if Samuel hadn't come back...

Turning, Wilber walked back over to where Clay was standing and when he got close, he hissed, "Ain't so tough now, are ya, ranger man." Then without warning, Wilber hit Clay on the jaw with his fist, then smashed his other fist into Clay's midsection and found both places, hard.

"No!" Loralie yelled. "Leave him alone!"

Wilber looked at Loralie and sneered, "Oh I ain't even hardly started, pretty lady. And when I get finished with him, you and me's gonna have us ah little fun."

Clay staggered back only two steps, then yelled at Wilber to get his attention away from Loralie, "That all you got? I know girls that hit harder than you do."

Wilber's temper went through the roof and he stepped over to hit Clay again but when he got close, Clay kicked Wilber between the legs that sent screaming pain rushing to his brain.

Wilber doubled over and had a hard time breathing. His breath was coming in short gulps and he held himself, hoping the pain would go away.

"Ya all rit, Viber? Ya vant me ta kill da rager?" Samuel asked in his almost inaudible way of speaking. His cheeks were swollen like a squirrel with his mouth full of nuts and the skin was the color of a crushed blueberry underneath the bandage around his cheeks.

Wilber shook his head back and forth, trying to make sense of what his brother had just said. "I'll be all right in ah minute. And no, I don't want-cha ta kill the ranger. I want thet pleasure ta be all mine," he said, gasping for air and finding it hard to talk.

Clay studied the two brothers and cursed his bad luck. He should have been more aware of his surroundings instead of thinking about Loralie and assuming the rustlers were running for the North Carolina border.

With his hands tied behind his back, he was hampered. While he struggled to try and get his hands free, from his peripheral vision he noticed the young brave standing next to Loralie staring at him and saw the young man's eyes moving to his right, indicating for Clay to move backwards toward the trees. At first he didn't understand. How far was he supposed to go and why? They were surrounded by trees, why that direction?

Glancing over his shoulder, Clay saw only a hand protruding from behind a tree some ten feet behind him and guessed it must be one of the other Indian braves. But why did they want to help him? They had been with the Mullins brothers all along. They had helped steal Loralie's horses. Were they now wanting to switch sides, and if so, why?

Before Clay could make a move, Wilber straightened up and blew air out of his lungs, then rushed Clay, pushing his shoulder into Clay's stomach, driving both of them to the ground.

Clay landed on his back and felt the wind being knocked out of him by Wilber's weight.

Wilber rolled off of him and climbed to his feet and began kicking Clay in the ribs and stomach.

Clay absorbed the first set of blows from Wilber's boots as best he could but knew he couldn't take much more without getting his ribs broken, which would take him out of the fight completely. Clay rolled over twice, then scooted around and kicked out with his feet, tripping Wilber as he came toward him, intent on kicking him some more.

Wilber landed hard and for the moment, lay there, stunned and trying to find his wind.

Clay rolled over next to the tree where the hand had been, and climbed to his feet.

As soon as he was erect, Clay felt a hand take a hold of his arm to hold it steady, then felt the sawing of a knife blade against the leather strap that bound his wrists.

Clay looked toward Samuel to see if he had any indication of what was going on and saw Samuel staring at Loralie, his mouth hanging open. Looking the other way, Clay saw Loralie smiling and motioning for Samuel to come to her. The Indian boy next to her must have told her what was happening and she was doing her best to distract Samuel.

When the strap was cut in two, Clay felt the handle of the knife being pressed into his hand.

Wilber struggled to his feet and stood, staring at Clay, who still had his hands behind him, pretending to still be tied.

"I've bout had it with you, ranger," Wilber said, drawing his pistol and pointing it at Clay.

"Wait a minute," Loralie called out. "Take the horses and go, but leave us alone and I promise not to come after you!"

Wilber looked over his shoulder and saw Loralie had taken a few steps toward him. He grinned at her and said, "Beggin' fer his life — thet's good, but not good enough."

His grin turned to an evil grimace. "I don't give ah damn bout yer horses. They's jest ah means to an end. I want yer land, jest like pa did. I only wanted yer horses so's I could sell 'm and get enough ta buy yer place when you go belly-up."

Loralie took another step toward him and said, "That's it? You want my land? What if I told you, you could have it if you let us go? What if I told you I would sign the place over to you and you'd never see me again?"

Wilber stood, looking at Loralie as his brain digested her words, then shook his head and said, "You'd say bout anything right now to get you and yer boyfriend free, but I ain't buyin' it. Soon as I'd let you go; you'd hightail it ta the nearest law and send'm after us."

Clay took a step toward Wilber, but Samuel raised his rifle to his shoulder and yelled, "Old it, rit thar!"

Wilber swung his head back around and grinned at Clay. "What'ya plannin' on doin', tryin' ta trip me again?"

"I promise, we won't go to the authorities. We can go to wherever you want and I will write out a paper, signing my place over to you," Loralie told him.

Without looking at Loralie, Wilber thought about what she'd just said. That would be an easy way to get possession of her place, but how legal would it be. He didn't know much about law, but he did know enough to know a paper like that needed to be witnessed by a lawyer, or judge, or banker or such – somebody of authority. Her name on a piece of plain paper wouldn't do it – too many questions would be asked and if she had to go in front of a judge, what would prevent her from telling the judge how she'd come to sign the paper. No sir, that wouldn't do, not at all. But, what if...?

"Well, what do you say? We have a deal?" Loralie asked.

Wilber yelled toward his brother, "Samuel, you keep yer rifle trained on the ranger. I got some explain' ta do with miss high and mighty."

When he was satisfied the ranger was being covered by his brother, Wilber walked over and stopped just in front of Loralie and wagged his pistol in front of her face. "You think jest 'cause I don't got much education, you can flim-flam me with yer lies, but I see right through yer schemin'. Yer jest bidin' yer time so's you can get us in front of the law so's you can tell'em what really happened."

Wilber looked over at Wolf, who had stepped up next to Loralie. "And you, you back stabbin' heathin', would blab yer head off ta save yer own skin."

Wolf started to say something, but before he could speak, Wilber reached out and slapped him across the face with the barrel of his pistol, cutting a gash just under Wolf's eye, then bringing the barrel down on top of Wolf's head and watched as Wolf's legs buckled and he dropped to the ground, blood running down across his face.

"Leave the boy alone!" Loralie yelled as she reached out and grabbed for Wilber's arm, but he stepped back and pointed his pistol at her.

"Hold on, missy. I ain't done with you, yet. No sir, not by a long shot - and I'd hate ta shoot ya afore I'm finished with ya."

Loralie straightened up and asked, "What more of me could you possibly want? I told you I would give you my horses and my land, what else is there?"

A leering grin appeared on Wilber's face and he stepped even closer to Loralie, then reached out and put his fingers under her chin, turning her face up toward his. "Honey, before I kill you, you and me's gonna have us ah real good time - and I'm gonna make yer boyfriend watch. Oncest you've had ah taste of a real man you'll be chasin' after me like ah fish ta bait, but thet's as fer as it goes. After I've had my way with you, I won't be of no need of you any longer and I've decided the best way to get yer land thout no law gettin' involved, is if'n yer dead. The state will take it over and I can buy it fer hardly any money atall."

Clay saw the fire flair up in Loralie's eyes and prepared himself for what would come next, and sure enough, Loralie jerked Wilber's hand away from her face with one hand and slapped him alongside his head with the other.

"Why you no good windbag. You think you can just lay your hands on me any time you want, well you're in for a big surprise."

Wilber staggered backward a few steps, his mouth contorting into a snarl and started to raise his pistol in Loralie's direction.

Two unexpected things happened at the same time. First, Wolf jumped to his feet and ran toward Wilber and jerked his arm up just as Wilber pulled the trigger, sending the bullet off into the air where it would land somewhere, harmlessly, then shoved Wilber down.

Second, Lives in The Woods, after cutting Clay loose from the leather straps, circled around behind Samuel and when the action began, he rushed out and hit him over the head with a piece of tree limb he'd picked up.

Wilber landed on his back, hard, but not hard enough to knock him out. He rolled over and came up to his knees and brought up his pistol, swinging it toward Wolf.

Just as it came level, Clay rushed over and kicked the gun out of Wilber's hand, then grabbed Wilber by the hair of his head and jerked him to his feet.

When Wilber got to his feet, he backhanded Clay along the side of his head, then bent over and pulled a long, double sided knife from his boot and held it out in front of him.

"Only thing I like better 'n a good knife fight, is takin' ah woman by force. Afore I do yer girlfriend, I'm gonna cut you up like I'd butcher ah hog, then whist yer still alive, I'm gonna take yer woman right in front of ya. How's thet sound?"

Clay pulled his hand around and held up the knife Lives in The Woods gave him and was surprised to see the quality of it. It was bone handled, but made from good steel and looked to be razor sharp. It had some weight to it and seemed to be well balanced.

Wilber was surprised to see Clay with a knife of his own. "Where'd you get thet pig sticker, ranger man?"

"You're not the only one to carry a concealed knife, Hillbilly," Clay said with a grin.

"Liar!" Wilber shouted. "It was one of them redskin brats what give it to ya!" he yelled.

"Doesn't really matter where I got it. I have a knife too, so that should even things up don't you think?" Clay said with a grin.

"Now, are we gonna fight or dance around til we get dizzy and fall down?" Clay asked, seeing the fluff go out of Wilber for only a moment, then a sly grin appeared.

Wilber looked over to his right and saw Samuel standing with his hands in the air and Lives in The Woods standing a few feet away, holding Samuel's rifle.

Loralie had picked up the handgun and rifle when Wolf attacked Wilber. When Wolf came back and stood next to Loralie and put out his hand, Loralie handed the rifle to him and holstered her handgun.

Wolf ran over to one of the horses and got a short piece of rope about six feet long, then came back and pointed the rifle at Wilber and said, "It will be a fair fight." Tossing the piece of rope between them, he continued. "Each of you will take an end of the rope and hold it in your free hand. You will not let go until the fight is finished, it is the Indian way."

Wilber reached down and picked up his end of the rope, then looked over at Clay. "You gonna pick up yer end or is this too up and close fer ya?"

Clay stooped down and took the piece of rope in his hand and had no more than closed his fist around it when Wilber yanked hard on the rope, pulling Clay off balance and face first down on the ground.

Rushing in, Wilber took a swipe at Clay, but Clay was already rolling out of the way and only took a small cut on his left shoulder.

Coming to his feet, Clay and Wilber circled each other, their eyes locked - each of them testing the balance of the other by tugging on the rope from time to time.

At one point, Wilber changed directions, then when Clay began to follow, he changed again and jerked hard on the rope, while at the same time, moving in toward Clay and lashing out with his knife, then ducking under the rope and moving away from Clay's counter swing.

The front of Clay's shirt right over his stomach turned red with his blood and he felt the sting where Wilber's knife had struck him, just barely breaking the skin.

Wilber grinned and said, been knife fightin' Injun style since I was ah youn'an and I ain't never lost yet. Could 'a done ya in but didn't want ta, not yet. I figure ta cut ya several times – make ya suffer some afore I do ya in. Makes it more fun thet way."

Clay realized he was more than likely outmatched with this style of knife fighting, which he had never done before. I need to be more cautious, he thought to himself as he tugged on the rope to test Wilber's measure.

Wilber laughed and danced around like an actor on the stage, then yanked hard on the rope and stepped to the side. As Clay was trying to gain his balance, Wilber cut Clay across the chest and slipped away again before Clay could react.

"I can stop this with one shot," Loralie yelled.

"No," Clay said, never taking his eyes off of Wilber.

Clay noticed that each time Wilber was about to attack, his eyes would get big and he would lick his lips, so he was ready for him the next time Wilber made a move and right before Wilber jerked on the rope, Clay beat him to the action and jerked hard on the rope, then moved in the opposite direction and swung his knife at Wilber's shoulder – the one Wilber held his knife with, and felt his blade connect.

Wilber came close to dropping his knife at the pain. "Damn yer hide, you got lucky but one little cut ain't gonna help ya none. I'm gonna kill ya and there ain't nuthin' you can do ta stop me."

And with that Wilber jerked on the rope with all his weight and at the same time, drove his knife toward Clay's oncoming stomach.

Knowing he was about to be stabbed with Wilber's knife, instead of trying to step aside, he slashed his own knife down across Wilber's knife hand and felt his knife strike bone.

Wilber yelled and dropped his knife, then tried to move away, but Clay followed him and when he got close, he punched Wilber in the face with his fist.

Wilber staggered back and before he could react, Clay had grabbed him by the hair and shoved the point of his knife against his throat just enough for Wilber to know he had lost the fight.

At that very moment, Wilber knew he had drawn his last breath, and gritted his teeth, waiting for the pain he was sure would come when his throat was cut.

Just then, a pistol shot rang out and a man's voice yelled, "Hold it right there. You cut him and I'll kill you where you stand."

Clay released Wilber's hair and stepped back, looking up at a man sitting on a dapple-gray horse, pointing a pistol at him. Letting his eyes swing from side to side, he saw six other riders behind the man, and all of them had guns in their hands.

Clay tossed the knife on the ground and asked, "Why's any of this your business?"

Before the man could answer, Loralie spoke up and said, "He's riding one of my horses which puts him in cahoots with Wilber. At least that would be my guess. Am I right?" she asked, looking at the man sitting on one of her horses.

The man turned his attention to Loralie and smiled. "Now what makes a pretty little filly like you think this horse might have at one time belonged to you?"

Loralie pointed and said, "Turn your head and look at the brand on her hip. I think you'll see a rocking LB, which stands for Loralie Benson, which is me. Wilber here stole her, along with several others from me and either gave that one to you or sold her to you, but either way, she was stolen from me and I want her back, along with all the other horses he stole from me."

"And I suppose you're going to tell me those horses down in the trees," he said, pointing in the direction of Loralie's horse herd, "also belong to you?"

"That would be correct," Loralie said. "Me and Clay, here," she said, indicating Clay, "we was trailing them when Wilber tried to bushwhack us."

The man looked at Wilber and his brother, then back at Loralie. "If those horses are yours, I want to compliment you on the fine job you did training them, but in the long run I don't care who they originally belonged to. I will have a bill of sale from Mister Mullins and that is good enough for me. And as far as getting any other of your so-called horses back, that would be nye onto impossible. You see, all but this one I'm riding, has been sold and shipped to Europe. And just for the record, I have a bill of sale from Mister Mullins for them too."

Loralie's face shrunk and she let out a sigh. "Well, at least I still have the ones down in the trees, yonder. I can start over."

The man tugged his coat around him a little tighter as a cold wind blew in from the north. "About that. There is a bit of a problem. You see, I have already given Wilber here, the first half of his money for those horses and they've already been promised to a man in Spain. Now you wouldn't want me to go against my word, would you?"

Loralie stood up a little straighter and adjusted her shoulders. "I don't much care what you do as long as you don't do it with my horses, and if you think you're just gonna ride in here and take 'em without a fight, you'd better guess again."

The man drew and fired his pistol and just missed shooting Loralie in the ear.

Loralie reacted by putting her hand up next to her ear, then looked at her hand to find it empty of blood.

"I'm not in the habit of shooting women, but if you try to do anything foolish, you will leave me no choice. You can stand still and do as you're told, or you can go for that pistol on your hip and I will kill you – makes very little difference to me."

Loralie looked at Clay who said, "Leave things be for now. I'd say we're slightly outnumbered."

Clay then turned and looked at the man, "What do you plan to do with us?"

The man thought for a full minute, then said, "Nothing. Unless you force me, I don't plan on killing you if that's what you're asking. What I am going to do is tie each of you to a different tree and once we're gone, you can do your best to free yourselves. In case you can't, then you can hope someone comes by who will untie you before the wild animals get to you. That would be a most gruesome way to die.

"Now hold on jest a gal-derned minute," Wilber yelled. "I got ah score ta settle with both of 'em and I ain't gonna be denied."

"Very well," the man on the dapple-gray horse said. My boys and I will start the horses toward the North Carolina border. You can catch up when you can."

"I'd like ta see 'm tied ta those trees you was ah talkin' bout, afore ya go. All of 'em cept the woman. I got plans fer her." Wilber said, looking up at the man.

"As you wish," the man said, and nodded to his men.

After picking up his pistol and knife, Wilber stood and watched as the ranger and the three young Indian boys were tied to trees. When they tried to get a rope on Ol' Son, he bit one of them, then ran off into the trees to the sound of bullets flying past him.

As the men rode away, Wilber yelled. "My brother an me'll catch up with ya real soon."

The man on the dapple-gray mare put his spurs to the mare's sides and galloped away without looking back.

When they were gone, Wilber told his brother to go fetch their horses while he tended to some last bit of business.

Samuel nodded, and without a word, headed off to round up their mounts.

Once Samuel had gone, Wilber pulled his pistol and pointed it at Loralie and told her to stand still. He walked over and pulled her pistol from her holster and stuck it in his belt, then tied her, loosely to a nearby tree. "I'll get back ta you shortly," he told her with a wicked grin.

Next, he checked the ropes on the three young Indians, then turned his attention to Clay to make sure he was bound securely. When he was satisfied, Wilber stepped around in front of Clay and drove his fist into Clay's stomach. "I should kill ya, but I'm not gonna. But I am gonna rough you up enough ta give the wolves and such other animals that are meat eaters, some blood ta smell." And with that he began beating Clay's face until he was bleeding from his mouth, nose and cheekbones.

Clay stood, tied to the tree, unable to do anything, his head drooping, trying to breathe through his mouth because his nose was filled with blood that was dripping down onto his chest and feet.

"Got nuthin' ta say, ranger man?"

Clay raised his head and spit blood onto Wilber's face.

Wilber wiped the blood from his face onto his shirtsleeve, then drove his fist into Clay's right eye, causing it to swell shut almost instantly.

"I'm gonna leave one eye open so's you can watch what I do to yer girlfriend," Wilber said, enjoying his power over the ranger.

Clay struggled to get loose, but he was tied securely to the tree. "You touch her and I swear, I'll kill you," Clay said as blood dripped from his chin.

"You do thet, Mister Ranger Man, yea, you do thet."

Wilber laughed and looked toward Loralie, licking his lips. "Now, Miss High and Mighty, it's time fer you and me ta have some…"

Loralie had been working feverishly to get herself untied and had been successful, and was waiting for the opportunity to do something.

Clay called out, "I'm warning you, Wilber. You touch her and I'll see you die a slow death."

When Wilber turned back to look at Clay, Loralie saw her chance and dropped the rope to her feet, then bent down and picked up a large piece of tree limb. She then rushed toward Wilber with the intent of hitting him in the back of his head.

Wilber heard the rushing of feet against the leaves and whirled around just in time to see the tree limb coming toward him and moved sideways just enough so he took the blow against his shoulder instead of his head.

The blow hit him on the shoulder and he felt his arm go numb, but was able to swing his other hand out and slap Loralie against the side of her head – sending her sprawling across the ground.

Clay and all three of the young Indians were struggling to free themselves, but to no avail.

"So, ya wanna play rough, do ya? Well, that's how I like it best," Wilber said, rubbing some life back into his arm.

Loralie rolled over and came back up on her feet and like a female lioness, she was ready to fight. She felt the stinging in her cheek, which just inflamed her temper. She would rather die than have the likes of him have his way with her.

Clay continued to struggle to get himself free, but in his condition, he couldn't do much.

Loralie was in a crouched position, circling Wilber, looking for an opening where she could strike. He was much larger than her and a lot stronger, but she'd been raised to stand up for herself and she wasn't going down without a fight.

Wilber's arm began to have some life, again, and he swaggered around, grinning at the redheaded woman who thought she could defy him. Before this was over, he would have her screaming for mercy.

He was feeling sure of himself when Loralie rushed him and kicked him on the shin, then stomped down on his foot. He felt severe pain rush up his leg. He reached out to grab her, but quick as a cat, she'd moved away and had picked up the tree limb, again and swung it with all her strength, hitting Wilber in the ribs, causing him to grimace.

Like a mad bull, Wilber rushed Loralie and smashed her alongside her head with his fist, sending her backwards. She landed on her back and lay there, trying to get the bright lights to go away. She hadn't been knocked out, but close to it.

With all her strength, Loralie climbed slowly to her feet and waved her hands toward him, indicating she still had some fight left in her. "Com 'on, you big tub of blubber."

Wilber backed up several steps and decided he'd had enough. He reached for his pistol, not realizing he'd backed up close to Clay.

Clay was awake enough to take advantage of Wilber being as close as he was, and swung his foot upward and kicked the gun out of Wilber's hand as Wilber pulled it from his holster.

"What the?" Wilber said as he turned to see who had kicked him. And when he did, Loralie took advantage of the distraction and rushed over and brought the limb down across Wilber's head.

The lights went out in Wilber's head and he dropped to the ground, unconscious.

Loralie tossed the limb to the side and reached down and pulled her pistol from Wilber's waist, then stepped back and pointed it at him. Her eyes were wild with anger and her hand was shaking, slightly. She was both angry and scared. If ever she wanted to kill a man, it was Wilber Mullins.

Clay spit a mouthful of blood from his mouth and said, "Don't do it. Not in cold blood. We both know he deserves to die, but not this way. We'll turn him over to the authorities."

Loralie stood for a long moment, pointing her pistol at Wilber's head – her blood running hot with vengeance. Clay's words finally made her come back to her senses. He was right. She would regret shooting Wilber like this, for the rest of her life. She took a deep breath and shoved her pistol down into her holster and turned her attention to Clay and the young Indian boys.

First, she went to Clay. His head was hanging down and she could see he was in bad shape.

As she stepped behind the tree to untie him, Samuel rode up with his and his brother's horse, and stopped just at the edge of the tree line. Samuel watched as Wilber regained consciousness and staggered to his feet. Samuel let out a hiss, which caused Wilber to turn and look in his direction.

Then, without hesitation, Wilber ran for the woods, where he met his brother holding the reins to his horse. He grabbed the saddle horn and as the horse began to move, Wilber swung his way up onto the saddle and kicked the horse in the sides with both heels.

Loralie jerked the pistol from her waistband and pointed it in Wilber's direction, but Wilber and his brother had disappeared into the trees, making it extremely difficult to get a good shot at either of them.

"Let 'em go," Clay mumbled through bloody lips. "We'll catch up to 'em soon enough and this time I'll make sure we have the advantage," he said, thankful she had not shot Wilber, earlier, even though she'd had every right to do so.

Loralie looked at Clay's beaten face and wanted to cry. Filled with rage, she glanced over her shoulder and looked in the direction the Mullin's brothers had gone. One part of her was angry for not shooting Wilber when she had the chance, but another part of her knew she couldn't shoot someone in cold blood, no matter what he was about to do to her. If he'd had a gun, that would have been different. They would have one less Mullins to worry about.

The three young Indians stood, still tied to the trees, wondering what would happen next.

After seating Clay on a fallen log, Loralie quickly untied the three young braves and sent Bullfrog to see if he could retrieve their horses while she tended to Clay.

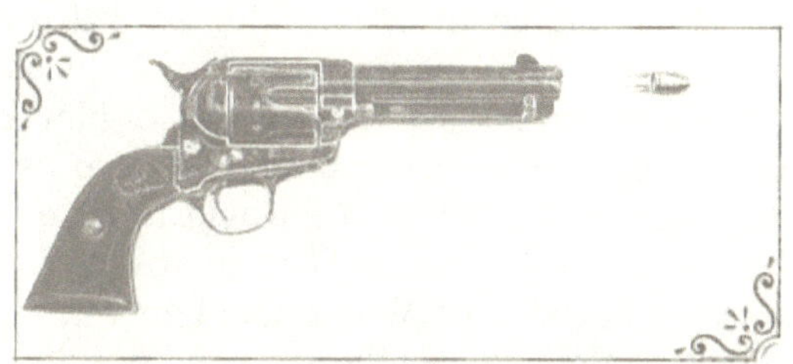

CHAPTER THIRTY-TWO

-

The sun was on the low side of the western sky and the temperature was dropping at a steady pace in the mountains of North Carolina when Wilber and Samuel rode up close to the outer rim of light from the campfire, and Wilber yelled, "Hello the camp. It's jest us Mullins brothers."

"Come," a voice from somewhere just beyond the fire, said.

After seeing to their horses, the Mullins brothers squatted next to the fire and each poured himself a cup of coffee.

"Well, did you kill them?" the man who had been riding the dapple-gray horse asked as he walked up next to the fire.

Wilber blew on his coffee, then took a sip before answering the man. "No sir Mister Reardon, I did not. I did somethin' even better. I left the Texas Ranger, tied to ah tree, unconscious and bleedin'. I reckon the wild animals will have themselves ah good time with him and the others. It'll be ah regular feedin' frenzy if'n a pack-o-wolves happens to get their scent. We jest might be able ta hear their screamin' afore the night is over," Wilber lied. He wasn't about to tell Reardon the truth and have him look down his nose at him.

He turned his gaze on his brother and gave him a look that said not to contradict him.

Samuel knew the look and squatted down and poured himself more coffee.

Alex Reardon was a man with little or no conscious, or scruples, but there was something about Wilber Mullins that grated on his nerves. Maybe it was because he was a crude hillbilly and he didn't like hillbillies. No matter, he planned to get rid of him and his idiot brother as soon as they got the horses to the holding pens and Wilber signed the bill of sale. Until then, he would tolerate him. In the meantime, he just nodded his head as if he approved of what Wilber said he'd done. He hoped what Wilber told him was the truth, but seriously doubted it. He'd noticed the wet spot on Wilber's pants.

"What if they somehow get loose and come after us," Reardon asked as he poured more coffee for himself.

Wilber looked over the rim of his cup and said, "First place, even if he was ta get loose, thet ranger ain't in no shape ta go chasin' after nobody; not after what I did ta him – and second they's tied real good. No sir you can take it ta the bank – they won't ever be leavin' that part of the woods."

"I hope you're right," Reardon said. "Well, we'd all best get some rest. Tomorrow we have a full day ahead of us."

Wilber watched as Alex Reardon stood up and walked over to the tent his men had pitched for him and climbed inside, drawing the flap closed behind him.

"I don't much care fer thet man," Wilber said in a low tone to Samuel.

"Sems ah mit upity, do't he," Samuel said, his cheeks still swollen and bloody.

"He is at thet, little brother. He is at thet. But he won't be so high and mighty as soon as we get our hands on his money. I got plans fer takin' over his business. Yes sir, I surely do," Wilber declared with a smug look on his face.

Samuel shook his head from side to side. He could almost feel sorry for Reardon. Almost, but not quite.

-

Ol' Son had been wandering back and forth in the woods, just beyond sight, and when the coast was clear, Ol' Son came walking back into the area where his master and the others had been tied to trees. He moved around slowly, sniffing the air for the evil men's scent. When he found nothing but their old scent, he went over to where Clay was sitting, and sat down on his haunches and began to whine.

Clay reached out and scratched him behind the ears and said, "You're the only smart one of us. You know when to get out of harm's way."

Wolf came walking over to them and when he saw Clay's face, he gasped. Clay's face was black and blue from his hairline to his chin and one of his eyes was swollen completely closed. Blood had congealed and was stuck to his face, looking like large, ugly scars.

Wolf sucked in a large breath of air and said, "You are a tough man, Mister Brentwood. I'm not sure I could have taken such a beating and still be standing," Wolf said, shaking his head.

Clay looked at Wolf, but said nothing, then nodded his head.

Suddenly, Clay was consumed with dizziness. He reached out and put his hand on the log he was sitting on, trying to summon enough strength to keep from falling. When he felt Loralie's hands take hold of his arm, he looked up at her and tried to smile.

"Here, scoot down and sit on the ground and lean your back against the log," Loralie said.

As she helped Clay sit down on the ground, she called over her shoulder, build us a fire and find some water."

While Lives in The Woods made a fire, Wolf ran over to the small creek nearby and filled a canteen, then hurried back.

Loralie was looking around for something to wipe Clay's face with when Bullfrog came riding back in with all their horses.

She ran over to her mare and rifled through her saddlebags and found some bacon and coffee and a rag she could use to wash the blood from Clay's face with.

"Where did you find our horses?" Wolf asked, astonished at seeing Bullfrog back so quickly, and sitting on his own horse.

"I was running toward where the horses had been, hoping to get them back when I saw them coming through the trees toward me.

They were following Mister Brentwood's big black horse. When he saw me, he ran up to me and stopped and whinnied at me. I jumped on my horse and here we are."

Wolf looked at the black stallion and shook his head. He was an amazing horse.

Loralie poured water from the canteen onto the rag and then gently wiped away as much blood as she could, making Clay look a little less damaged. No much, but at least enough to be presentable.

Thirty minutes later, they were sitting around the fire, drinking coffee while the bacon sizzled and popped in the skillet.

One of Clay's eyes was still swollen closed and the other was bloodshot red, but at least Clay could see out of the one eye.

He turned his head and asked Loralie, through still swollen lips, "You want to explain how these young braves are now on our side?"

Loralie looked at the three braves and smiled. "Wolf told me the only reason they stole my horses is because Wilber threatened to do bad things to their families if they didn't do as they were told. Plus, Wilber paid them ten dollars for each horse they brought to them and he said their families could use the money," Loralie told him.

Clay looked at her and nodded his head. "And you believe them?"

"I do," Loralie said, matter of factly. "So much so that I offered them jobs on my ranch if they help us get my horses back."

"And of course, they agreed," Clay said with as sheepish a grin as he could make.

"I think they're basically good boys. It's all very simple. They were afraid of Wilber and their families needed money. All of the Indians I've ever heard of, are poor. Plus," she added, "If they're working for me, they won't need to steal horses."

Clay nodded his head and sipped his coffee. She just might be right. He glanced over and watched as all three of the young Indians sat, sipping their coffee, staring at the fire.

Clay knew he was in no condition to ride just yet but was anxious to get back on the trail of the horse rustlers. So, with Loralie's help, he went down to the creek, stripped off his clothes and waded in. The icy water quickly revived all his senses.

Loralie sat on a fallen log and watched, giggling at Clay's reaction to the icy cold water.

CHAPTER THIRTY-THREE

-

Come sunrise, Reardon was anxious to get the horses moving and prodded everyone until they were in the saddle heading south. Wilber volunteered to ride drag, which surprised Reardon. He didn't trust either of the Mullins brothers and didn't cotton to the idea of having them behind him, so he told one of his men to ride drag with Wilber and keep an eye on him.

Wilber had two reasons for riding drag; one so he could keep an eye on Reardon. He didn't trust the man any more than an angry rattlesnake – and two, it gave him time to formulate his plan. When one of Reardon's men came back to ride drag with him, Wilber became even more suspicious.

They drove the horses at a pace faster than Wilber thought they should, especially with the weather conditions being what they were.

Within an hour of leaving their camp, more dark clouds rolled across the sky, blocking out the sun. The temperature began to drop and large snowflakes began to fall, which was accompanied by heavy wind.

Between the heavy snowfall and the wind blowing it in all directions, they could barely see twenty feet in front of them.

Wilber rode up next to Reardon and yelled over the howling wind, "We need ta get the horses in outta this," he said, moving his arm around.

"No!" Reardon yelled back. "We keep going! The border is just up the trail a few miles."

"What's thet got ta do with anythin'?" Wilber asked.

"There's a place where we can hide them until I'm ready to ship them," Reardon yelled back.

Wilber rode back to the rear of the now slow-moving horse herd, his mind running at full speed and when he pulled up next to Samuel, he noted his brother didn't look well. His eyes were glassy and he was sitting a bit wobbly on his saddle. He had a piece of cloth wrapped around his swollen jaw to protect it from the storm that was turning red.

"You all right?" Wilber asked as he rode up next to Samuel.

Samuel turned his head and looked at Wilber, then said through the cloth in a muffled tone, "Um fin."

"Well you don't look fine," Wilber said back to him.

With that, Samuel shrugged his shoulders and fell sideways off his horse.

Wilber pulled his horse to a halt and jumped off. Samuel was laying in the snow, shaking violently from head to foot.

Wilber laid his hand against Samuel's forehead. It was scorching hot.

Samuel opened his eyes and looked up at his brother for a brief moment, then took his last breath, his body was no longer shaking.

Wilber looked down at his brother in disbelief, then stood up, watching as the herd disappeared into the swirling snow.

Wilber knew there would be no use asking Reardon to stop the herd long enough to bury his brother. He could care less. Besides, with the ground frozen as hard as it was, they couldn't dig a grave anyway.

Wilber reached down and pulled his brother up enough to get him over his shoulder then carried him off into the nearby trees, where he put him down in a sitting position against one of the trees.

"Sorry little brother, but this is the best I can do. Maybe I can come back in the spring and give ya ah proper buryin'. That is if'n the animals don't get to ya first."

Wilber took a last look at his brother and walked back over and climbed aboard his horse, then took up the reins of his brother's horse and sat there, wondering if he should go back to make sure the ranger and the woman were dead. Him and that woman had killed another one of his kin; the last one, and he hated them more than anything on earth.

After a couple of minutes, Wilber decided his best bet would be to go after the herd and Reardon. If the ranger and the woman did survive, somehow, he could come back and kill them after he had taken the herd and his pockets filled with the money they would bring.

-

Fortunately for all concerned, it was lucky that Wilber had not chosen to come back, looking for Clay and the others. Had they suddenly met in the snowstorm, who knows what might have happened.

As it was, the small group had been riding for two hours when Clay raised his arm and called a halt. "We can't see the trail in all of this. And the wind blows away any tracks as soon as they're made. We need to find some shelter and hole up until it blows over."

No one could argue with Clay's decision, especially the three young braves who had no heavy winter clothes and were nearly frozen.

With their limited sight, they missed three places before Clay saw a large outcrop of rocks off to his left and led the small party in among them and was surprised to find a ledge sticking out of the mountain and the ground beneath it completely devoid of snow and protected from the wind.

Within a few minutes they were all sitting around a blazing fire, enjoying its warmth and the fresh coffee Loralie had made.

"Do you suppose they're holed up someplace, too?" Loralie asked.

"If they aren't, they're even dumber than I give 'em credit for," Clay said looking out at the raging storm.

Loralie turned her head and looked at Wolf. "I'm guessing you boys know this country pretty well by now. Any idea of where they might be holding the horses to get them in out of this storm?"

Wolf looked at Lives in The Woods who knew the mountains between where they were and Ashville best of all, and asked, "Where do you think they might be?"

Lives in The Woods thought for a minute, then said, "There is a place, but you would have to know where it is or you would ride right passed it in this weather. Even in good weather, it is not easy to see."

"Do you think Wilber or the other man might know of this place?" Loralie asked.

Again, Lives in The Woods thought for a short while, then said, "Maybe, but I do not know. To the best of my knowledge, not many people know of it – mostly just Indians."

******

It was nearly midnight when they rode out. The storm had passed by and the sky was clear with a full moon so bright lighting their way it almost seemed like daylight. The air was still very cold. The horse's breaths could be seen as they trudged through the deep snow.

Between Clay and Loralie they came up with enough clothing to help give the young braves a fighting chance at not being frozen during the trip.

******

Only a few miles further on, Loralie's horse herd was having a hard time of it and had taken it on their own to stop and bunch up with their hindquarters facing the icy wind.

Even with Reardon screaming and hollering at them - slapping them on the rear with his coil of rope, the horses held their ground and wouldn't budge.

Wilber, sensing an opportunity, rode up next to the cowboy riding drag with him and shoved the end of his pistol barrel against his coat to muffle the sound and pulled the trigger.

Wilber rode on, leaving the man laying in the snow where he fell, and within an hour, he had lowered the odds by three.

Reardon was the one Wilber really wanted to see dead, but Reardon became wary of him every time he came near him, so, he settled with killing Reardon's men.

Suddenly, just like it had come, the storm was over and Wilber knew he would have to bide his time to kill Reardon and steal his money and the horses.

Reardon pulled his horse to a halt and looked around, then rode over next to Wilber. "Where's the rest of my men? There should be six of them, but I only count three."

"What 'a ya askin' me fer? You think I got 'em hidden in my pockets?" Wilber answered.

Reardon eyed Wilber with doubt on his face. "I don't trust you, Mullins – not any more than I do a woman scorned."

Reardon looked around again and asked, "Where's your brother? Wasn't he riding back there with you?"

"He's dead. Died in the saddle and fell off his horse. I carried him off the trail and set him up next ta ah tree. I plan on comin' back come spring and bury him," Wilber said in a calm voice like it was an everyday event.

Reardon studied Wilber for a long time and said, "You're a hard man, Wilber Mullins. And you're telling me you don't have any idea where three of my men disappeared to? Is that your story?"

Wilber didn't like the way Reardon's questioning was going and eased his hand close to his pistol. Maybe he would have an opportunity to kill Reardon after all.

"With the way the wind was blowin' snow all around, I guess they could 'a wandered off, but who knows, maybe they jest got tired o workin' fer you and left."

Reardon looked at Wilber and said, "If I thought you had anything to do with their disappearance, I would kill you right now."

If that wasn't a challenge, Wilber had never heard a better one and he pulled his pistol and shot Reardon dead center in the chest, driving him from the saddle.

In the clear air, the gunshot filled the night, causing Reardon's other three riders to turn and look at Wilber and their dead boss.

"He killed my brother and tried to kill me!" Wilber yelled at the three men staring at him. "I had no choice but ta defend myself."

The three men rode over and looked at their boss. "He ain't got no gun in his hand," one of the riders said.

Thinking quickly, Wilber said, "He went fer his gun, but I was ah mite faster. So now I reckon you work fer me."

The three men eyed Wilber before one of them asked, "How much you payin'?"

Again, Wilber's mind sought just the right answer and asked, "How much was Reardon payin' ya?" knowing loyalty meant nothing to these gunslingers. They were only here for the money.

"Ah hundred ah piece," the tallest one of them said.

"Well, I'll give ya ah hundred and twenty-five apiece when I get the horses sold," Wilber said.

The tall cowboy looked at his two partners, then back at Wilber. "You want us ta take 'em to the same place as Reardon wanted ta go?"

Not knowing where that place was, Wilber nodded his head and said, "Yea, I reckon thet's where the men who's buy 'm will come ain't it?"

The tall gunslinger with a droopy mustache and leather looking skin, nodded his head and said, "Yeah, I reckon it is. Men come and look 'em over, then we drive 'm ta where ever they want us to – usually the train station down in Ashville.

Wilber smiled to himself. Now he knew the holding place was somewhere not too far north of Ashville.

After going through Reardon's pockets and taking the money he found, Wilber looked at the three men and said, "Drag Reardon over off the trail and then let's get these horses movin'. We got buyers waitin' fer us."

One of the three gunslingers, the one who was short and squatty, with a cigarette hanging from the side of his mouth loosened his rope and lassoed one of Reardon's feet and dragged his body off to the side of the trail. He gave the rope a flip to loosen it from the dead man's leg, then coiled the rope up and hung in back on his saddle.

Wilber watched in fascination. The whole process had taken less than three minutes.

CHAPTER THIRTY-FOUR

-

The sky was cloudy, the wind had an icy bite to it and everyone was anxious to be on the trail. The horses seemed to be just as ready as the people, as they danced around trying to keep warm.

As he put a foot in the stirrup and swung up on Midnight, Clay asked Loralie's three new ranch hands, "My guess is, they've moved on. You wouldn't happen to know where they're taking the horses would you?"

They all shook their heads, no. Wolf looked at Clay and said, "In the other times, we only took three horses at a time and we always took them to a spot along the river just west of town. They would look them over, then leave our money on a tree stump and leave with the horses. We had never actually seen their faces or knew who they were until this time. And the other man, we know nothing about him. I'm sorry. And with so many horses, this time, I don't think they would take them to the place near the river."

Clay looked at Loralie and said, "Well sir, I guess it's up to us then. He turned and looked down at Ol' Son and said, "You ready to go find Loralie's horses, boy?"

The word "go", sounded good to Ol' Son and he raced off a short distance, barking and jumping around – as much as a three legged dog in deep snow can jump around.

As they started off down the trail, Clay said, "We'll follow their tracks as best we can and if the tracks disappear, we'll have to rely on Ol' Son's nose."

He looked back at Loralie and winked. "One way or another, we'll get 'em back."

As they rode along, Clay tried not to worry about what would happen when they caught up with the rustlers. There would be nine of them and all of them had guns – and from what he'd seen, none of them would give it a second thought when it came time to killing him or Loralie, or even the young Indian boys.

While they were five, they had only three guns and he wasn't sure how the young men would react if it came to a shootout. And he didn't want to find out if he could help it. They were still young, with their whole lives ahead of them. To begin killing at this stage of their lives would not be a good thing.

As they topped over the hill and saw Ashville down towards the bottom, Clay sat his horse and tried to see the whole picture. He felt confident they wouldn't take the horses into Ashville, so they would need to hold them somewhere where they wouldn't draw suspicion.

Clay leaned back and reached into his saddlebag and withdrew his binoculars and held them up to his eyes, turning the focus wheel until he was satisfied.

Off to his left - a few miles northeast of Ashville, Clay detected movement. He adjusted the binoculars a little to bring things a little more into focus and could see Loralie's horses being driven into a corral. Swinging the glasses, a little, he was able to see a barn and a small building that, because of the chimney, looked like a house. There was no smoke coming from the chimney, but he guessed there soon would be.

"There they are," Clay said, pointing in the direction he'd been looking. "I'd guess about an hour and a half, or so. That seem right to you?" he asked as he turned and looked at the three boys.

Wolf reached out and took the binoculars from Clay and put them to his eyes and after a moment, he handed them back and said, "Yes. That is a good guess."

Clay looked at Wolf and said, "You boys know this country better than either me or Loralie, so you can lead the way. Only thing is, let's stop and look things over before we go rushing in and get our heads blown off.

A short time later, they found the bodies of Samuel and the three rustlers Wilber killed.

"Well, that evens the odds a bit," Clay said as he swung his leg over his saddle and settled down on it.

"Aren't you going to bury them?" Loralie asked.

"Can't," Clay told her. "The ground is frozen solid."

CHAPTER THIRTY-FIVE

-

Wilber felt secure in the knowledge that the ranger and the Benson woman would not be able to get loose, and even if they did, they would be afoot. Even so, he continued to have a bad feeling in his stomach. Once they had the horses in the corral, Wilber sent one of the men to the hayloft of the barn to keep watch.

Inside the small house, Wilber found a cash of food and half a case of whiskey. They were all hungry, but eating could come later. One of the men took the man in the barn a bottle and then joined the others in the house in a game of cards and after a few drinks, Wilber forgot about the ranger and the Benson woman.

-

It was close to four o'clock in the afternoon when Clay, Loralie and the Indian boys got within sight of the corral and hauled up.

All of them dismounted and tied their horses to the nearby trees, then crept up to a spot where Clay could take a closer look with his binoculars.

After a short survey, he lowered his binoculars and said, "There's a man in the hayloft of the barn who is supposed to be the lookout, but we shouldn't have much of a problem with him. He's got a bottle of whiskey and doing his best to empty it.

"The windows have no curtains and I got a look inside. Wilber and the other two are in the kitchen playing cards and doing their share of drinking, also."

"So, do we raid the house while they don't expect us?" Wolf asked, excitement in his voice.

"Don't be so eager for a shootout my young friend. From what I can see, our best bet is to wait for nightfall and while they're passed out from drinking too much, we can just waltz in and hopefully take the horses back without any trouble."

"What about Wilber Mullins?" Loralie asked, pointing toward the house.

"Let's ride back a ways to where they can't see our fire and make some coffee and we can talk about him," Clay said, giving Loralie a gentle pat on the shoulder.

"Don't you want him to pay for what he's done?" Loralie asked.

Clay looked at Loralie and smiled. "Of course, I do, but first things first."

"What's that mean?" Loralie asked.

"Over coffee," Clay said as he mounted Midnight.

Even though he was feeling the effects of the whiskey on an empty stomach, Wilber was not yet drunk.

Standing up from the table, he walked to the door and opened it. "See anything?" he yelled to the man in the hayloft and when he got no response, he yelled again. "You, idiot in the barn, I'm talkin' ta you! I asked ya if 'n ya 'd seen anythin' and you'd better answer me! Don't make me come out there!"

Wilber had always run roughshod over most people and with the amount of whiskey he had in his belly he was feeling his oats.

Murphy was a man of forty and had been riding the outlaw trail for nearly twenty years and hated every boss he'd ever had — even killed a few of them for no more reason than he didn't like being yelled at, so when Wilber yelled at him and called him an idiot, the whiskey in him began to boil. Drawing his pistol, he took careful aim and squeezed the trigger.

The bullet slammed into the doorframe close to Wilber's head, causing him to duck back inside.

"Nobody yells at me and I don't cotton ta bein' called an idiot! I tole ya I'd give ah yell if somebody shows up and I will, so leave me be!"

"What's the matter with him?" Wilber said as he sat back down in his chair and grabbed the bottle of whiskey, and took a long pull.

The tall one was called Carl and he grinned. "He's a mite touchy sometimes, 'specially when he's been drinkin'. He'll be alright though; don't you worry 'bout that."

The short, squatty rustler was appropriately called, Stump, and he was getting drunk.

"Hell," Stump said, sticking the butt end of a cigar between his teeth, "I can hardly remember the last time Murphy shot his boss. He must not ah been too mad attcha 'cause he shot the door frame insteda' you."

Wilber looked at the two men across the table from him and made a decision. Once they were passed out, he would kill them and worry about the ranger when and if the time came.

-

Over coffee, nearly a mile away from where Wilber and his bunch were holed up, Clay made camp behind some outcrop rocks that hid their fire and gave them protection from any cold wind that might come up.

"Now what's this plan of yours?" Loralie asked as she sat sipping hot coffee and eating some beans and bacon.

"Simple enough I guess," Clay said, as he rolled a cigarette and lit it with a piece of stick he'd pulled from the fire. "Later, oh say, around midnight, they should be passed out - dead to the world. I plan on going in real quiet like and have the boys here lead the horses out and away from the corral and head them back toward your place. The boys know the way and they can be herding them back while you and I go into Ashville and see the sheriff. You can file charges and we can lead him and his deputies back out here and let him arrest them."

Clay blew a smoke ring and then looked over at Loralie. "What'a ya think?"

"My first instinct was to shoot him down like the dog he is, but now that my temper has cooled down, I can see where your plan sounds better. I just hope it works."

"You have every reason to want him dead, and I mean to see that he stretches a rope for what he's done, but I want it done legal like,' Clay said, snubbing out what was left of his cigarette and tossing the paper in the fire.

"More coffee anybody?" Clay asked as he poured himself another cup.

Everyone declined and Clay set the pot back down on the rock sitting at the edge of the fire.

"It's been a full day and I suggest we get a little rest; we've got a long night ahead of us."

-

It was a little after midnight when Clay awakened everyone and poured them each a cup of hot coffee.

"Didn't you get any sleep?" Loralie asked, taking the cup of coffee from him.

"Some. I've got a natural alarm clock in my head," Clay said with a grin.

Clay had laid the saddle blankets close to the fire so they would feel warm against their horse's backs when it was time to leave.

Half an hour later they hauled up just short of the place where the horses were being held.

"We go on foot from here," Clay said.

Looking at Wolf, he said, "You boys sneak in there, real quiet like while I take care of the man in the barn. When you see me wave, you can start leading the horses back to the campsite we just left. I think if you take that tan brood mare and one other, the rest will follow."

"What about me? What am I supposed to do, sit here like some willy-nilly female and wait while you men have all the fun?"

Clay looked at Loralie and smiled. "There is no way this side of heaven or hell that you could ever sit by, willy-nilly, it's just not in you. Besides, you've got the most important job of all. I want you to take your rifle and find a spot where you can see the house and if anyone comes out, I want you to put them back inside so we can get away."

Loralie nodded and watched as Wolf, Bullfrog and Lives in The Woods headed toward the corral and Clay circled around to come up on the barn from the backside.

"Be careful," she whispered to his back.

Wolf and Lives in The Woods found some rope hanging on the corral gate – enough to make two lead ropes and climbed through the fence, seeking the two horses they wanted, while Bullfrog went around to the back of the corral. Once the gate was opened it would be his job to move the horses along, quietly.

Clay came up to the back door of the barn quietly, and as gently as he could, he opened it just enough to slip inside. Even so, the rusty door hinge made a squeaking noise that caused Murphy to come awake with a jerk.

Climbing unsteadily to his feet, he weaved his way over to the edge of the hayloft and looked down. He couldn't believe what he saw – the ranger was climbing the ladder to the hayloft. Lifting his pistol, Murphy began firing in the general direction of the ranger, but in his drunkenness, his bullets were only coming close to their target.

Clays only recourse was to pull his pistol and shoot back. It was dark in the barn and he was shooting at an awkward angle but he must have gotten lucky because one of his bullets caught Murphy in the knee and when his leg went out from under him, he fell head first over the edge – landing headfirst on the barn floor. Clay heard the man's neck snap and knew he was dead. Clay hurriedly scrambled back down the ladder and ran for the front door of the barn.

Wolf had just opened the corral gate when he heard the gunshots. Turning, he leaped aboard the horse he was leading and yelled, "Get them out of here, now!" And with that, he yelled, "Yiiiieeee!" and kicked his horse in the sides with his heels and sent her at a dead run toward where Loralie was hiding.

Hearing Wolf's outcry and seeing his friends ride out of the corral, Bullfrog grabbed the mane of a passing horse before she got up much speed – took two bounces with his feet and swung up onto her back, yelling at the other horses as they followed Wolf and Lives in The Woods down the road.

Inside the house, between the sounds of gunshots, Wolf's yelling and loud hoof beats of the running horses, Wilber bounded up from his chair where he'd fallen asleep and grabbed the edge of the table to support himself until he could get his bearings.

Carl and Stump were already on their feet with guns in their hands. Carl was the first one out the door and saw the three Indian boys escaping with the horse herd. Stump was only a step behind him and both men began firing their pistols.

Loralie had her rifle against her shoulder and saw the two men come running out of the house and begin shooting at the young Indian boys. More than fear of the boys being shot, instinct for survival took over and with two quick shots, dropped both outlaws where they stood.

Wilber watched in horror as his horses fled the area, and saw both his men go down. He stumbled out of the door and began firing in the direction of the rifle flashes.

One of Wilber's bullets came whizzing by Loralie's ear with a loud buzzing noise that caused her to flinch and bang her head on the tree limb she was crouched beneath.

Suddenly, just like that, it all came back to her – her memory returned and her anger flared up like a raging inferno.

Seeing Wilber standing there, shooting at her, she saw nothing but a mean, no good outlaw that was trying to kill her. Pulling her rifle to her shoulder, she put a bullet dead center in his chest.

At the same time, Clay saw Wilber shooting at Loralie. He reacted by pulling his pistol and sending lead into Wilber's side.

Clay's and Loralie's bullets met each other inside Wilber's heart and blew it apart. He was dead before he hit the ground.

Clay ran for Loralie, who was crossing the yard with the rifle still held tightly against her shoulder.

"It's alright, he's dead," Clay told her as he took the rifle from her grip.

Loralie looked at Clay and as tears began to run down her cheeks. She put her arms around his neck and drew him to her. "Oh Clay, I remember! I remember it all!" she said, planting kisses all over his face.

Clay put his arms around her and held her, speaking softly into her ear. "Everything is going to be alright, now."

When Loralie was finished crying, they dragged the bodies inside the house and closed the door to keep any animals away.

CHAPTER THIRTY-SIX

-

Back at the campsite where the boys were holding the herd, Clay asked Wolf, "How far is it to Ashville?"

"An hour, maybe less if you ride hard," Wolf told him.

With instructions for the boys to wait there and keep watch over the herd, Loralie and Clay rode into Ashville and went straight to the sheriff's office.

Clay presented himself as a Texas Ranger, far out of his jurisdiction and stretched the truth some by saying he'd followed Wilber and his brother all the way from Texas and went on to explain what had happened and where the bodies were, should the sheriff want to go collect them.

The sheriff, a man of sixty some, listened and when Clay was finished, he said, "Yeah, I know of them boys. Bad to the bone, both of 'em. Their pa and brothers weren't any better. There's no reward for 'em that I know of, so I don't see any reason to waste my time bringing them in just to pay somebody to bury them, but thanks for letting me know I won't be having any more trouble out of 'em."

As Clay and Loralie turned to go, the sheriff spoke up. "Are you looking to sell those horses, ma'am? There's a horse buyer here in town, saying he was supposed to meet a man named, Reardon, who was supposed to have some quality horses for sale. Would those be yours?"

On the way down to Ashville, Clay and Loralie had talked about marriage plans and her raising her Tennessee Walkers in Texas, along with turning her forest into a park with hiking trails and campsites so that it would be preserved forever.

Loralie looked at Clay, then back to the sheriff. "Where can I find this buyer?"

After selling all but two of her best brood mares, they went back to the house where the dead men were, and set it on fire.

Once they got back to her ranch, Loralie dug up a box containing ten pounds of gold nuggets. "I didn't trust the bank with all my money," she said, laughingly.

"That and what you've got in the bank, makes me marrying a rich woman," Clay said.

Rolling his eyes, he said, "What will folks say?"

When they got down to Cinch Mountain and was headed for Clay's train, the telegraph operator ran up to Clay and said, "I'm glad you're back. You received a telegram several days ago."

Clay took it and read –

NEED YOU BACK HERE – PRONTO - RILEY

"Is something wrong?" Loralie asked.

"I don't know for sure," Clay answered, handing the telegram to Loralie.

Before leaving, Clay sent a telegram to Riley saying –

SHOULD BE THERE WITHIN FIVE DAYS – CLAY

After looking at Clay's face to make sure nothing was broken, the doctor said, "You took quite a beating, but I'm happy to say that there's no permanent damage other than a couple of small scars."

The young Cherokee braves were both fearful and thrilled to be riding on a train.

During the return trip, Loralie said, "About what happened…"

Clay reached over and put his finger against her lips and said, "Nothing more needs to be said.

\-

When Clay's private train pulled to a stop on Clay's ranch, he looked out the window and saw most of the people who worked for him running toward the train.

Loralie said, "You go ahead. I'll be out in a minute."

Clay nodded and left the car and hurried down the steps to find out what was wrong.

Riley walked up to him and said, "Now afore you ask, it ain't the kind of trouble yer ah thinkin' bout."

"Then what kind of trouble is it?" Clay asked

Riley turned and pointed.

Victoria Ontiveros, owner of a large ranch down in New Mexico and his one-time boss, came walking through the crowd. She was beautiful and carried herself with the pride of the aristocrat she was.

When she got up close to him, she looked at his still battered, black and blue face.

Reaching up, she touched his cheek, gently and said, "When we are married you will stay home and run the ranch. You will have no more need to chase banditos."

Clay swallowed and looked over his shoulder and saw Loralie stepping off the train.

THE END

FROM THE AUTHOR

Thank you to all my readers. Your reviews and requests for more Clay Brentwood books is an inspiration to me. I'll keep writing them as long as you keep requesting them...

Jared McVay

MEET THE AUTHOR

At the current time, Jared McVay lives in Oregon where he writes his books, does storytelling, book signings, speaking engagements, and gets in a little fishing from time to time.

Before becoming a novelist, Jared was a professional actor – stage, film and television, and a ghostwriter for screenplays.

As a young man he worked as a cowboy, a rodeo clown, a lumberjack, barker for a carnival and a truck driver. During the 1950's he rode the rails as a hobo and during the 80's, a blue water sailor. He spent his military time in the US Navy Sea Bees, where he learned his electrical trade as a power lineman, then spent ten years as a lineman for Kansas Gas & Electric. But it was his love of entertaining people that led him into acting and writing.

Jared has five children, eleven grandchildren, fifteen great grandchildren and four great, great grandchildren.

When not writing or talking about writing, or answering e-mails from his fans, you can find him enjoying life with his girlfriend, Jerri.

THANK YOU FOR READING!

If you enjoyed this book, we would appreciate your customer review on your book seller's website or on Goodreads.

Also, we would like for you to know that you can find more great books like this one at

www.SixGunBooks.com

Stories so real you can smell the gunsmoke.™